21st BIRTHDAY

For a complete list of books, visit
JamesPatterson.com.

21ˢᵗ BIRTHDAY

JAMES PATTERSON
ᴀɴᴅ MAXINE PAETRO

GRAND CENTRAL
PUBLISHING

NEW YORK   BOSTON

Copyright © 2021 by James Patterson

Hachette Book Group supports the right to free expression and the value of copyright. The purpose of copyright is to encourage writers and artists to produce the creative works that enrich our culture.

The scanning, uploading, and distribution of this book without permission is a theft of the author's intellectual property. If you would like permission to use material from the book (other than for review purposes), please contact permissions@hbgusa.com. Thank you for your support of the author's rights.

Grand Central Publishing
Hachette Book Group
1290 Avenue of the Americas, New York, NY 10104
grandcentralpublishing.com
twitter.com/grandcentralpub

Originally published in hardcover and ebook by Little, Brown & Company in May 2021
First oversize mass market edition: December 2022

Grand Central Publishing is a division of Hachette Book Group, Inc. The Grand Central Publishing name and logo is a trademark of Hachette Book Group, Inc.

Women's Murder Club is a trademark of JBP Business, LLC.

The publisher is not responsible for websites (or their content) that are not owned by the publisher.

The Hachette Speakers Bureau provides a wide range of authors for speaking events. To find out more, go to hachettespeakersbureau.com or call (866) 376-6591.

ISBNs: 9781538752869 (oversize mass market), 9780759555693 (ebook)

Printed in the United States of America

OPM

10 9 8 7 6 5 4 3 2 1

In memory of Philip R. Hoffman
Counselor and friend

21st BIRTHDAY

PROLOGUE

CINDY THOMAS FOLLOWED Robert Barnett's assistant down the long corridor at the law firm of Barnett and Associates in Washington, DC.

This meeting could be the beginning of something terrific, and she had dressed for the win; sleek black dress, tailored leather jacket, a touch of lipstick, and an air of confidence that came from the material itself.

As a senior crime reporter for the *San Francisco Chronicle,* she had dominated the inside track, investigating and reporting on the vilest and most audacious serial murders of our time.

Bob Barnett, a lawyer and a literary agent, had represented her true-crime epic, *Fish's Girl,* making a very respectable sale to a good publishing house. Then, as was said, "It debuted to great reviews" and had briefly touched the hem of the *Times* Best Seller list.

Fish's Girl was the real-life story of a psychopathic serial killer with an equally deadly and immoral girlfriend. Reporting for the *Chronicle,* Cindy had helped the police catch "Fish's Girl," and the finale in the book—and in real life—had been a shoot-out. Cindy had been winged by a 9mm bullet and then returned fire, bringing down the psycho killer herself.

The entire *Fish's Girl* experience had been extraordinary, but now it was old news. Industry press reported that book sales were down in all categories, and Cindy had been busy with her all-consuming day job.

Then, last week, Bob Barnett called her at home, saying, "I've been following your Burke serial avidly. Great work, Cindy. If you craft it into a proposal, I believe I can sell it."

He'd asked her to write a treatment of the story; an introduction, a chapter outline, and at least one fully written chapter to show off her style for those potential deal makers who didn't read the *Chronicle*. He had offered her a plane ticket and a room at the Ritz if she would fly to DC and meet with him about her recent coverage of the serial murders. Cindy had allowed herself to hope that Barnett would work his magic again.

"Call me when you're ready," he had said.

It hadn't taken long.

Now, Barnett's assistant led her into the corner office, told her that the boss was running a little late, and said, "Make yourself at home, Ms. Thomas. I'm right outside if you need anything."

The office looked just as Cindy remembered it. The carpet was grass green. A slab of green marble was set into Barnett's desktop, and potted orchids, most in full bloom, stood proudly on every flat surface. The floor-to-ceiling bookcase at a right angle to Barnett's desk held every book he'd sold; Cindy saw *Fish's Girl* was at eye level slightly out of line, as if Bob had taken it out to review before this meeting.

Cindy loved seeing it fitted in between the big

author names, and after snapping a selfie with her
book to show Richie, she took a seat on the sofa in the
meeting area.

She was ready for Barnett when he strode into
his office, saying, "Cindy, I'm so sorry I kept you
waiting."

"Not a problem, Bob."

He shook her hand with both of his and took the
chair at an angle to her seat on the sofa. He was a
nice-looking man, designer glasses, natural tan, thick
gray hair, and he was easy to talk with.

"I've been enjoying the view," Cindy said. "And
the orchids."

"I'm a genius with orchids," he said. "And not too
bad at picking winners, either."

She smiled appreciatively, and leaning forward, he
got to the point.

"I read your proposal in one sitting. This story is
right up there with *Helter Skelter, Black Dahlia,* and
In Cold Blood. I'm dying to hear the up-to-the-minute
conclusion. We get the right people on board, this story
could be a monster, Cindy. An absolute monster."

PART ONE

FIVE MONTHS EARLIER

CHAPTER 1

CINDY THOMAS WAS at work in her office at the *San Francisco Chronicle* on Monday at 5:30 p.m. when she heard a woman calling her name.

More accurately, she was *screaming* it.

"Cinnn-ddyyyyyyyy!"

Cindy lifted her eyes from her laptop, looked through her glass office wall that faced the newsroom, and saw a tall, nimble woman zigzagging through the maze of cubicles. She was taking the corners with the deftness of a polo pony as a security guard with a truck-sized spare tire chased her—and he was falling behind.

As a reporter, Cindy had a sharp eye for details. The woman shrieking her name wore yoga pants and a Bruins sweatshirt, a knit cap over chin-length brown hair, and mascara was bleeding down her cheeks. She looked determined—and deranged. The woman, who appeared to be in her mid-forties, didn't slow as she raced toward Cindy's open door, but a moment later, the lanky woman was inside Cindy's office, both hands planted on her desk, black-rimmed red eyes fastened on hers.

She shouted at Cindy, "I'm Kathleen *Wyatt*. K.Y. You remember?"

"Your screen name."

Wyatt said, "I posted on your crime *blog* this morning. My *daughter* and her little baby *girl* are missing and her husband *killed* them."

Security guard Sean Arsenault pulled up to the doorway, panting. "I'm sorry, Ms. Thomas. You," he said to the woman who was leaning over the desk. "You come with me. Now."

Cindy said, "Kathleen, are you armed?"

"Be serious."

"Stand by, Sean," Cindy said. "Kathleen. Sit down."

The guard said that he would be right outside the door and took a position a few feet away. Cindy turned her attention back to the woman now sitting in the chair across from her desk and ignored the inquisitive eyes of the writers in the newsroom peering through her glass office wall.

Cindy said, "I remember you now. Kathleen, I had to take down your post from my blog."

"He *beats* her. They're *gone.*"

Cindy's publisher and editor in chief, Henry Tyler, leaned into her office. "Everything okay, Cindy?"

"Thanks, Henry. We're fine."

He nodded, then tapped the face of his watch.

Cindy nodded acknowledgment of the six o'clock closing. Her story about a shooting in the Tenderloin was in the polish phase. Henry had a word with Sean and then closed the door.

Cindy turned back to Kathleen Wyatt, saying, "You accused a man of murder and used his name. The rules are right there on the site. No vulgarity, name-calling, or personal attacks. He could sue you for defamation. He could keep the *Chronicle* in court until the next ice age."

Wyatt said, "You come across as such a nice person, Cindy. But like everyone else, you're all about the money."

"You're doing it again, Kathleen. I'm going to have to ask you to leave."

The woman folded her arms over Cindy's desk, dropped her head, and sobbed. Cindy thought Kathleen Wyatt seemed out of her mind with fear.

Cindy said, "Kathleen. Kathleen, do you know for a fact that this man murdered your daughter and granddaughter?"

Kathleen lifted her head and shook it. "No."

Cindy said, "Another question. Have you called the police?"

This time when Kathleen Wyatt raised her head, she said, "Yes. Yes, yes, yes, but have they found the baby? No."

CHAPTER 2

WHILE KATHLEEN WYATT dried her eyes with her sweatshirt, Cindy retrieved the post she'd deleted this morning and read it again.

Kathleen had written about her son-in-law, Lucas Burke, using ALL CAPS to shout that Burke had abused her daughter, Tara, and that he'd even been violent with their baby, Lorrie. Kathleen had written that she was terrified for them both and trusted her gut.

Cindy had seen the post a few minutes after Kathleen had submitted it. The screaming capital letters, many misspellings, and the nature of the post unloaded on a newspaper blog made the poster sound crazy. Or like a troll.

Now that Kathleen had told Cindy the story to her face, her credibility had risen. But, damn it, Cindy couldn't know if Kathleen was paranoid or in an understandable panic that her loved ones could be in danger—or worse. Her fear was relatable and the idea of a murderous husband *plausible*. It happened too often. And that it may have happened since Kathleen posted her cri de coeur this morning made Cindy feel awful and guilty. And still, there was nothing she could do to help.

Kathleen slapped the desk to draw Cindy's attention.

Her voice was rough from yelling but she said, "I called the police as soon as I couldn't locate Tara. And after you call the police once or three times, you have to beg them to pay attention. But I did it. My daughter's twenty now. An adult. The cops called in the K-9 unit, put out an Amber Alert on my granddaughter. Or so they say. It hasn't come through on my phone."

Cindy said, "The missing baby—what'd you say, she's a year old?"

"Closer to a year and a half."

"They're looking for her."

Kathleen reached into her fanny pack and pulled out a picture of mother and child. Tara was a brunette like Kathleen, and Lorrie was a redhead. They both looked very young.

"Lorrie is sixteen months old to be exact. My daughter is always home all day with the baby. I went over there. The house is empty. Her car is gone. I've called her and called her and we always, *always* speak in the morning after Lucas has gone to work. That baby could be dead already. If you'd run this picture in the paper six hours ago—"

"I'm a reporter, Kathleen. I need confirmation, you must know that. But, still, I feel sorry—"

"Don't you dare tell me how sorry you are. Sorry won't help my daughter. Sorry won't help her baby girl."

"Sit tight," Cindy said. She reviewed her story about the shooting in the Tenderloin, changed a few words, and then rewrote the last-line "kicker." She addressed an email to Tyler, attached her story, and pressed Send.

Deadline met, Cindy turned back to Kathleen. "No promises. Let me see what I can do."

CHAPTER 3

CINDY SPEED-DIALED the number, then drummed her fingers on her desk until Lindsay picked up.

"Boxer."

"Linds, I need some advice. It's important."

"What's wrong?"

"No, I'm fine. Can you give a couple of moments to a woman with a missing daughter and grandchild?"

"Me?"

"Thanks, Linds. I'm putting you on speaker. I'm here with Kathleen Wyatt. I'll let her tell you why. Kathleen, this is Sergeant Lindsay Boxer of Homicide."

Lindsay said, "Kathleen. What happened?"

"They've disappeared into a black hole."

"Say again?"

Kathleen said, "My daughter, Tara, and her baby disappeared this morning and her husband has threatened to kill them."

"You say they disappeared. Is there any indication that they were hurt?"

Kathleen paused before answering, "Tara has run away with the baby before."

"From her husband?"

"Tara has told me I don't know how many times that he's said that he hates her. He's hit her, but not so it shows. He wishes Lorrie had never been born. And yes, I've called the police."

Lindsay asked, "Had Tara taken out a restraining order on Lucas?"

"She wouldn't do it. She's only twenty. She's too young. Too dumb. Too needy. She doesn't work. She's *afraid* of him, and also, oh, God help her, she loves him. At seventeen, she begged me to consent to their marriage, and God help *me,* I did."

Horns honked over the phone line. Lindsay was in her car. She raised her voice over the clamor and asked Kathleen, "What was the police response?"

"Today? They say they talked to Lucas but he had an alibi. A girlfriend, probably. You should see him. Smooth as ice. He denies threatening her, them, of course. They have some units searching and they have dogs now in the vicinity of the house. And drones. And they say Tara will come home. And, Lindsay—if I may—I really think it may be too late."

The words "too late" tailed up into a heart-wrenching howl. Kathleen was crying as if she were sure they were dead. As if she knew. The security guard reached for the door, but Cindy put up her hand and shook her head.

Lindsay said, finally, "Who was the officer who took your report?"

"Bernard. Officer Bernard."

"Okay, Kathleen," Lindsay said, "I'll check with Officer Bernard. Give Cindy your number and I'll get back to you. If a baby has been missing since eight this morning, that's a police matter. Call the SFPD and ask for Tom Murry in Major Crimes. He's the head of Missing Persons. Keep your phone charged."

"I've met Lieutenant Murry," Kathleen said. "He doesn't take me seriously."

"I'll call him, too," said Lindsay. "See how the investigation—" she broke off. "Sorry, I've got to go."

Cindy said good-bye to Lindsay, watched Kathleen write down her phone number with a shaking hand, muttering, "You should help me, Cindy. Lorrie is dead. I feel it in my heart."

Cindy said, "It's almost dark. Go home and call the police, again. Did you call Tara's friends? What about her neighbors? If you hear anything at all, let me know. Wait. Let me see that picture."

Kathleen handed the picture of Tara and Lorrie to Cindy, who snapped it with her phone. She told Kathleen that she could run it with a request for information as to the pair's whereabouts without mentioning Lucas Burke.

Tugging at her watch cap, Kathleen muttered a thank-you as Cindy walked her out to the elevator. Cindy walked back to her office, wondering why Kathleen Wyatt had come to her. Was she right about her son-in-law? Or was Kathleen Wyatt just paranoid?

CHAPTER 4

I'D BEEN AT MY DESK since seven Tuesday morning.

It was now eight thirty. I wanted to get some answers for Kathleen Wyatt before the 9 a.m. all-hands meeting Lieutenant Jackson Brady had called. As the mother of a daughter myself, I felt an extra urgency.

My partner, Inspector Richard Conklin, and I sit at facing desks, at the front of the dull gray Homicide bullpen. He'd just arrived, but when Rich heard me talking to Lieutenant Murry over the phone, he went to the break room to get coffee.

Rich knew I was doing a favor for Cindy, his live-in love and my friend. When he got back to his desk, I thanked Murry, hung up, and Conklin pushed a fresh mug of mud over to my desk. It was black, three sugars, just how I like it.

"Boxer. What did Murry say?"

"He said that Lucas Burke is a bad dude, but he doesn't think he's a killer."

"How bad?"

I blew on my coffee, then referred to my notes.

"Last year, Lucas threatened a female motorist after a fender bender, grabbed her shoulders, called her names, and shook her. He was taken in for assault and battery but the motorist didn't press charges.

"A few months later, Lucas took a chain saw to a neighbor's tree he claimed was on his property. It was not. He got fined eight hundred dollars. End of that.

"Then, Kathleen reported him for domestic abuse of her daughter, but Tara denied it, said her mother was nuts. Kathleen is a little loosely wrapped, Richie. Which makes her hard to read. But it's also true that abused women often deny the abuse.

"Anyway, that's Lucas Burke's record. He's at least combative."

I called Cindy and sipped coffee while Rich walked over to Sergeant Cappy O'Neil's desk, sat on the edge of it, and traded what-ifs with him and Sergeant Paul Chi. I could hear them opining on the upcoming meeting, but there was little controversy. We were all of the same opinion. Brady was going to announce his future plans. But what had he decided to do?

The root of the matter was the scandal that had devastated the Southern Station, our station, not long ago. Lieutenant Ted Swanson of Robbery had enlisted two teams of bad cops to knock off drug dealers and payday loan joints for cash. Eighteen people died in several shoot-outs, and even Swanson took enough lead to kill him two or three times over. But he survived his injuries and was now serving out the rest of his worthless life at Chino, a maximum-security prison.

Warren Jacobi, our friend, my former partner, and at that time chief of police, had to take the fall. He was retired out, and Jackson Brady, our good lieutenant, picked up the slack for Jacobi, simultaneously running Homicide and the Southern Station. When asked to choose which job he wanted, he'd put off the decision. Maybe he took too long. Lately, rumor had it that the mayor was having talks with Stefan Rowan, a heavyweight organized-crime commander from New York.

I loved working for Brady. He was smart. He never asked anyone to do anything he wouldn't do. He was brave. And he was loyal to the people who reported to him.

What scared me most was that the rumor might be wrong. That Brady was going to step up to become chief of police, and the hard-ass New Yorker would replace *him* as Homicide CO.

Maybe a promotion would be good for Brady, but speaking for myself, it would break my heart.

CHAPTER 5

I LOOKED PAST CONKLIN and saw Brady leave his office in the back corner of the squad room. He put on his jacket and headed up the center aisle toward the front of the room. Conklin got up from Cappy's desk as Brady passed and joined me at our desks.

Brady took the floor, his blond-white hair pulled back in a pony, his denim shirt tucked in, his dark jacket unbuttoned. I couldn't read his expression.

Brady took center stage at the front of the squad room, facing the dozen Homicide cops from the day shift, another dozen cops from the night shift, and more were coming in. Cops from other departments leaned against the walls, sat in empty chairs, or perched on the corners of desks, all quietly waiting for Brady to drop a bomb.

When the anticipation had stretched so thin it was starting to thrum, Brady said, "I know the wait time has been hard on everyone. I did my best to hold things together with your help. My wife says I look like I've been dragged behind a car. To tell the truth, I feel a little like that, but I was of two minds.

"Now, y'all know I've been running up and down the stairs, changing hats in the landing. I was asked to choose, fourth floor or fifth, but if I coulda kept doing both jobs, I woulda done it. But in the interest of safety, public good and welfare, and living to see my forty-fifth birthday, I've decided to hang my hat in Homicide."

Big sigh of relief from me, and a spontaneous round of raucous applause and hooting from the squad.

I said loud enough for Brady to hear, "So glad, Brady. That was a sacrifice."

"No," he said, "it was selfish. I just couldn't move into Jacobi's swell office and push paper. I'm a street cop and I like being part of the action."

Laughter came up all around the room and it was like sunshine breaking through the clouds. Then I realized we hadn't heard the rest of the story.

Who was our new police chief?

Anticipating the question, Brady said, "And that leaves the last shoe. I make it to be size eleven medium wide, currently filled by a former Homicide cop from LA and Vegas who for the last dozen years has been heading up our forensic lab, ably, with good humor. Not prideful, but we know he's a first-class CSI."

It took a minute for the parts to come together, and then I got it. I had just never considered Charlie Clapper as chief of police, but damn, he was an excellent choice.

Brady was saying, "At this point, I'm supposed to draw back the curtain and say about a former cop and highly respected forensic scientist, 'Round of applause for our own Charlie Clapper, now police chief, SFPD.'

"But I forgot to get a curtain, and Clapper isn't here. He's going to be across the street at

MacBain's—second-floor private room reserved for alla us, from noon to two. No cover charge, beer's on the house. If there are any questions, we'll get ya answers all in good time."

Conklin got to his feet and said, "Brady? If you had anything to do with recommending Clapper for the chief job, I just want to say, hot dog. Good choice and all in the family. And I'm glad you're staying with us."

CHAPTER 6

CONKLIN AND I WALKED across the street at the appointed time, still stunned by the breaking news. But pleased.

We both liked Clapper. A lot. He was a solid pro, never a showboat. I remembered so many cases where he'd been the forensic specialist; when hamburgers had become bombs, when we dug up a dozen decapitated heads in a backyard, when he'd gone through the exploded science museum where my husband, Joe, had been almost killed. He'd taken us through crime scenes and pointed out things he thought we ought to know.

The bottom line: Charlie Clapper had never let us down.

Richie held the door for me at MacBain's and we entered the favorite watering hole for Hall of Justice workers, from court stenographers to the motorcycle police. At lunchtime, the ancient jukebox was cranked up and the place was packed to the walls, but we didn't have to look for a table. We headed straight up the stairs to the second floor, where it was clear that the party had already started. A buffet had been set up with hot plates and servers, tables were arranged around the room, and a lot of cops were in attendance, not just from Homicide but from every section at the Hall.

Altogether, a hundred people were there, including Brady, everyone with a glass in their hand. I waved to Clapper as we passed and he waved back. When everyone from Lieutenant Tom Murry from Major Crimes to Lieutenant Lena Hurvitz from Special Victims to DA Len Parisi had a plate and was seated, Brady clinked his glass with a spoon.

He had our attention. He said, "Charles Clapper, former director of our Forensics unit, needs no introduction. Most of you have hung on to his shirttails as he ran a crime scene, questioned him on the witness stand, relied on him for his wisdom when a crime was so unbearably awful you didn't know whether to puke or bawl your eyes out.

"Starting tomorrow morning, Charlie is going to take over as chief of police and move into the fancy office on the fifth floor. You all are stuck with me heading up Homicide.

"Charlie, please take it from here."

There was applause and shouts of "Way to go, Charlie!" and a minute later Clapper had a drink in his hand. As always, Clapper was perfectly dressed, his hair cut and combed, a mirror shine on his shoes. He stood with one hand in his pocket as he said, "Thanks, everyone, for that very kind welcome to a job none of you want or would take on pain of death."

When the laughter died down, Charlie went on.

"As Lieutenant Brady said, I've known some of you for more than fifteen years, and I'm glad that I had that much time to learn the SFPD and be of help to putting the wicked behind bars.

"Now I've got a different job and the number one task the mayor has given me is to rebuild the Southern Station. Most of you have lived through the corruption of our good name. Our Robbery and Narcotic departments are thin. I have some major recruiting to do.

"I'm a perfectionist. I do things by the book. That's how I pulled CSU back from the brink and why I was drafted for this job. Here's what it means to you. The by-the-book rules are in effect; color within the lines, button every last button, stay in your own lane. Keep thorough notes, keep your phones and radios on, and keep your eyes and ears open. Stay in touch with dispatch or your CO. I love you all, but effective immediately, love's got nothing to do with it.

"I have to be the enforcer."

CHAPTER 7

AS THE PARTY WAS breaking up, I checked in with Lieutenant Tom Murry, head of Missing Persons.

Tom sounded hoarse and worn-out as he told me that now that his search had passed the twenty-four-hour mark, he was expanding his canvass.

"Tara Burke and her kiddo are still missing. We're following every dumb-ass lead. The hounds alerted on a dead cat, but that was all. We're running plates around the Burke house and Lucas is cooperating, has offered other places we can look. We'll be at this all night."

I commiserated. Asked if he wanted any help.

"Yes."

I called Joe to remind him that I was having dinner with the girls tonight, then I researched Lucas Burke. My search was limited to the internet and our police files, but there was some new background from a bio he'd given in a speech I found online.

I learned that Lucas's mother and sister had died when Lucas was in grad school, but his father, Evan

Burke, was still alive and had not remarried. Lucas taught at Sunset Park Prep, a private girls' school in the Sunset District. Three years ago, Burke divorced his wife of ten years and married Tara Wyatt. Lorrie was Burke's only child.

I highlighted names and places, saved the research into a file, and went to go find Brady.

Brady wasn't in his office. It was second nature to head up to the fifth floor. I asked squad assistant, Brenda Fregosi, to let Rich know I'd be back in a few.

I found Clapper in his new office, an office I'd been in so many times I was on first-name terms with the dust bunnies under the sofa.

I said, "Gotta minute, chief?"

Clapper waved me in.

Piles of papers covered his desk. There were cardboard bankers' boxes stacked along the window wall, labeled by date in marker pen, lids taped in place.

Those would be Clapper's papers, yet to be filed.

Charlie looked harried, a change from his usual benign countenance. But I got it. The man was organized. His job in Forensics had been a perfect match for his personality type.

Brady had been overwhelmed and not organized by nature.

It would take Clapper a few days to see the desktop and get his files up to speed.

I pulled out a side chair and sat down.

I briefed him on my last case in two sentences and we commiserated in one. Then, I said, "Chief, a woman came to Cindy Thomas's office yesterday claiming that her daughter and sixteen-month-old grandchild were missing. She believes that her son-in-law is violent and could have killed them."

"Thomas called you?"

"Yep. I spoke with the complainant and I spoke with the officer in charge, Lieutenant Tom Murry, and he hasn't turned up anything yet. Hounds are out. Drones, too. Canvass of the neighborhood and school where the husband works. Now, over twenty-four hours have passed."

Clapper sat back in the desk chair. He said, "I'm aware, Boxer. And know Lieutenant Murry to be thorough. What are you asking?"

"I want to bring in the husband for questioning. See if I detect a falsehood, and maybe I can break him—"

Clapper cut me short.

"Correct me if I'm wrong, but this isn't your case."

"Uh."

"Murry interviewed the husband?"

"Yes, but he didn't get anything from him."

"Boxer, it's Murry's case. He's working it. What did I say earlier today?"

"Many things."

"I said stay in your lane. If your board is empty, it won't be for long. Don't call me, Boxer. Have Brady call me. That's the chain of command."

I was insulted and hurt. I felt my cheeks heat up as I stood from the chair and went to the door. Clapper didn't look up, didn't say good-bye or thanks or see ya around.

When I got back to the bullpen, Brenda had a message for me. She said softly, "That lady over at your desk is looking for you. Name is—"

Without seeing her, I said, "Kathleen Wyatt."

"Bingo," said Brenda. She made a little circle with her index finger next to her temple, universal sign for crazy.

I clenched my fists and headed toward my desk.

CHAPTER 8

CLEARLY, KATHLEEN WYATT was in yesterday's clothes.

My guess was that she'd been driving around the city looking for her daughter and granddaughter since then. She seemed out of it, but I put it down to stress and exhaustion.

I took her to the break room, got her coffee and a leftover donut, waited for her outside the ladies' room.

Given the Clapper rules, I told her that Lieutenant Murry was working the case full-bore. I quoted the record: that at ten after eleven Monday morning, Lucas called his wife from his cell phone and she answered. Their call lasted just under three minutes. Then I moved on to reassurances: that most likely Tara wasn't ready to be found, and she would be in touch. And then I heard myself say that I would drive out to Sunset Park Prep and talk to Lucas personally to assure myself that he hadn't hurt anyone.

She gave me a disbelieving look.

"Kathleen. Either trust me or leave me out of this."

"Okay. I trust you."

"Good. Go home and get some sleep."

I walked Kathleen down to the street, watched as she drove off in her ancient Fiat. Then I went to the day lot across Bryant and got my car out of stir. I'd thought that I had a decision to make, but I'd already made it. Something was drawing me to this case. I can't explain it, but I felt attached and that maybe I could bring Tara and Lorrie Burke home safely.

It was half past two. School was still in session.

I called dispatch, told them I had to take a half day lost time, texted Rich that the less he knew the better and I'd call him later. Then I called Cindy.

"This is so off the record, it's in a different time zone," I said to her.

"What've you got?"

"I'm taking a flier. Gonna talk to the husband. Don't tell Richie. I'm disobeying the new chief."

"Love you, Linds."

Sunset Park Prep was located on Thirty-Seventh Avenue and Rivera Street, and this was where Lucas taught English to eleventh- and twelfth-grade girls. I knew of the school, which was reputed to offer a college-level experience in a day-school environment.

I parked the car on Sunset Boulevard, clipped my badge to the inside pocket of my jacket, and tucked my gun into the back waistband of my chinos.

I looked up Lucas Burke's class schedule again—and, yes, from three to four he had an office hour in the Academic Building.

Couldn't have timed it better if I'd tried.

I put my phone in my breast pocket and got out of my car.

Ready or not, Lucas Burke. Here I come.

CHAPTER 9

I WAS DEFYING a direct order, but I felt justified.

In three out of four cases of familial homicide, the husband was the killer. Dozens of cases came to me; bludgeoned wives and smothered children, buried in shallow graves or put through wood chippers, entire families shot and tucked into their beds, the husband displaying grief, begging the real killer to come forward, or leaving the country. Often they remarried in under a year.

I hadn't given up on Tara and Lorrie Burke after less than a day and a half. This was still a presumed missing persons case, even if the chance of finding the two alive was heading toward zero. I needed to get a take on Lucas Burke, the man at the center of it.

I parked in the lot at Sunset Park Prep. The ten-acre campus had grounds like clipped green velvet. The main building was imposing, built of white stone in the early twentieth century. Athletic fields and smaller buildings stretched out beyond it.

I'd just flashed my badge at the visitors' check-in when

the bell rang and students exited classrooms, chattering as they walked the broad corridor to their next class.

I stopped a group of young ladies and asked where I could find Mr. Lucas Burke's office.

One said, "You just passed it."

I reversed course, saw "Mr. Burke" on a nameplate to the left of an office door. I knocked and heard "Come innnn."

Burke looked up when I entered his office.

He was a good-looking fortyish man sitting behind a desk heaped with neat stacks of paper. His hair was a thick and wavy auburn, and he wore tortoiseshell glasses, a blazer over a blue shirt, a red tie, and a wedding band on his ring finger.

I showed him the badge clipped to my inside jacket pocket and introduced myself. We shook hands and he offered me a chair. I took it and started talking.

"You know that Kathleen Wyatt filed a report against you," I said, in a neutral tone. I didn't want to anger or alarm him. I wanted to come off as a friendly neighborhood cop, checking out a complaint.

Burke took off his glasses, swiped his face with his hand, and sighed at the same time. "Sergeant, you've met Kathleen?"

"Yes. She's distraught. Very."

"I've already made a statement to Missing Persons about this," said Burke. He picked up a business card from his desk and read the name, "Lieutenant Tom Murry. You should check with him, but since you're here, I'll repeat myself. Kathleen Wyatt is—how shall I say this? Eccentric. Paranoid. Off her rocker. She calls me at all hours and I'm afraid to turn off the phone in case Tara tries to reach me."

"She still hasn't called?"

"No, we haven't spoken since I called her yesterday

morning, but I'm not having a panic attack. Tara, like her mother, is high-strung. We had a fight. I don't even remember what it was about."

"Really?"

"Okay. If you must know, she ran through our credit line on frivolous purchases. I bought her a Volvo when Lorrie was born, and that wasn't enough. Underwear and makeup and some stupid gadget to calm her mind. She bought a chair. From England! Never even saw the chair. Four thousand dollars plus shipping. I work my butt off and she gets high on online shopping sprees, so I took her credit card and ran it through my shredder."

Burke did look annoyed. Highly. I could see his point. Then again, he was providing motive. He might be innocent or could be a killer. My instincts weren't making a call.

He said, "Sergeant, I can tell you everything I know right now. I last saw Tara yesterday morning at about seven thirty when we had our fight. Shouting and name calling only. I walked out and was on time for my eight o'clock class. An hour or so later, Kathleen began calling my cell every ten minutes."

I was looking for tells as I sat across from him. He wasn't sweating or avoiding my gaze. There was a framed photo on his desk. I moved it toward me. Tara and Lorrie at her first birthday, about four months ago. Visible on the inside of Tara's wrist was a small heart-shaped tattoo lettered "LuLu."

He said, "Help yourself. Anything else you need to know about my personal life?"

"You're not my concern, Mr. Burke. There's a state-wide Amber Alert out for your daughter. Help us out, will you? You must have some thoughts about where Tara and Lorrie might be."

Burke waved away the implied question.

He said, "You know Tara never even locked the doors on our house, right? And she's done this before. This time, she emptied our safe, but she won't get far on a few twenties. The baby's diaper bag is gone. Here's an idea. Why don't I file charges against *her*? How about kidnapping, for starters?"

"Good idea. Come with me to the station," I said. "You can make a statement, file your complaint. And we can have a longer talk. Mr. Burke, let's get Tara and Lorrie home."

He scoffed and then he laughed and said, "Tara's just pissed off at me. She's a doting mother. Nothing will happen to Lorrie."

A young woman appeared in the doorway. She had a long blond braid and blue-painted fingernails that matched her school uniform.

"Mr. Burke, when should I come back?"

"Give me ten minutes, Misty."

She said okay and left.

"Another thing," Burke went on. "Sergeant, here's something you should know. Tara's doctor prescribed antidepressants. They're still in the medicine chest and the bottle is full."

"She's gone off her meds?"

"Yes. And in my opinion, that's why she's telling stories to her friends, spending like crazy, running away from home, and do you want to know what worries me?"

He was ranting, and I wasn't going to stop him. I actually found him believable, but I wished I'd had this on tape.

"Tell me," I said.

"What worries me is that Tara is unhinged, Kathleen is unhinged, and if this is genetic, I worry Lorrie will be, too. Okay? Give me your card and I'll call you when I hear from my wife."

CHAPTER 10

FIVE MINUTES LATER, I was back in my car and still deeply disturbed about the missing wife and child.

Kathleen Wyatt had gotten to me, and I believed in my heart that Tara and Lorrie were in danger. I couldn't walk away, despite Clapper's direct order, until they were safe.

Lucas Burke hadn't raised my hackles. I didn't feel that he had killed Tara and Lorrie, but he hadn't seemed very worried, either. Where were they? Had Tara run off, as her husband insisted? Or had something happened to them, as Kathleen feared?

I thought about Tara and Lorrie Burke. I swear I heard them calling out to me. If they weren't home by morning, I wanted to get this damned case from Missing Persons and work it. Get search warrants. Interview Burke's coworkers, students, neighbors, and friends.

My tension turned physical. My neck and shoulders were cramping. It felt like the restraints Clapper had put on me were tightening.

I got back to the squad room at just after five

and found a note from Conklin weighted down by my stapler.

I'm with the search team. Call you later. R.

I gulped Tylenol dry and called Richie. He picked up.

"Where are you?" he asked.

"At my desk. How's it going?"

"I've got that feeling like when you've put something down in your house and can't find it. But you know it's there. It's gotta be there."

We talked more. I told him about my interview with Burke, warming myself up for an unpleasant meeting with Clapper, and told Rich I'd report back. I took the stairs up to the fifth floor, headed for the corner office facing Bryant.

I knocked. And then, I wriggled the doorknob. Stupid. What if Clapper opened the door in my face and said, "What do you want, Boxer?" But his door was locked.

At around 6 p.m. I drove to the edge of the Financial District, parked on Jackson Street, and walked toward Susie's Café, where I was looking forward to seeing my three best friends. Cindy had named our gang of four "the Women's Murder Club" and it had stuck.

We'd claimed Susie's Café as our clubhouse. Cindy, Claire, Yuki, and I loved the place for the "don't worry, be happy" crowd at the bar, the steel band and occasional limbo contest, the tasty Caribbean food, and that everyone knew our names.

We try to meet here every couple of weeks for the laughter and camaraderie, and we also pool our mental resources and apply them to cases that refuse to crack.

Tonight, we were getting together because three weeks had passed since we'd last seen Claire.

A chill breeze blew down the empty street. I buttoned my jacket but I still felt cold.

Then I saw the lights coming from the café windows. If anything could warm me, it was Susie's Café and a huddle with my best friends.

Maybe one of us would have a bright idea.

CHAPTER 11

AS I CLOSED IN ON Susie's front door, a small crowd streamed out to the street. A gent held the door for me and, as always, the roar of laughter and the aroma of curry washed over me.

I stood for a moment inside the entrance, mapping out my path, then edged between the standing-room-only patrons banked at the bar and the clump of customers waiting for tables. I exchanged hellos with Susie and crossed to a corridor at the rear of the main room. This narrow passageway led past the kitchen, then emptied into the quieter, smaller, and cozier back room. No music, no bar back there, just Jamaican street art on the walls and a dozen tables and booths, including the one we thought of as ours.

Claire was at the far end of the banquette, the seat next to the window. Yuki sat across from her and both smiled hugely as I came up to the table. I slid in next to Claire and high-fived Yuki over the table.

"Cindy's on the way," she said.

I grabbed Claire's hand.

She had been diagnosed with lung cancer and had undergone surgery that cost her half a lung. The surgery was successful, but there'd been no promises as to her life expectancy. That scared the hell out of me and everyone else who knew and loved Claire. Still on leave from her post as the city's chief medical examiner, she was seeing her own doctor every three months for checkups until further notice.

Sitting next to her, I noticed how thin she'd become. She'd wanted to drop a couple of dress sizes for years, but cancer was no one's idea of how to lose the weight.

Yuki had just come from her office at the DA and was wearing a sharp black jacket and pants, hair falling to just below her chin with a blond streak in front. She looked good, but sleep-deprived.

She leaned in and said, "Dr. Terk told Claire that she's doing better than expected. That is to say, she's doing great."

Claire cracked a grin. "No secrets, right? I'm cleared to go back to work, although I had to swear on my daughter's pet bunny I would not pull all-nighters."

We all started laughing. Claire's daughter Rosie's rabbit was a big-eyed flop-eared thing named Hoppy who sleeps with Rosie on her pillow. Then Claire asked about the new commander of the Southern Station and the laughter stopped.

"Clapper's kind of a brilliant choice, isn't he?"

Yuki, who was married to Brady, said, "Hmmmm."

Claire said, "Not so enthusiastic, Yuki-san. What is it?"

"Uh. Well, Brady is moody. Bad moody. Didn't sleep last night. That's odd for him. He likes Clapper a lot. It's more like he'd almost decided he didn't want the promotion to chief, but you know, he's pissed that the mayor made the decision for him. Feels to him like a slight. Or a vote of no confidence."

Before I could say that I'd already gotten a big fat demerit from Clapper, our favorite waitress, Lorraine, came to our table. Her red hair was pulled up in a knot; she had pencil and pad in hand.

She asked, "Is Cindy coming?"

Yuki said, "Any minute."

On cue, Cindy blew into the back room.

She wore denim all the way and her curls were tight from the damp wind. Her big blue eyes were shining, and after she slid in next to Yuki, she said, "Sorry for making you wait. I was stuck behind an oil truck."

Lorraine greeted her and recited the specials.

Claire asked for steak, black beans, and rice. Yuki ordered a crab salad, and Cindy said, "Conch, deep fried."

"We're out of conch," said Lorraine.

"Chicken feet dredged in spicy flour."

"So, by that you mean blackened snapper and fries."

"Exactly!" said Cindy. "And a salad."

"Me, too," I said.

"Yuki. You need a margarita?"

"Just beer," said our dear friend who had no tolerance for tequila at all.

"So that's beer all around," Lorraine said.

"Hear, hear," I said.

Beer came. We lifted our frosty mugs and toasted as one.

"To Claire."

"To us," said Claire.

We clinked mugs.

Lorraine brought plates of food lined up and balanced on both of her forearms, and when dinner was on the table she asked if we needed anything else. We all said we were good. After taking long slugs of brew, Cindy leaned forward and said dramatically, "Well, girlfriends. I've got news."

CHAPTER 12

"LET ME PUT a drum roll under that," Cindy said. "I've got *Burke* news. But first, I've gotta eat something."

We booed and hissed and Claire said, "You're gonna pay for that."

Cindy laughed, saying, "Seriously, I'm starving."

As she doused her fries with hot sauce, I said, "I guess I'll spill my own Burke news. I went to Sunset Park Prep today and had a chat with Lucas Burke."

"Linds," said Cindy. "You trying to scoop me?"

"I needed to get a fix on him," I said. "Your friend Kathleen got to me. She hooked me good." I told my friends about my impromptu meeting with Burke, how he claimed that he'd had a fight with Tara Monday morning and that she'd taken off with the baby in retaliation.

"Oh, and he said she's off her meds. He offered to come down and file charges against her for kidnapping the baby, but when I took him up on it he said, no, she'd be home soon. He said he destroyed her credit card."

"Could you have arrested him on suspicion?" Claire asked.

"I have nothing on him. And Clapper would probably suspend me from duty. Missing Persons is on the case. So that's what *I've* got. Cindy? You're up."

Cindy put down her fork, dabbed her lips with her napkin, and gave us all a little smirk.

"This is off the record. Hear me?"

All of us were guilty of swearing Cindy to the same promise, so we laughed, raised our right hands, and agreed. Then, using topic sentences, complete paragraphs, and an occasional subhead, Cindy told us what she knew.

"Misty Lee Fogarty is a senior at Sunset Park Prep," she said. "She's eighteen, taking English Lit from Lucas Burke and also sleeping with him. He told her that he's leaving his wife for her."

Claire said, "I guess when you're eighteen, you've never heard that before."

"Who told you this leaving-the-wife story?" Yuki asked.

"Friend of Misty. And then I spoke to Misty, myself. On the record."

"Long blond hair in a braid?" I thought of the girl who'd come to the door when I was in Burke's office.

"That's her," said Cindy. "And Misty says, yah, Lucas put it in writing."

I asked, "And you believed her?"

Cindy reached for her bag and pulled out a note hand-printed on a pink index card. She flashed it so we could see the writing and then, read it out loud.

"Dear Misty, I'm in love with you. I promise that I will be free and we will be able to get married by the end of the school year.

"Love, Luke."

I said, "Is it dated?"

"Nope."

"Well, take a picture of that, will you, Cindy, and send it to me. Off the record." I winked. "I want to compare it with his signature on his DMV file."

She growled playfully, took the picture and sent it to me. I wondered if she would show it to Rich later, how my partner would react to my cutting him out.

Then I asked our so-called girl reporter, "So what do you think, Cindy? That Lucas killed his wife to be with Misty?"

"What do *you* think?" she asked me.

"I think it's lechery," Yuki said with conviction. "It's not evidence of anything criminal. But it could be a match to a fuse if Tara got wind of it. Or what if Lucas flat out told her? If he even needed to— Tara is only twenty years old."

"If I'm Tara," I said, "that's grounds to clear out the safe, grab the baby, and just take off."

Cindy said, "And doesn't tell her mother? I'll tell you what I think. Lucas Burke needs a good cop-beating under hot lights."

Claire said, "Too many old cop movies, Cindy."

"Yeah, yeah. Okay. Here's my plan. We're running Tara and Lorrie's photos in the paper and online tonight. Tyler's putting up a twenty-five-thousand-dollar reward for information leading to finding them. I'm just letting you know, Linds. There may be a lot of phone traffic tomorrow."

"It's okay," I said. "Whatever it takes."

"Is there anything you can do to turn up the heat?"

I sighed, shook my head no, thinking again of Clapper telling me to stay out of it.

Then I thought of the report I needed to write. "Can you send me the photos?"

Cindy picked up her phone and then it got so quiet at the table we could hear every conversation in the room. Quarterly meeting in the booth behind us. First date in the booth in front. Drunken laughter at the table to the left.

I have a young child at home and so does Claire, so we asked for the check and broke up dinner early, no excuses required. We all hugged and said good night.

I thought about the Burke family during the entire drive home.

CHAPTER 13

JOE WAS IN HIS big chair with Julie in his lap, lying against his chest. Our aging border collie, Martha, was at his feet.

I said, "Don't get up."

Sweet Martha got up anyway and then Julie squirmed to her feet and I hugged them both on the way to my husband. I leaned down and kissed him and he pulled me down into his now empty lap.

"What's wrong?" he asked.

"Nothing. I'll tell you later."

Julie held up a greeting card with a hand-drawn rainbow and a dog that looked a little like Martha on the front.

"Mommy. Lookit this!"

"Let me see."

"It's from Franny!"

"Oh, wow, honey. That's so cool."

Franny is Francesca, Joe's adult daughter from his first marriage. She lives in Rome, and after her mother died recently, she came here to see Joe, and to meet her little half sister, Julie. Big surprise to us all, but a good one.

My little girl showed me the envelope with her name and address printed in blue. When I took a closer look at the card, I saw a few Italian words between the bands of the rainbow.

"Can you read this, Mommy?"

"It says...*Ciao Bella.*"

She said *"Ciao Bella"* along with me and I had to laugh. I said, "It means, 'Hello, pretty.' Sweet, huh?"

She nodded vigorously.

They'd had spaghetti and meatballs for dinner, a favorite meal at the Molinari household. Now Daddy needed some computer time, so after I showered and dressed in pajamas, I snuggled up with my little kiddo, a glass of Chardonnay, and a pint of pralines and cream and we watched a sitcom on TV.

I sneaked looks at her, wondering at her innocence and easy laughter, trying to remember if I had been like Julie when I was her age. Nothing came to me. By the first commercial break her eyelids closed, and I whispered, "Time for bed, Julie Bugs."

She yawned and put her arms around my neck and I carried my nearly four-year-old to her bed. She wanted water, but by the time I returned she was asleep, breathing deeply under the stars and moon mobile hanging over her big-girl bed.

I found Joe in the kitchen with his hands in dishwater. I grabbed a towel.

He shot me a concerned look. "Start talking, Blondie."

"Grrr. Must I?"

"You know you want to."

"Ohhh-kay. Clapper told me to stay out of the Burke case but I decided to go interview Lucas Burke by myself. Kept Richie out of it, which, as we all know, shows consciousness of guilt."

He handed me a wet dish. "How'd it turn out?"

"Nothing to show for it. Burke plausibly denied having anything to do with his missing wife and child."

"He has an alibi?"

"Said he was on time for class the day she disappeared. That may be true but doesn't account for the night before. What he says is that in the morning, they had a fight about money. He destroyed her credit card. He left for school, and his theory is that Tara looted the safe, took the baby, and drove off to piss him off. He says she'll be home when she runs out of cash."

"He didn't express concern about the baby?"

"Not so you could tell. According to Cindy, Burke has a girlfriend."

"Motive enough for some men to off their wives."

"Yup. And I would like to get into this for real. I'd like to interview the girlfriend. But. It's not my case, says Clapper in an uncharacteristically stern tone of voice."

"What're you going to do?" Joe asked.

"What would you do?"

"I asked first."

I sighed as I dried and put away the last of the dishes. Then I said, "I'll write up my interview notes, tell Clapper what I did, say 'sorry,' and make a case for him not to treat me like a rookie. I mean, come on. I ran Homicide not too long ago. I've closed more cases than...than anyone."

"That I know, Blondie. I hope he's secure enough in his new job to cut you some slack."

"Cindy's running photos of Tara and Lorrie Burke online tonight and in the morning print edition—"

"It's already on the tube," said Joe. "I had to change the channel so 'big eyes' didn't see it."

"Hunh. Well. Maybe Tara Burke will see it and step forward. That would be a happy conclusion, and would get me off the hook with Clapper. Oh, man, if only Tara phoned in. Or someone else with a tip leading to her and the baby. Or even a credible sighting, confirmation that they were still alive."

Joe said, "Either way, I think you're covered."

I wasn't so sure. I emptied the remains of the Chardonnay into my glass and drank it all down.

CHAPTER 14

I WAS AT MY DESK by 7:30 a.m., the third time this week, and it was only Wednesday.

The message light on my phone console was blinking impatiently. Cindy had warned me that her story about the missing Burkes with the headlined reward was going to set our hotline on fire. But I had a hunch that this call was something different.

I picked up the receiver and stabbed the red button. As I'd thought, the message was from Charlie Clapper, chief of police.

"Boxer, it's Clapper. Call me when you get this."

Sometimes I just hate to be right.

Conklin wasn't in yet because, unlike me, or any parent, he could still get seven hours of sleep. I looked around the squad room. Brady's office was dark. Paul Chi came in, threw his coat over his chair, and waved hello as he passed my desk on his way to the break room.

I followed Chi and stood by as he filled the coffeepot. He asked, "How ya' doing, Boxer?"

"Five on a scale of ten."

"Sometimes I wish for a five," he said. "I'm getting arthritis in my right shoulder."

"Sorry, Paul."

"Nah, it's okay. I need to take some Advil, which I'm gonna take with the coffee. What's it going to take to get you up to a seven?"

"You've seen the news?" I said.

"Yeah. If Tara Burke has hit the road with her baby, I hope she's in Canada."

Someone on the night shift had stuck the morning paper on top of the microwave. I grabbed it and read the front page. **Missing. REWARD FOR INFORMATION.**

The subhead was *25k Reward for Information leading to return of Tara Wyatt Burke and her baby daughter.*

I looked again at the photo but didn't bother to read the article. I knew it by heart, both sides of the story. I poured myself a cup of hot java, took my mug back to my desk, and called Clapper.

"Chief, it's Boxer."

He didn't bother to say hello.

He said, "I just got off the phone with Tom Murry. He says you interviewed Lucas Burke. I don't see a report from you. Is that right?"

"Yes, sir. Murry asked me to help."

"That meant he was looking to you for support, not inviting you to take over his case."

This was really killing me. I've had nothing but an excellent relationship with Clapper since my first days in Homicide. I knew him. I liked him. I admired him. Sometimes I thought of him as family.

"Charlie, I was wrong to do it. Sorry. But there's a baby missing. *A baby.*"

"Stop right there, Boxer. You have probable cause?"

"No," I admitted. "Charlie. I mean, chief. Why do you want to bust my chops—"

"We have eyes on Burke. I hope to God you didn't crowd him into making a move we're all going to regret."

He hung up on me.

Conklin pulled out his chair and sat down across from me. "What the hell was that?"

"That was Clapper handing my ass to me. You've never heard me say this before, Rich, but I don't know if I can work like this. I don't know if I can stay in this job."

CHAPTER 15

I REACHED FOR my coffee but hit the mug and knocked it over. A small lake of black coffee spread across my desk and cascaded onto Richie's desk as well.

Chi dropped off a roll of paper towels, and Rich and I had the spill mostly contained when I heard my name.

It was Brady, and he was standing right there.

The look on his face was terrible; eyes scrunched up, mouth turned down. He looked like he was in pain. I didn't need a hunch. It was obvious Clapper had called him and I was about to be disciplined. I was ready.

"I can't believe I did this—" I sputtered.

Brady said, "A red-haired baby girl, tentatively identified as Lorrie Burke, has washed up on Baker Beach."

My thoughts scrambled. I had thought I'd be prepared for this, but it was too much, too fast.

Brady continued, "Uniforms at the scene say the

body is waterlogged. That'll have to be confirmed. The ME has been called."

My hands were shaking as I dropped coffee-drenched paper towels into the trash can.

I asked Brady, "So you're thinking she's been dead for a day or two?"

"I'm not calling it, but that's prob'ly right."

"Any sign of Tara?" Conklin asked.

"Not yet."

"Clapper knows?" I said.

"I just told him."

I said, "I spoke to Lucas Burke in his office yesterday. I've got notes and was just going to work up a report."

"What did you think of him?"

"He seemed pissed off at Tara but not worried or too calm."

Brady nodded, said, "Undercovers are watching Burke in case he runs. I'll see you at Baker Beach."

Brady took a call and turned away from us. He was walking back to his office when Conklin said, "Lindsay. Let's go."

I nodded, glanced back at the mess on our desks, and grabbed my jacket. I did a quick inventory to make sure I had my badge, my phone, my gun.

Conklin watched me with concern in his eyes. He wasn't going to say, "Everything's going to be all right."

Instead, he put his hand on my back and guided me toward the door.

"I'll drive," he said.

No objection from me.

CHAPTER 16

THIRTY MINUTES AFTER speaking with Brady, Conklin and I arrived at Baker Beach, a curving acre of sand on the Pacific Coast with the Golden Gate Bridge to the east rising into the morning sky.

The night shift had taped off the parking lot, excluding all but law-enforcement vehicles. I badged the uniform at the cordon. Richie parked the car. I turned off the radio and got slowly out of the car.

Vehicles are not allowed on the beach, but in this case, Claire's team had bypassed the beach ban on vehicles and driven across the sand to the horseshoe of yellow tape, the primary perimeter that took in a section of beach around the victim at the water's edge.

I saw the stoop-shouldered form of Gene Hallows, Crime Lab Director and Clapper's new head of Forensics, standing just outside the tape watching his team take photos, sketch the location, but that's all of the crime scene they'd be processing. No footprints. No car tracks. No other body in the surf.

Four detectives from Northern Station interviewed the growing crowd of surfers and beachcombers and early-morning nudists in the parking lot, towels around their waists. The detectives would be asking people for any information they might have about anyone or anything out of the ordinary.

Good luck with that.

The baby could have been dumped into the water anywhere along South Bay.

Lieutenant Tom Murry came over to me and unofficially passed the baton from Missing Persons to Homicide.

He said, "Freakin' tragedy. I've sent my preliminary report to the chief and copied Brady. We'll keep searching for the child's mother."

I mumbled something like "Monstrous. Keep in touch"—and just then Brady pulled into the lot next to an unmarked police vehicle. Probably Clapper's ride. I saw him crossing the beach below, walking toward Hallows and the CSIs.

Richie and I headed out, crossing the asphalt and walking down a path to the primary scene.

Claire was hunkered down near the body but not touching her. Her techs stood by their vehicle, each holding something; a sheet, a body bag; two of the techs had a stretcher.

Claire was waiting for us to view the body in situ and then she'd take the deceased to the morgue.

Rich headed for the tape and I stood watching the little girl's red hair moving with the action of the surf.

Claire stood up. Of all days to return to a job she loved, her first case was a young child. The grief I felt for a baby I had never known was mirrored in Claire's face.

I reached for Claire and we went into each other's arms.

There would be no happy ending for this dead child. All we could hope for were answers to how, why, and who had ended her precious life.

CHAPTER 17

I STOOD WITH CONKLIN and Hallows outside the barrier tape, only yards from the shoreline where the little girl was in danger of being reclaimed by the tide.

A clean white sheet had been laid out above the waterline, and as I watched the almost living surf bathe the little girl, Clapper broke away from the crowd of CSIs and waded into the water and lifted the child's body out of the ocean.

He walked a dozen yards up the sand and gently placed the little girl on the clean white sheet. If there was any doubt in my mind that this was the same Lorrie Burke I'd seen in the photo Kathleen Wyatt had shown us, it was gone.

Clapper stepped back to let the CSIs take more photos.

He glanced at me and said, "Boxer. You've got your case."

When I didn't answer, he said, "Brady's here, on his way down."

I looked up and saw Brady making his way along the path to the beach. A few yards away from where I stood, Bunny Ellis, Claire's lab assistant, folded the sheet around the child, left side, right side, tucked up over her feet, then turned down over her face.

Hallows unzipped the size small body bag and laid it down next to the sheet. Claire picked up the shrouded body, laid it inside the body bag, and Hallows zipped it, then carried the dead girl's body to the rear doors of the ME's van.

These were solemn moments. No one spoke. Even the people watching from the parking lot up on the bluff were quiet—and then a scream shattered the silence, a woman crying out, "*L-orrrrr—eeee!*"

I looked up toward the parking lot, flicking my gaze over the bystanders. Then I saw her.

Kathleen Wyatt was wearing a blue sweatshirt, a black watch cap, leggings. Even from where I stood a hundred yards away, I could see the anguish on her face.

I started running across the beach, taking the upward path to the parking lot, and Kathleen started running to me. Kathleen was only a few yards away from me. I called her. I meant to comfort her, to let her know that I would tell her everything I learned, as soon as I could. But I didn't get the chance. The doors to the ME's van had closed, and it started up the service road used by the park employee vehicles.

Kathleen evaded me and ran in front of the van. The van squealed to a stop and Wyatt went to the rear and banged on the doors, calling her granddaughter's name.

I pulled her away from the van. Much stronger than Kathleen, I was able to hold her and signal the driver to go.

"I can't leave her alone!" Kathleen wailed. "I have to stay with her!"

"Kathleen, Kathleen," I said, spinning her around so that she was facing me. She looked so stunned, I wasn't sure that she was actually seeing me.

"Kathleen, the medical examiner is one of my best friends. Dr. Washburn is a great woman. She has three kids including a young daughter. Lorrie will be in the best of hands. If we're going to find out who did this to her, we have to know everything we can about her death."

The word "death" was too much. I understood that she couldn't yet absorb the truth.

I said, "Kathleen, I'm the lead investigator on Lorrie's case. I'm going to find out what happened, and I hope to God that we can find Tara alive."

As I held on to the sobbing woman, I wondered, where the hell *was* Tara Burke? I knew little about her. According to her husband, Tara was off her meds, crazed, and had run away with the baby before. According to her mother, Tara had married a bad man. He was unfaithful, and brutal to her and to the child. That he had a girlfriend had been validated, as had his temper, seen in small explosions with strangers. Had Tara actually killed her child? Or had Lucas killed his daughter—and maybe his wife as well?

I was still holding Kathleen, and had cued up the words "I'm going to let you go now. Don't run." But I was stopped by the sound of a racing car motor. I looked up the bluff and saw a silver Audi skid to a halt on the side of the road. A man got out of the driver's side and began gesticulating to the uniformed cop blocking his way.

I couldn't make out the words, but I knew him.

Lucas Burke.

CHAPTER 18

THE SIGHT OF LORRIE BURKE lying dead at the water's edge had infuriated me.

Someone had maliciously killed that helpless little girl, and I was outraged—but I couldn't show it. When I saw Lucas Burke, our number one and only suspect, arguing with a cop in the parking lot, I wanted to throw him down and arrest him.

But I couldn't and didn't.

I kept my grip on Kathleen's biceps as I looked around for my partner, Conklin. Then I saw him far down the beach, conferring with Clapper and Hallows, the three facing the ocean. Clapper was making circular hand motions, no doubt describing the tidal patterns.

Lucas spotted me and called down from the parking area.

Still holding Kathleen by the arm, I turned to look at him. He'd made a megaphone with his hands.

"Sergeant! Is it Lorrie? No one will tell me! This is insane!"

I shouted back, "Hang on! I'm coming up."

Kathleen and I were alone on that footpath. I didn't want to bring her into proximity to her son-in-law and maybe set off a confrontation. Turning to face her, I said, "Kathleen. Wait for me here. I'll be right back."

I had a plan.

I'd get a couple of uniforms to drive her home, and two more would take Lucas to the Hall and hold him until Conklin and I could settle him in the box with a cup of coffee and sweat him until he gave up everything.

My big idea fell apart instantly.

Kathleen jerked away from me and ran up the footpath to the parking lot. She was fast, even at a forty-five-degree uphill sprint on sand. She ducked under the tape, raging, screaming accusations at Lucas. She reached him before I could catch up.

The lot was still filled with sightseers who backed away from Kathleen as she closed in on her son-in-law, cursing him for killing her granddaughter. There was zero proof of this, but it didn't matter to her. She had all the evidence she needed inside her grieving heart.

Lucas yelled back, telling her she was *crazy,* that he had nothing to do with this fucking *tragedy.* To *get the hell away from him* or she would be sorry.

I was still a car's length away from her when she kneed her son-in-law hard in the groin.

He howled, grabbed himself while yowling in pain. But Kathleen wasn't finished. She pulled back her arm and socked him hard in the face.

There was so much ambient sound coming from the lot—talking, shouting, sirens—I didn't hear the impact of her fist connecting with Burke's nose. But I saw it.

Burke cupped his face with his hands and screamed *"Get away from me, you maniac!"* even as Kathleen pulled her fist back, teeing up to punch him again.

I yelled, "Hey, hey," got between them, and at the same time a pair of uniforms pulled Kathleen away. This time it took both strong cops to hold her.

I said to the closest officer, "Drive Ms. Wyatt to her home and sit on her until further notice."

CHAPTER 19

THE TWO UNIFORMS muscled Kathleen Wyatt toward the rear seat of a cruiser, but she was manic, struggling and even biting, until the larger of the two cops said firmly, "Ms. Wyatt. Stop this crap right now or I'm going to cuff you. You're not going to like that."

Those were the magic words. Kathleen sagged and allowed herself to be folded into the back of the car.

Lucas Burke, the "injured party," was pacing, head down, blowing his nose onto the asphalt, blood and tears dripping onto his shirt. I put my hand on his shoulder so that he would look at me.

I said, "I'm sorry, Mr. Burke. The victim is a child who matches Lorrie's description."

He groaned and covered his face with both hands.

"This can't be true," he said. He sobbed that he didn't believe it, that Tara would never let anything happen to Lorrie.

"There's nothing you can do here, Lucas. Come with me. I can answer some of your questions and you can help us, too." I looked at him appraisingly. "Is your nose broken? Do you want to go to the emergency room?"

"No. No."

I suggested taking his car back to the Hall. I would drive. He would sit in the passenger seat.

But again, my brilliant plan fell apart.

The show was over. The tourists were getting into their vehicles. A cop was directing them out of the lot onto Bowley Street, but a traffic jam had formed both inside the lot and beyond, where vehicles had slowed to get a look.

Part of the logjam was caused by a sound truck marked "WKOR." Not even two hours had passed since we got the call. Topside, I saw the press leaving their cars and trucks double-parked and at odd angles, making the road impassable as they stampeded toward the crime-scene tape.

I recognized several of the reporters; they were the A team. The standout of course was Cindy Thomas, tape recorder in her hand, pointing it at Lucas Burke.

It was up to me whether to let the reporters surround Lucas. I let them.

Burke bit.

He stepped up to the barrier tape separating the parking lot from the road.

"I haven't seen her," Lucas was saying to Cindy and the mob in general, "but I've been told that my baby girl is dead. Tell my wife—she has to come home."

It was too much for him. He turned, searched for me among the reporters, and together we pushed our way out to the road.

"Keys?"

He handed them over and got into the passenger seat. If Burke was innocent, if he had truly believed that Lorrie was fine and that he would see her and Tara again soon, he was shocked and horrified and deep in some hell seeing images too awful to bear.

But if he'd actually killed his child, *killed her,* then he was an extraordinary actor. Which some killers are. I needed time with him to figure out which one he was. I needed time to chip away at his story, nail down a timeline. I would need Conklin to befriend him, coax out Lucas's story if I felt my own rage taking over.

I was outside the driver's side of Burke's Audi, on the phone with Conklin, when Lieutenant Brady walked to the tape and addressed the press.

"A child was found dead in the water at six fifteen this morning. Y'all have heard this before. We have no comment on ongoing investigations. Chief Clapper will call a press conference when he has something to tell y'all. Please help us by moving your vehicles out of the road. That's it. Thank you."

Brady ducked under the tape and cleared the lane. We took off toward the Hall.

There was no police radio in the car to distract from the sound of Lucas Burke crying.

God help me, I felt sorry for him.

CHAPTER 20

TWO HOURS AFTER LEAVING Baker Beach, Cindy and art director Jonathan Samuels met with publisher and editor in chief Henry Tyler in his office.

Samuels was a good videographer for a print guy. He had shot and cut the chaotic parking lot melee with Cindy's stand-up Lucas Burke interview into a neat three-minute spot that could be picked up by the media with credit to the *Chronicle*.

Tyler sat behind his desk facing the laptop. Samuels stood behind him, leaning in to bring up the light, push in on Burke or on Cindy at Tyler's direction.

The video would shortly be on the air. Maybe there'd be a miracle. Maybe Tara Burke would see it and step forward.

Cindy sat in the side chair across from them, her elbows on Henry's desk, her chin in her hands. She was aggrieved about the baby, but glad that she and Samuels had scooped other media. She didn't need to see the video again. She could picture it, knew it by heart.

The video began with their arrival at Baker Beach.

The camera was focused on a couple dozen members of the press charging across the road to the parking lot on the bluff overlooking the crime scene.

Cindy had fast-walked beside Samuels, recording her voice-over. "We've just learned that the body of a small child washed up on Baker Beach about an hour ago. Sources tell the *Chronicle* that it is suspected to be that of Lorrie Burke, age one year and four months, last seen alive with her twenty-year-old mother, Tara Burke, forty-eight hours ago.

"I believe the man just beyond the police tape wearing the herringbone jacket is Lucas Burke, Lorrie's father," Cindy said.

The crush of media bumped into Samuels, repeatedly jostling the camera lens. When it steadied, the angle was on Cindy's profile as she called out to Lucas Burke, who was visibly injured. *Broken nose?*

"Mr. Burke, Cindy Thomas, the *Chronicle.* Has the identity of the child—"

"I haven't seen her," Lucas replied.

Samuels had zoomed in on Burke, capturing the bloodied nose, the cheeks slick with tears. And he got the background sounds: police ordering the gathering crowd to stand clear of the tape; competing car horns; the squawking of seabirds protesting the intrusion. Sirens wailing as more law-enforcement vehicles streamed up the road, braked outside the tape, and were then admitted to the parking area.

Cindy heard Howard Bronfman from the *Examiner* shout, "Who found the child?"

"Someone taking a walk," Burke said. "That's all I know."

The background sounds continued as Lieutenant Brady, the senior officer at the scene, appeared.

Samuels had closed in on Brady. He'd been scowling, authoritative, but his slight southern drawl softened his speech. He gave the predictable "no comment at this time" statement, then told all bystanders to clear the road.

Samuels said to Tyler, "I was getting ready to shut down the camera, but Cindy saw Sergeant Boxer walk Burke to this car over here." He pointed to the figures at the top right of the screen. "So, I got this closing shot."

On the video, Burke got into the passenger side door of a late model Audi sedan. Boxer went around to the driver's side, stood outside the door, speaking into her phone with her head down. She tipped her chin up in greeting to Cindy, then disappeared into the car, which headed north on Beach Road.

"Nice," Tyler said.

He watched the last section of the video. Cindy stood in a secluded spot with the ocean and the silhouette of the bridge at her back. She brought the viewers up-to-date on the story as she knew it, adding, "Tara Burke has not been seen or heard from since Monday morning when her husband left for work. If anyone has seen Tara Burke or knows of her whereabouts, please contact this paper and the SFPD hotline.

"All calls will be kept confidential."

Phone numbers appeared on a black screen and then faded out.

Tyler said to Cindy and Samuels, "Well done, both of you. Cindy, write it up and we'll get it on the front page. Samuels, I want to see two or three compelling images to accompany the story. I'll choose one. Upload the video to our YouTube channel and have promo send it to the network affiliates."

"Can and will do," said Samuels. "Give me ten minutes."

He left in a hurry.

"So what do you think happened?" Henry Tyler asked Cindy. "Did the mother do this? Or was it the father? Or some random maniac who didn't even know them?"

Cindy had a strong feeling that the death of Lorrie Burke was going to be a big story, whoever had killed her. She remembered awful crimes that appeared to be like this one, unjustified killings of small children by one parent who'd snapped. Or worse, had made plans to kill the child or children because of mental illness, psychopathy, desire to send the child to God, where the precious one would be safe from earthly harm. Or just because being a parent was too damned much trouble.

"God willing," she replied to Tyler, "whoever did this will be caught, tried, and locked up in a cell the size of a walnut shell for life."

CHAPTER 21

I HAVE A CLEAR VIEW from my desk of everything in the bullpen, including Brady's office and the front entrance.

Brady and Clapper stood together just outside the doorway, speaking too softly for me to hear.

Something had happened. I was sure of it.

I heard Clapper say, "You'll take care of it?"

After Brady nodded, the chief headed upstairs to what I still thought of as Jacobi's office. Brady came through the gate, stopped at Brenda's desk, picked up Wednesday-morning messages and mail, then came over to me.

"Got a minute?" he asked.

I nodded and directed his attention to the TV on the wall overhead. "You're on the tube."

Brady sat down in Conklin's chair, swiveled it, and tilted it back so he could see the TV on the wall overhead. He punched up the sound, watched himself telling the media gaggle that he had no information for them at this time.

"I look awful," he said.

He did. There were sweat stains under his arms, sleep in the corners of his eyes, and his hair was mussed, not throwing off its customary platinum sheen. But mostly, he looked depressed. Brady picked up the remote, muted the sound, and asked me where Conklin was.

"Burke had to clean himself up. Conklin's getting him a clean T-shirt."

Brady picked up Conklin's desk phone and called Brenda.

"Brenda, when you see Conklin, call me," Brady said.

To me he said, "Come on back to the executive suite."

"Sure."

I followed Brady along the center aisle of the empty bullpen to the lieutenant's glass-walled bread box of an office at the bullpen's rear corner with its dingy view of the elevated freeway. This office used to be mine, but I'd been glad to give it up and everything that came with it. I've never regretted that decision.

Brady opened a desk drawer and slid a pile of yellow legal pads off the desktop into the drawer. He inserted a flash drive into his computer, no doubt photos of the crime scene, then folded his hands on his desk.

What had I done now? We had Burke in custody. Claire was doing her workup on the victim. Parisi was getting warrants so we could search Burke's house and car and grab his computer while we were at it. I'd started writing up our reports, and I'd spoken with Lieutenant Murry, who had expanded his search area and was still looking for Tara Burke, alive or dead.

Conklin and I were on track so far.

"Something wrong, lieu?"

"Cookie?" he said. He offered me an open tin of sugar cookies, all different shapes. I picked a squiggly one with a jelly button in the center.

Brady picked one with sprinkles.

He shoved the whole thing into his mouth and washed it down with cold coffee. After he swallowed, he said, "I'm setting up a task force in the interest of finding Tara Burke. You and me, Boxer, we're partners again, at least for a while until we solve this case. Or maybe longer."

"What? I mean, whatever you say, Brady, but what about Conklin?"

I like and trust Brady, and we'd been partners for a short while years ago. But at that time, I was the senior partner. Now, Brady outranked me and would have the first and last word. I reported to him and he wasn't asking for my opinion. But I didn't like the way this new arrangement felt. A dark thought occurred to me.

Was this Clapper's idea of keeping me on a leash?

Brady said, "We're adding a new person to Homicide. Name is Sonia Alvarez and she's coming here from Las Vegas PD. Clapper knows her, thinks highly of her, introduced her to Conklin by conference call, let them know they're going to be partners."

"Yikes."

"It's too soon to say how it will work out," Brady said. "So back to what I was saying. Task force. You and me, Conklin and Alvarez, and Missing Persons. If Murry's team doesn't turn up Tara Burke and fast, you and I will be point men for every other cop in the department. Any questions?"

"Does Conklin know?"

"I'm gonna tell him. You and I will interview Burke. Conklin will observe, and as soon as Alvarez gets here, we'll start breaking her in."

It felt like I was supposed to salute.

But I kept my wits about me and went back to my desk to wait for Conklin. I had just a few minutes to digest this sour news and get back to work.

Tara Burke was still missing and suspect number one was in the house.

CHAPTER 22

CLAIRE PLACED HER HAND on the dead child's forehead.

"Sorry," she said. "Sorry that this happened to you, little one."

She took another photo of the baby girl's face and tucked the drape around her. Then, Claire shucked her gown, cap, and mask, dropped them into the laundry bin, stripped off her gloves and disposed of them in the trash.

The autopsy suite was kept at fifty degrees, and Claire was cold inside and out. The unnatural and premature deaths of children made her sick. Even after all the decades in med school followed by work at Metro Hospital, followed by the time and bodies she'd autopsied as chief ME, she still couldn't get used to it. If she were alone right now, she would cry.

Bunny Ellis, Claire's morgue tech, was dropping the instruments into the autoclave.

"Doctor, ready for me to put the patient away?"

"Only if you want five gold stars and lunch on me."

"Stars, yes. Lunch, maybe some other day."

"Gotcha," said Claire. "Thanks, Bunny. I'll be in my office."

Claire pushed open the swinging doors, and when she was outside in the corridor, she leaned against the wall for a moment to collect herself, then headed to her office. She sat in her swivel desk chair and called Lindsay's cell.

Lindsay picked up.

"Claire. Can I call you back? This is a bad time."

"I need thirty seconds. Just give me that."

"Go."

Claire said, "Lorrie Annette Burke was a well-nourished Caucasian female about a year and a half old, twenty-two pounds. The manner of death is pending.

"This part is not for dissemination. Lorrie Burke's death appears to be consistent with homicide. There's some bruising around the mouth, petechial hemorrhaging in and around the eyes. She was smothered, Lindsay. Looks like with a hand over her mouth and nose. There are fingerprint bruises on her right upper arm as though she was jerked or possibly held down.

"There was no water in her lungs. She was dead when she went into the ocean, and I can't establish time of death with real accuracy due to the water temperature and bloating of the body, but I'm estimating thirty hours ago more or less. Enough time in the water for sea predators to nibble at her fingers. Her blood is going out to the lab now. She looks very much like her photo, but you may need to identify her by DNA.

"How many seconds was that?"

"Just the right number. And you've got me thinking that Lorrie was alive for about a day after going missing. Thanks, Butterfly."

After they ended the call, Claire went to the washroom and splashed water on her face.

She was having some just discernable pain in her chest, which was to be expected after her recent surgery. She had been told not to exert herself by her surgeon, her husband, her best friends, and her oldest child, and here she was worn out before noon. She needed to take a nap.

Back at her desk, Claire opened the intake folder and looked at the list. There were three patients needing her attention. None of them, thank God, were children.

If she did one more post now and called in her backup pathologist, barring complications she could be home in bed in four hours.

Yeah, right.

Going by past experience, that would never happen.

CHAPTER 23

BRADY AND I WERE in Interview 1, sitting across the table from Lucas Burke.

It's a small room, ten by twelve with gray-painted cinder block walls, a camera in one corner of the ceiling, two chairs on each long side of the gray metal table, and a shelf under the one-way mirror inset into a wall. There's a narrow observation room behind the glass.

Richie Conklin was observing. I liked, trusted, and respected Brady and we had done many interrogations together. But I felt for Conklin. When Brady informed him about the task force and that he would be working with a new partner, he'd said okay, but he couldn't have taken this news as anything but a demotion.

I felt Clapper's hand in this shake-up, but right now I had to focus on this critical opportunity to interview Burke while he was vulnerable. Burke would have a hard time lying to us without being called out.

A tried-and-true method of police interrogation

involved manipulation of the suspect, namely to make him comfortable. Make him your friend. Give him a way out so that he would tell the truth before the hammer came down.

There were rougher, more intimidating methods, but "Let's be friends" seemed appropriate protocol with this man in this circumstance.

I asked Burke if he needed anything.

"Coffee? Tea?"

"I can't stay here," he said. "Call me when you know something."

Brady said, "Mr. Burke, I know you'd like to be anyplace but here. Understand that the more focused we are during these critical first hours, the better our chances of finding Tara alive and maybe Lorrie's killer. Okay?"

Burke sighed deeply and said, "I can barely think straight, but go ahead. Ask me and make it fast."

"Now I'm sorry, but I have to show you a picture."

"Of Lorrie?"

Brady nodded at me.

The morgue photo Claire had sent me was on my phone. I took the phone out of my jacket pocket, brought up Lorrie's image, and passed my phone across the table to Burke. He looked at the photo, rocked back in his chair, cried out "Noooooooooo," and then slapped my phone facedown on the table.

"That's her," he said, weeping. "I need to go home."

Brady said, "You're free to go, Mr. Burke. But, did you understand what I said? A half hour answering our questions may help us get the bastard who did this. We need your help."

Brady and I took turns tossing questions; softballs at first.

Who were Tara's friends? Names of her relatives? Did

you have a housekeeper? A nanny? Can you account for your time on Sunday, Mr. Burke? What were your movements on Monday after your fight with Tara?

And then Brady started pitching hard balls right across the plate. *Can anyone confirm your whereabouts on Sunday? On Monday?*

Do you know of anyone who wanted to hurt her? Who do you think killed your child?

Assuming she's alive, where could Tara be?

Isn't it true that you have a girlfriend and you want to marry her?

"Mr. Burke," said Brady, standing at the table, throwing a menacing shadow over Lucas Burke. "Isn't it true that you wanted to move on with your life and Tara was in the way?"

"You can go straight to hell," said Burke. He pushed back his chair and moved toward the door.

CHAPTER 24

I WAS THE SO-CALLED good cop in this setting.

I headed Burke off and stepped between him and the door, saying, "Come on, Lucas. We're on your side. We're frustrated, too. You don't want to leave us without a lead to Lorrie's killer, do you?

"Come on. Sit down. Look," I said, "I still have your car keys." I dug into my pants pocket and showed him his car keys. I stepped away from the door and put the keys on the table.

Burke glared at me, at Brady, at the keys, and then sat back down and angrily answered our questions.

"I don't know who killed Lorrie. If I did, I'd kill him myself and happily go to prison. The last time Tara ran away she went to the outlet mall out in Livermore, but by now she's probably run out of cash. So where is she? I don't know. But you know what I think? I think a total stranger kidnapped Tara and killed my little girl."

I asked, "Have you received a call or a note from anyone asking for ransom?"

"No. But that doesn't mean she's not a captive. Tara is a big flirt," he said with a growl. "She flaunted her wild side. Makes total sense to me that she caught the attention of a psycho. She could have been buying all that makeup and underwear to show herself off. She's trusting. Naive. Maybe she has a boyfriend. Maybe Lorrie wouldn't stop crying. Oh, God. I don't want to think about that. Is this what you want to know?"

Lucas's ramblings made no rational sense, except as a glimpse inside his clearly conflicted mind.

I said, "Back to you, Mr. Burke. We've been told that you're seeing one of your students."

The photo of the note was on my phone. I found it, showed it to Burke. I read it out loud.

"Dear Misty, I'm in love with you. I promise that I will be free and we will be able to get married by the end of the school year. Love, Luke."

"Look, it's a fling. Misty is in my creative writing class. She's very dramatic and we were playing at elopement. It was stupid of me, but as God is my witness, I had no intention of leaving Tara. Misty knows it wasn't real. Ask her."

"I intend to do just that," I said.

"Tara is a terrible pain in the ass," he said, "but I still love her."

Brady said, "I had a bad marriage once, and I understand the pressure you've been under. But you have to come clean with us. Maybe something with you and Tara got out of hand. Did she attack you? Come at you with something heavy? Point a gun? Did you have to protect yourself? Is that how it happened? Because if that's the story, we can help you, Mr. Burke."

"No. No, no, no."

Brady said, "Your mother-in-law has filed reports against you for abusing Tara. Any truth to that?"

"No, damn it. I was not charged. Tara didn't accuse me; it was her nutty mother. Tara and I had a fight about money, that's all. Shouting and door slamming. Both of us. I left her in the kitchen crying and that's all I know."

Brady was still standing.

He unhitched a pair of cuffs from a belt loop and told Burke to stand up and put his hands behind his back.

"We're holding you as a material witness while we check out your story."

"I don't get it. You said I could leave," Burke said, not moving.

"Changed my mind. You have a right to have an attorney," Brady said, and then continued reading the man his rights. "Do you understand your rights?"

"You're not charging me, but you're holding me?"

"You're a material witness, sir. Last one to see your wife and daughter. We have to verify your story, and as soon as we're satisfied we'll either charge you or release you. Hands behind your back."

Burke looked up at the two of us. He wasn't a big man, while Brady's arms are massive and I'm a fit five foot ten. The door was locked. Burke didn't stand a chance of getting out.

He stood and put his hands behind his back. Brady cuffed him and left me with Burke while he went to get guards to take Burke to holding on the sixth floor.

"This is for your own good, Mr. Burke. If we don't find evidence of your involvement in murder or kidnapping, you'll be in the clear. Meanwhile you'll have a cell of your own. I'd advise you to sleep. Do you have a lawyer?"

"Divorce lawyer, that's all."

Interesting. "You want to call him or do you want a—"

"Harold Tish. Number's on my phone."

I used Burke's phone, tapped on Tish's saved number, and when a receptionist answered, I said that Lucas Burke was calling. When Tish got on the line, I put him on speakerphone and held Burke's phone up to his face so he could hire his lawyer. When the arrangements were made, Burke was escorted to his cell.

What did all of this boil down to?

We had nothing on Burke. But we had *him*. And we were just getting started.

CHAPTER 25

RICH CONKLIN AND HIS new partner, Inspector Sonia Alvarez, sat in Brady's glass office, waiting for him to arrive. Conklin had met her at the elevator a minute earlier and walked her back to the corner office. He sized her up as they waited together in awkward silence.

He guessed she was mid-thirties, about five six, 130. Looked strong. Had an efficient haircut, no makeup, but her great big eyes made up for it. She wore Dockers and a man-tailored shirt, serious cross-trainers, a necklace with a little charm: horseshoe, presumably for good luck. No other jewelry that he could see. His impression was of a good-looking girl in a tough job with no interest in drawing attention to herself.

Conklin said, "So, Vice, right, Alvarez? Was this sudden? Or you've been planning to make a change?"

"Sudden, yah. Chief Clapper calls me Monday and makes me an offer. I mean, took me a couple of days to process, but it's time to switch things up. I've been living in Vegas most of my life. My cousin is putting me up for a while. You like it here?"

"San Francisco? Or SFPD?"

"How about both?"

"God, yeah on both."

Alvarez said, "Anything you think I should know?"

"I mean, it's hard and we've been stretched for a while, but it's a clean operation."

Christ. What was he supposed to tell her? He didn't know what Clapper had in mind for him. Brady, either. He glimpsed Brady through the glass wall as he strode up the center aisle and came through the open door.

"You two have met. Good."

Brady closed the door, introduced himself to Alvarez. They shook hands and he told her to sit back down and he'd take her through a four-minute orientation. After that, Conklin would bring her into the loop.

Alvarez sat erect in her chair as Brady gave her a shorthand introduction to the Homicide squad, the new organization, and the case she would be working on as part of the Burke investigation task force.

"Conklin will give you the case details."

He drew boxes on a yellow pad with a red grease pencil, connected the boxes with lines. An organization chart. He turned the pad to Alvarez.

Conklin noticed that the box around Alvarez's name was drawn with a dotted line. He gave her a quick look and she returned it.

Brady saw the looks and fielded them.

He said, "When I came here from Miami PD I was in rotation until it all came together. I worked with Conklin as a matter of fact, worked with his partner Sergeant Boxer, and also with the lieutenant, Jacobi. So, it's a two-way street, Alvarez, up to a point. We'll try to make a good fit, but most important, right now is to find Tara Burke, wherever she is."

Conklin knew that he and Boxer were ideal partners. They picked up on each other's verbal and visual cues, knew when to step forward, stand back, draw their guns.

This was just too sudden.

He heard Brady ask him to take Alvarez back to his desk and summarize the case of the missing wife and child, the discovery of Lorrie Burke, and the interview with Lucas Burke, now on the sixth floor in holding.

Alvarez said, "Thanks for the opportunity, sir."

When his phone rang, Brady took the call.

"Okay, Brenda. I'll tell them."

He hung up and said, "Young lady by the name of Johanna Weber is wanting to talk to us. She says she's Tara Burke's bestie. Welcome to Homicide, Alvarez."

CHAPTER 26

BEFORE ENTERING INTERVIEW 2 with Conklin, Alvarez said, "What do we know about Tara Burke?"

"Very little, but I'll take the lead and feel our way."

"Okay, but I reserve the right to jump in anytime." She grinned, but she meant it.

"No problem," he said.

Conklin opened the door and saw Johanna Weber, Tara Burke's self-described best friend, sitting at the table. She was dressed in jeans and a T-shirt, had blue-streaked hair, and was tapping on her phone, fingers flying.

She looked up and Conklin made the introductions. When he and Alvarez were seated, he said, "Ms. Weber, you have something to tell us about Tara Burke?"

"I hope," she said. "Anything I can tell you to help find her, I will. She was like my sister and we shared everything."

Conklin said, "You mind if I ask you some questions, get them out of the way?"

"No, go ahead."

"Do you know where Tara is?"

"I wish I did. I'm very, very worried. I haven't heard from her since the weekend. Her mailbox is full."

Alvarez said, "Okay to call you Johanna?"

The young woman nodded.

"What can you tell us about Tara?"

"We've been friends since the sixth grade. Like, close. We used to double date, and I was her bridesmaid—"

"What's her marriage like, Johanna?" Alvarez asked. "Do you have any idea?"

"They definitely have problems. Lucas is like, what, twenty years older than us? To be honest, I think she may have been hooking up with someone on the side. And no, she never told me who. She was teasing me, with like 'Ooooooh, someone likes me.' So, why was she saying that? I don't know. I really don't know."

Conklin watched as Johanna pulled her hair back from her face and twisted it and then kept talking. "I really think Lucas loves her and Tara tortures him. She just thinks faster, like, runs circles around him and whatever. And Tara told me that she thinks Lucas has a girlfriend, so like that's not cool, either."

Alvarez said, "I'm new to this case, Johanna, so tell me more about Tara. Why would she have a boyfriend when she's only been married for a short time? Three years?"

"Three years and two months. She might do it to get Lucas mad. That's the kind of thing she might do, like the way she never locks the doors on their house. And she showed me a bruise on her wrist once. I don't know if Lucas did it, but I asked her. Listen, she's very cute. You've seen her picture? Then, you know. Guys were always hitting on her."

Conklin said, "I just want your opinion, Johanna. Do you think Lucas would hurt Tara?"

She shook her head no, vigorously. Johanna said, "If anything, he loved her too much."

"You know that the baby was found today. Lorrie's dead."

Johanna Weber's eyes filled with tears. Her mouth quavered. Alvarez said, "Okay, okay," while Conklin found a package of tissues on the shelf under the mirror.

Alvarez said, "In your opinion, could Tara have hurt her baby, say in a fit of anger, or even by accident?"

"No, not ever. She loves LuLu. If something happened, Tara would take her to the hospital so fast." Johanna dried her eyes and then said to Conklin, "Tara's dead, isn't she? She's been killed."

Conklin said, "We're looking for her. Every cop in San Francisco is looking for her."

She thanked him and he thanked her, gave her his card, and told her to call if she thought of anything, heard anything, anything at all. He told her he'd walk her out and said to Alvarez, "I'll be right back."

Conklin returned with his laptop and loaded the video of Brady and Lindsay's interview with Burke. He played it for Alvarez.

"Let's see the Burke interview. I need to hear him, watch him."

Conklin hit a few keys and the video came up. Brady and Lindsay started by going easy on Burke, then working him over. The video ended with Burke in cuffs on his way up to holding.

Conklin said, "So what are you thinking?"

Alvarez said, "He's believable. If he's lying, he could be a movie star."

Said Conklin, "Academy Award. At least a Golden Globe."

Alvarez said, "So, what now, partner?"

"Let's see what Brady wants us to do."

CHAPTER 27

BRADY AND I WAITED in an unmarked Chevy in front of Lucas and Tara Burke's house on Dublin Street.

It was a fairy-tale house: small, baby blue with gables, bay windows, and a white picket fence. It didn't look like even mice were killed here.

We'd gotten all we could get from Lucas Burke as a material witness, and his attorney had sprung his client from our humble jail in under twenty-four hours.

At that time, Burke had given us his verbal consent to search his house, even turned over his keys. But if we found evidence, Burke's attorney would move to exclude it because we'd had no warrant. I could hear it now. *My client's baby had been murdered. The police say, "Okay if we go through your house? See if Tara left a note, anything like that. Clear up some questions?" Mr. Burke should have said "Get a warrant," but he was grieving. And he was not under arrest. Because he's innocent and the police had no probable cause.*

Clapper said, "We have no choice. Brady, keep

eyes on him. Night shift. Swing shift. We do what we can do."

Meanwhile, three days after she'd left home with Lorrie, Tara was still missing. On that basis, most judges would approve a search.

We'd been waiting in our car for hours.

If I were a smoker, I'd have gotten out of the car and lit up. But I didn't smoke, and Brady and I both stink at small talk. So we listened to radio calls and stared out at McLaren Park across the street, a rolling 320 acres of grassy heaven. (Assuming you didn't know about the bodies buried in that park that once went undiscovered for decades.)

I thought of the murdered baby and her young missing mother and asked myself if, by the end of the day, we would have probable cause to charge Lucas Burke for the murder of one or both.

My phone buzzed and I grabbed it off the dash.

"I'm ten minutes out," Yuki said.

"Good. And thank God."

"Thank me later," she said with a laugh.

I told Brady and he grunted, looked at his watch. The CSI van appeared, flashed its lights at the reporters blocking the way, and pulled up to the curb bordering the park. Crime Lab Director Hallows and CSI Culver got out of the van as ADA Yuki Castellano's Toyota pulled up behind us.

"Record time," I said to Brady.

Yuki passed papers through the driver's-side window to my CO, who was also her husband. Brady unfolded the warrant.

"Judge Hoffman signed here, here, and here," Yuki said, then she summarized. We had twenty-four hours to go through Burke's house. We could open closed closets, cabinets, drawers, and doors. Could confiscate electronic devices and weapons. Without knocking out walls or otherwise damaging property, CSU could test for anything that might indicate evidence of crime.

Brady and I got out of the car. He put an arm around Yuki, squeezed her shoulders, and kissed the top of her head. Then he crossed the street to speak with Hallows. Yuki and I leaned against the Chevy while I phoned Conklin, who was at the top of the street, our outer perimeter.

I watched him duck under the tape and hold it up for Inspector Sonia Alvarez. Conklin introduced Alvarez to Yuki, and from the way she walked, talked, and handled herself, I thought Alvarez seemed all right. A straight shooter.

Brady joined us to say, "Hallows and Culver are ready for the walk-through. Any questions?" he asked Alvarez.

"No, sir. I've done this before."

Brady sent Conklin and Alvarez to cover the rear door of the small two-story house. I peered through the front window and saw no sign that anyone was home. But to be on the safe side, Brady pulled his gun.

He said, "Are we feeling lucky?"

"Very."

I stepped forward, knocked on the dark blue front door, and announced. When no one answered, I did it again. This time, I heard footsteps and the sound of the chain lock coming off the door, its brass knocker shaped like a fist. The door swung open. And there he was in the doorway, Lucas Burke.

"What do you want?"

Brady said, "We have warrants to search your house, Mr. Burke. This could take a long time, probably overnight. Is there somewhere you can stay? Or I can have an officer drive you to a hotel."

"The hell you will. Do you understand? My baby girl is dead. I have to make arrangements. I'm in mourning. And look at this mob outside. Reporters, for God's sake. My neighbors are seeing this. You're ruining my life!"

Brady said, "We're very sorry, but we need to go through your house. For your sake as well as ours, you shouldn't be here."

Burke slammed the door in our faces, but just before Brady kicked it in, it opened again without the chain. Burke brushed past us, strode angrily to his vehicle. He revved his engine, honked his horn at the press, and when he had an opening, he hit the gas and his car shot up the street like it was a lit fuse.

CHAPTER 28

BRADY HOLSTERED HIS GUN and deployed us from the entranceway; Conklin, Alvarez, and Hallows headed up the stairs while Brady, CSI Culver, and I clung to the ground-floor perimeter.

The living room was small and tidy but not obsessively so, with an ExerSaucer visible in the center. A slate blue corduroy three-seater couch, with matching chairs, was angled toward the fireplace and the TV mounted above it and there were framed family photos on the mantel. To the left, Lorrie was pictured with a stuffed animal, with Lucas and Tara to the right in a traditional just-married pose.

I turned away from the photos and looked for signs of violence, but saw none. No holes in the walls, no blood spatter on the ceiling, no bloody smears on the edge of the coffee table, no wet spots on the carpet. The fireplace tool caddy looked full. The bookshelves didn't swing open to reveal a hidden room.

I took notes. Culver documented the living room with his Nikon, then stood in the doorway to the den as Brady and I went inside.

"This is depressing," he said.

"How so?"

"I'm seeing phantoms, Boxer. Burke getting dressed for work. Tara making breakfast. Not speaking."

"And Lorrie?"

"I just see her beached."

Me, too.

We took opposite sides of the room, and did a search for weapons or incriminating messages, like a note from Burke's girlfriend saying, "*It's now or never.*" Or from Tara. "*It's over, you jerk. Drop dead.*" Found zip. The desk drawers and file cabinets held graded classwork and warranties for household maintenance. Insurance policies. I took a look: whole life, quarter of a million each on Tara and on Lucas Burke. No policy on the baby. If Tara was dead, Burke was in the chips unless he killed her. I confiscated the policies.

"No laptop," said Brady. "He stashed it somewhere. Work? In his car?"

"I say it's with Burke. Let's see the kitchen," I said. "Knives live there."

Along the way, I stopped to talk to Culver, who was crouched half in, half out of the hall closet.

"Lookit this," he said, smiling brightly. "We've got video."

"Show me."

I saw what looked like a DVR for an old security system.

Culver said, "Just the one camera over the front door. Low-tech, motion activated, and it was running."

"Good catch."

Culver reversed the recording so I could see what he'd already watched.

He narrated.

"So here's Burke on Monday morning. He leaves

the house alone at seven forty a.m. The camera is not positioned to show me Burke's expression, but he's in a hurry, carrying a computer bag. Car keys in his hand."

As Culver talked, I watched Burke come out of the house alone, not locking the door, carrying only a laptop bag. He got into his silver Audi and zoomed out of the frame.

Culver said, "And here comes Tara."

He forwarded the video. The time stamp read 8:12. Tara was wearing a denim dress, low heels, bouncing the baby against her right hip, her handbag in her left hand. As Tara's friend Johanna had said, the young mother was pretty. Her car, a red Volvo, was in the short driveway.

Tara put her bag down on the asphalt, strapped the baby into a rear-facing car seat, then returned to the house and came out again carrying a diaper bag and an overnight case, which she put in the trunk.

Tara got into the driver's seat. I could see her checking on the baby, then carefully backing out and making a reverse K-turn on Dublin Street. She headed downhill in the opposite direction her husband had taken.

As with Lucas, the camera angle was all wrong for seeing faces, but her actions and body language were clear.

She was not distressed or in a panic. And the carry-on showed Tara Burke had planned to be gone for *some* period of time.

Maybe not forever, but surely overnight.

CHAPTER 29

CONKLIN SHOUTED DOWN to us from the top of the stairs.

"I need you to see something!"

I followed Brady up the staircase and found Conklin at the closet across from the bathroom. It was filled with linens and cleaning supplies. Conklin pointed to a crumpled-up blanket on the closet floor. It was crib-sized, pink, and patterned with bunnies.

Conklin said, "That blanket must have been there since Tara and Lorrie left the house on Monday. I want to see inside of it."

Culver took a few shots of the blanket and then Rich carefully unfolded it with his gloved hands. A little pile of feces was in the center of the folds, like the fortune inside the cookie.

Kathleen Wyatt had told me that Tara and Lorrie had been abused, that Lorrie was sometimes locked in the closet for crying. The soiled blanket was suspicious—but by itself proved nothing.

"She could have taken it out of the baby's crib and

thrown it into the closet," I said, but I made note of it in my book.

This dollhouse of a home had no basement, no attic, the eaves were enclosed with sheetrock. So, after checking out the upstairs rooms and finding no bodies or signs of any, we cops left the house to CSU, stood near our cars, and brainstormed, theorized, hypothesized.

Where had Tara gone? Had she left Burke? How had she gotten separated from Lorrie? Had she and Lucas been in touch since Monday morning?

That was an interesting thought but took me nowhere.

The trees in the park were alive with the light rustling of leaves and the sweet sounds of birdsong. It was the kind of day that made you think that nothing bad could ever happen here.

And then Brady's phone buzzed.

He answered, "What's up?"

His face went rigid. He said, "I got it. I got it. Wait, let me get the coordinates again." He slapped his shirt pocket, got back into the car, opened the console, and was reaching for the glove box when I handed him a pen and my notepad. Brady scribbled and said, "Thanks. See you later."

He clicked off and went into deep thought.

I said, "Brady? What happened?"

"That was Teller."

"Teller?"

"A CSI. A body was found on the eastern side of the park. Female."

"Is it Tara?"

"Don't know. Lady walking her dog found a girl's body in a shallow grave. Throat cut. I've called for backup."

What the hell was this?

Had Burke killed Tara and buried her in the park? And now that bastard was loose? My mind was ranging, trying to take in this new information and make sense of it.

I needed to see the victim.

I stuck with Brady as we all followed Hallows along a trail into the lush greensward. We'd walked for no more than five or six minutes when we reached a half dozen CSIs who'd roped off the area around the body.

My heart was pounding, but Brady was a brick. He had a quiet word with the CSIs that boiled down to "We'll take it from here."

I edged close enough to the deceased to see that she was partially covered with soil and leaves. But she was exposed enough that I could see that she was naked. Her throat had been cut on an angle and her breasts had been sliced, in no discernible pattern. From where I was standing, only her profile was visible.

I stared up as a news chopper hovered overhead. Then Clapper drove up in his car, lights flashing.

Ready or not, this gruesome murder was about to go public.

CHAPTER 30

CLAPPER LOOKED OVER the partially exposed and mutilated body and made a general announcement.

"Listen up, everyone. You know the rules. Play dumb. Do not speak to the media or anyone else. I'll make an announcement after the vic has been identified and next of kin notified."

I decided to get out ahead of the ID I knew was coming. I said, "I can notify her mother. I know her."

This would be a horrible job. Kathleen would go insane, but I thought it better for me to deliver the news than a stranger. Just then, a CSI appeared at Clapper's elbow saying, "Sir, we found something."

"Go ahead. What is it?"

"A pile of women's clothes. All folded neatly. I looked in the handbag. Here's her license."

Clapper took the license by the edges from the CSI's gloved hand. As he looked at it, a muscle twitched in his cheek.

"This license belongs to a Wendy Franks," said Clapper. "She resembles Tara Burke. But, her nose.

The width of her forehead…" Clapper stooped down and held the driver's license, containing the requisite California state seals and holographs, near the dead woman's face.

"Unless her prints say otherwise, the victim is Wendy Franks."

Things went a little crazy about then, everyone talking at once, firing off opinions, comparing the DMV photo to the victim's face. I looked at the license in Clapper's hand and said, "Wendy Franks had brown eyes and was five nine. From her description, Tara Burke has blue eyes. She's five six."

Alvarez said, "So, is Franks's death a mistaken-identity situation? Or was her death totally unrelated?"

The CSI said, "I took a shot of the clothes."

I peered at his image on his phone, saw a folded green striped dress, sandals, a brown shoulder bag. Not the clothes Tara was wearing on the video from Monday morning.

More confirmation.

The dead woman wasn't Tara. Period.

Claire and several of her techs joined us graveside. She greeted those of us she knew and began shooting pictures of the deceased in situ, while Hallows's team did the same.

I paced away from the body, looked at my watch every five minutes. Conklin and Alvarez were talking together under a tree. Brady stood with Clapper and Culver, and so forty-five minutes passed.

When the scene had been photographed from every angle, Claire and a tech carefully lifted the dead woman from her shallow grave and placed her onto a sheet.

I stooped next to Claire as she wrapped the body.

"Can you estimate time of death if I don't hold you to it?"

"Swear it's between you and me, Lindsay. Because I'm not ready to retire."

"Promise," I said.

"The young lady is out of rigor. I'd say she died twenty-four hours ago and you don't need me to tell you cause or manner of death. Once I've got her on my table, I'll do a preliminary workup."

Brady joined us.

Claire said, "You're gonna want a cheek swab from Burke. Maybe she scratched the bastard as he was killing her. Maybe he left a trace behind. Or maybe he didn't do it."

Leaving Brady at the scene, I hitched a ride back to the Hall with Conklin and Alvarez. I slumped against the back seat, just thinking. Lucas Burke had been released more than twenty-four hours ago. He'd had time to kill her, barely. Maybe.

But had he done it?

And if so, why?

Had Franks witnessed something she wasn't supposed to see?

CHAPTER 31

CINDY WAS AT HER DESK, laser-focused on her work, when a static storm crackled over her police scanner.

The signal faded, came back strong, and she could make out a few words. Piecing sentence fragments together, she gathered that a deceased female had turned up in McLaren Park. She listened, hoping for more information. A voice over the radio sputtered the name "Tara Burke."

Cindy fell back in her chair.

She righted her chair, spun around to where the radio sat on the windowsill, and fiddled with the channel dial in search of a clear signal but didn't get it. She ran out to the newsroom, found Jonathan Samuels at his desk and told him what she'd heard. He opened a file drawer, grabbed his camera, and said, "All set."

The two had picked up the portable scanner, left the *Chronicle* building, and gone directly to the underground parking garage across the street. By the time they were strapped in and heading toward the park, the name Tara Burke had been withdrawn.

"Correction...vic...unidentified."

Cindy said, "That's messed up. How'd they get that so wrong?"

"Overexcitement," Samuels said, "and bias confirmation. Slow down, will you?"

Cindy eased up on the gas. Her urgency had cooled, but who, what, where, when, and why was still news. According to the scanner chatter, this was likely just another homicide who'd been buried in the greens and brambles of McLaren Park.

Traffic flowed and soon the car was closing in on the Burkes' gabled house.

Samuels said, "Up ahead."

She said, "Good catch," and turned down the radio. Two blocks away, police vehicles were pulling away from the curb near the park, streaming toward them, then, passing them.

"There's our story," she said. "We just have to get it."

Cindy parked the car on the street opposite three marked CSI vehicles, a K9 transport vehicle, and some cruisers.

Samuels hung his press pass on a cord around his neck, Cindy pinned hers to her jacket, and together they crossed the street toward the law-enforcement vehicles. Cindy picked out the youngest of the uniformed officers who was standing alone, thumbing his phone.

"Hi there," she said. "I'm Cindy Thomas with the *San Francisco Chronicle*."

He said, "How can I help you?"

"I'm covering this crime. What can you tell me about what happened here?"

"I'm not authorized to do that."

"Okay, but, if I don't know your name . . . ?"

"Hah-hah. No. Sorry."

"Okay then. Mind if we just take a walk in the park?"

"Not in the crime scene, uh, Cindy. Off-limits until CSU is done here."

That's when Cindy noticed a woman sitting on her porch across the street, watching all of it.

Cindy said, "Thanks anyway," and she and Samuels crossed to the wood frame house with a small porch and front garden.

Calling up to the woman in the rocking chair, Cindy said, "Hi there. We're from the *Chronicle*. May we talk with you for a minute?"

The woman answered, "Come on up. See the gate latch? There you go. I'm in no rush."

Introductions were made. It seemed Ms. Milissa Goeden, retired social worker, knew of Cindy, read her column, and was, in fact, a fan.

"I'm the one who found her," said Ms. Goeden. "Well, Sparky did." She petted the head of her cocker spaniel lying at her feet. "That poor girl."

Ms. Goeden used her finger to mimic a blade slashing across a neck.

Samuels said, "That's awful. You didn't by chance learn her name?"

"I was there when they found her driver's license. She's somebody Franks. Candy. No, no. Wendy. Wendy Franks. After that, it was 'Thanks for being a good citizen, ma'am. Now get out of our crime scene.'"

Cindy said, "We're familiar. But thank you from us. You helped us a lot and maybe we can help find Wendy's killer."

"You be careful, Cindy. Be very careful," said Ms. Goeden.

CHAPTER 32

I WAS WORKING at a desk outside of Brady's office. We faced each other through his wall and he could still close his door for privacy. At the opposite end of the squad room, Alvarez sat at my desk and Conklin was at his. They were engaged in animated conversation.

Looking hard for the bright side, at least I still had my own computer.

I put two photos up on my computer desktop; one of Tara Burke next to the morgue close-up of Wendy Franks's face. I compared them, scrutinized them, confirming what I already knew. They didn't match. So who was Wendy Franks? I was restless. She was haunting me. Why had she been murdered? Why hastily buried in McLaren Park? The park had a history as a dumping ground for inconvenient corpses, but the coincidence of a fresh body in close proximity to the Burke house bothered the hell out of me.

Except for matching her home address to the one on her driver's license—she had moved to Sausalito from Santa Barbara two years ago—three databases had turned up a big pile of nothing so far. She had no record, not even a parking ticket. She'd graduated from UCLA. She was single, painted and sold seascapes, according to an article in a local paper that had covered her one-woman show. Sausalito is in Marin County and, accordingly, Clapper had tossed the case to Marin PD.

He had done the right thing, to be honest. Our task force still had Lorrie Burke's open murder and her missing or dead young mother, and our Homicide squad was still responsible for any homicide investigation in both the Southern and Northern Districts.

I heard a booming voice and looked up to see DA Leonard "Red Dog" Parisi striding down the center aisle, the floor vibrating as he marched past me and into Brady's office.

He closed the door, but I could hear him bellow, "Tell me I got this wrong. Tell me we didn't lose Burke."

I didn't dare watch them through the glass walls, but I heard most of the back and forth. Burke hadn't returned after his dramatic flight from his house. We'd kept him for less than a day and he'd been gone for one. That was enough to alarm the DA.

Brady said, "We're looking for him, Len. We. Could. Not. Hold him."

Brady's office door opened. Parisi stepped out and said, "Clapper wants to discuss."

He noticed me. "Boxer," he said in greeting. Then, he kept going toward the exit.

Brady said to me, "Clapper wants us. Grab the tip lines, will ya? We've got to follow every lead."

"Ten-four, boss."

Four other cops in the bullpen were also at their desks taking calls. I stabbed a button.

"Sergeant Boxer. Homicide."

"I saw Tara Burke," a man's voice said. "And I took her picture. Before I post on Instagram—"

"Right," I said. "Send it to me. Your name please?"

He didn't give me his name, but did stay on the line while he texted me a night view of a woman in a crowd.

"You're sure this is Tara?" I said. "I can't make out much of her face."

"I could be wrong," he said. "I want to help."

"Where was this taken?"

"Fresno," he said. "Last night."

I thanked Mr. Anonymous, printed out the photo. It was hard to tell from the photograph if the subject was Tara or some other pretty young woman.

"Last night? Did you approach her?"

Line went dead. More calls came in and piled up. It got to be that within a couple of seconds I could tell if the caller was having a good time at our expense or sincerely thought they knew where to find Tara Burke. But none of the many calls I took in the next half hour gave me any real hope at all.

Brady stopped by my desk on his return from his meeting with Clapper.

He said, "Hallows found nothing in Burke's house that indicates a violent death. Or the cleanup of any kind of crime. Or even the *thought* of a crime. He allows as smothering a baby might leave no trace. So. Square one by process of elimination. And that means weekends and holidays are canceled."

I just hate square one. I also hate coloring within the lines, staying in my lane, and doing it by the book.

Risking the wrath of Clapper, I called Claire.

CHAPTER 33

CLAIRE ANSWERED HER PHONE, "Washburn. What do you need?"

The snappish greeting told me to get right to the point.

"I'd like to see you about Wendy Franks."

"No good, Linds. Her parents are coming in to identify her. Any minute."

"Ah. Whatever you can tell me on the phone. I just need the basics."

"Well, first of all, it's a damned shame."

"Right. More, please."

"Okay. Unofficially. Healthy white female, killed by a deep knife slash across her throat by a common hunting knife approximately twenty-four hours before she was found. So there's your cause, time, and manner of death.

"It appears that the killer took her from behind and cut left to right."

I said, "Like, she was sitting, and the killer puts a hand on her shoulder and draws the blade across with the other hand?"

"Could be. He used considerable force. She'd pretty much bled out before the douchebag who did it dumped her."

"So, you're thinking she was killed somewhere else, then dumped. Possibly the grave was pre-dug. Which would make this premeditated."

"That's for you and the DA to decide. So, here's the final flourish. The knife work I call serial killer gibberish. He made those cuts in her breasts while she was still alive, but probably unconscious. No defensive wounds on her arms, no bruising, no blood or tissue under her nails. Wendy never saw it coming."

"Sick, sick, sick," I said. "A fetish thing?"

Cappy walked by, overheard me. Gave me a look, patted my shoulder. I nodded to him, then, stared down at my desk.

Claire was saying, "Maybe, but I'm thinking he didn't kill her for sexual pleasure."

"Because?"

"She wasn't raped. Still she was naked. I'm swabbing her neck, shoulders, face. See if that wretch left any DNA on her. Her blood's on the way to the lab," Claire said. "Where should I send the results and the autopsy report?"

"Send it to Captain Brevoort, Marin County PD."

I thanked her and let her go back to her work. It was only three in the afternoon. I walked to the washroom, splashed my face with cold water, and stared at my reflection. I looked bad but I felt worse. I wanted to work this case, find Wendy Franks's killer and put him where he could never hurt anyone again. There was no proof, but I also felt sure there was a connection between Wendy Franks and Lucas Burke.

I knew what I had to do.

I wanted to talk with Misty Fogarty, the girl with

the long braid and blue-painted fingernails who had come to Burke's office doorway while I was interviewing him on Tuesday afternoon.

I called Cindy and sweetly asked for Misty's phone number.

"Why?" she said.

"If I tell you, you'll have to tell Richie, so just give me the number, hmmm, girl reporter? If it pans out, if I can tell you—"

"If, if, if. I've heard this before. I must really love you."

She read out Misty's number and blew me a kiss. After we hung up, I duly dialed it.

Misty answered with a cheerful "This is Mis-teeee."

Luckily for me, the current headlines had zero impact on her yackety-yak personality, the kind detectives just love. She talked about herself and volunteered to meet me at a diner called the Comfy Corner at four.

An hour from now.

I called Joe and we exchanged brief news bulletins. Then I left a message for Brady. "Following up on a lead." I threw on my jacket, waved good-bye to all the deskbound cops and Brenda, and then I left the building.

CHAPTER 34

I FOUND MISTY FOGARTY waiting for me in a booth at the front of the diner.

"Hiiii, Sergeant Boxer."

I slid into the banquette across from the eighteen-year-old high school student. She was pretty, a natural blonde, wearing the same blue-and-white school uniform I'd seen her wear three days ago. Her phone was on the table, faceup.

"Misty. Nice of you to make time for me. I wonder if you can help me out. I'm trying to find Tara Burke."

"Oh. I thought you were going to tell me how Luke is doing. He hasn't been at school for two whole days."

"We were holding him as a material witness but—"

"What's that?"

"It's someone who may have direct knowledge of a crime."

"Like a suspect?"

"No, no. More like he was the last one to see Tara

and Lorrie, so we were keeping him safe and hoping he would have some ideas for us," I soft-pedaled.

"But he's not in jail, anymore?"

"He was released around lunchtime yesterday."

"Oh," said Misty. She was visibly shaken. "He must be disoriented after being in jail, right? He's very sensitive. But I guess . . . I guess you know that."

The waiter came by. Misty ordered green tea. I ordered coffee. Gave myself a little reminder. *Make her your friend. Let her talk.*

"You're close to Luke, huh?" I said.

She nodded, wiped a tear away with a blue-tipped finger.

"He's wonderful. The best."

"In what way?"

"The way he looks at me. Talks to me."

She shook her head and I felt a real meltdown coming.

Misty said, "I know he's married. I know that what I'm doing is wrong, but I love him so much. And now he's all alone and I don't know how to help him."

"It's okay, Misty. He's okay."

"I'm worried," she said. "Whoever killed Lorrie and took Tara could have hurt him, too."

"When was the last time you and Luke were...alone?"

"Sunday night. For a couple of hours."

"Where'd you go?"

"My car."

The beverages came. Misty poured her tea.

"He should have called me," she said. "Look." Misty turned on her phone, started scrolling through her pictures, found the one she was looking for, and held up the phone for me to see.

It was a selfie with cars whizzing past in the background, Misty and Lucas grinning in the foreground.

"Can I see?" I said.

She handed me the phone and I looked at the time stamp on the photo. It was dated Sunday at 8:13 p.m. I scrolled through the picture file, saw other pictures of Misty with her friends, and a few where she was with Burke, her face lit with love-light.

I sugared my coffee, took a sip, commiserated with Misty about how much she missed Lucas, and then edged in some questions about Tara, asking Misty how well she knew her, if she had any theories about her disappearance or on Lorrie's death.

Her answers were long, discursive, and thoughtful. I couldn't have been more interested.

In sum, Tara was only two or three years older than Misty; they'd even overlapped at Sunset Park Prep for one year. She thought Tara was bratty and not very smart, but sexy and attractive to men.

I said, "I heard that she might have a boyfriend. A boyfriend would be a good suspect."

"If Tara had a boyfriend everyone at Sunset Park Prep would know it," Misty scoffed. "And Luke would have been justified in getting a divorce."

Misty leaned across the table and told me just above a whisper that Luke complained about Tara, said that she was whiny and cold. Misty said she wouldn't be totally surprised if Tara had killed the baby just to hurt Lucas and then taken off, never to be seen again.

I asked for and paid the check, gave Misty my card, and told her to call me anytime. "I'm here for you," I said.

She stood up to give me a hug.

"I don't know what to do. What should I do?"

I stood with her in the aisle at the front of the diner as other customers brushed past us.

"Misty, what do *you* think you should do?" I asked her.

"I should break up with him, right?"

"If I was your friend or family member, I would say so."

She nodded, hugged me again, hard, and I hugged her back.

I was only fifteen minutes from home, and as I drove, I thought about Misty with Lucas Burke, sneaking time with him in her car, the rest of the time on the sidelines.

My own theory of the crime was starting to gel.

CHAPTER 35

IT WAS THE FIRST calm moment of the day.

I sat at the kitchen counter while Joe loaded the dishwasher and filled me in on the domestic tranquility on Lake Street.

Julie was across the hall with Mrs. Rose, who was showing her how to make cookies. Martha was sleeping on the rug in our bedroom, one of her favorite places. As he talked, Joe brought me a slab of lasagna and a glass of Chianti and sat down at the counter beside me.

This was as good as life got.

I kicked off my shoes and asked my sweet husband to brainstorm with me about heinous bloody murder.

With his decades of experience in America's Secret Service, he was an excellent brainstormer, and he didn't have to be sworn to secrecy. He also enjoyed it.

He poured himself a glass of wine and we clinked glasses, said "Cheers" in unison, and I started talking.

I recapped for Joe how Lucas Burke had resisted

our search warrants, had sped away, and was currently missing. That DA Parisi was in an uproar, that Chief Clapper was facing media coverage and increasing the pressure on Lieutenant Brady, which didn't solve anything.

I went over discovery of the body of Wendy Franks, who was found murdered in McLaren Park, and how she was briefly misidentified as Tara Burke.

"Possibly Franks's death is unrelated. But my gut says otherwise."

"Hmmm. Tell me more."

I dug into the lasagna, which was hot and tasty. Joe made the best lasagna in the world, and I told him so.

"Good. Thanks. So keep talking, Blondie. You have about ten minutes before this place fills up with Julie, Mrs. Rose, and a pan of cookies."

"A timeline is forming in my mind."

"Go."

"On Sunday night, before we've even heard of Lucas Burke, he nips out, and according to Misty has a 'date' with her in her car—then, fresh from his teenage rendezvous, he goes home. Tara lights into him the minute he walks in. The fight picks up again in the morning."

Joe nodded and I went on.

"Burke leaves the house at seven thirty, we have that on video. He arrives at Sunset Park Prep on time. That's been verified. Tara leaves soon after Burke with the baby and an overnight bag. Also on video."

"Where's she going?"

"Don't know. No sign of her car or of her. When she walked out the door, her attitude tells me she's defiant. Either she's getting back at her cheating dog of a husband—'You're not the boss of me.' Or meeting her rumored but not verified boyfriend. Or she's taking the baby and running away from home. Or she's doing all three. Giving her husband the finger and running away from home with her boyfriend. Any which way, she hasn't been seen or heard from since."

"Got it," said Joe. "I'm with you so far."

"Okay," I said. "So continuing the timeline. Same day, Tara's mother, Kathleen Wyatt, breaks the glass on the fire alarm. She posts bloody murder on Cindy's blog, calls Lucas Burke a killer, and storms Cindy's office. Cindy gets me involved, and on Tuesday afternoon, I talk to Lucas about his still missing wife. He says, 'She's run away before. I destroyed her credit card. She'll be back when she runs out of gas. There's nothing to see here.'"

Joe said, "Then Wednesday morning, his daughter washes up dead on the beach."

"Correct."

I checked my watch to be sure of the date.

"Yes, that was Wednesday. Claire estimates that the baby had been dead for about thirty hours. Asphyxiation. The story is a media bomb, and still no sign of Tara."

"So, who killed Lorrie?" Joe asked.

I slugged down some wine, pushed my plate to the side.

"I feel strongly that Tara is dead, which means she can't have killed Lorrie and skipped town. My sketchy theory? Lorrie and Tara are killed together by Tara's unknown rumored boyfriend. Or—track me here. Lucas meets Tara somehow, somewhere, after classes on Monday. He tells her all about Misty, and when Tara goes off on him, he kills her and smothers the baby with his hand. He wants nothing to do with this family."

Joe was nodding, saying, "Yep, yep, yep," so I kept going.

"Burke tosses the baby into the ocean. Maybe he doesn't expect her to wash up so quickly, to be identified so soon. He takes longer to get rid of Tara. If I'm right that she's dead, then I feel certain that when her body is found there will be marks on her body indicating murder."

Joe said, "As theories go, yours works for me. If he killed the baby, he'd have to kill Tara and vice versa. If he had killed them at home, you'd have evidence, so that speaks to luring Tara to some location, remote probably—"

The doorknob turned and Martha got her old haunches under her and trotted to the foyer.

"To be continued," said Joe. He went to the door and a grinning Julie stepped in, Gloria Rose behind her holding a tray of chocolate-chip cookies that smelled a hundred percent delicious.

"See the faces?" Julie said, pointing to how the chocolate chips formed smiles, frowns; some cookies looked like they were laughing and some seemed very stern. Cracked me up. I grabbed Martha's collar and said to our lovely neighbor and nanny, "I'll fire up a pot of decaf."

"I'm all coffeed out," she said, "but dying to taste the cookies. Got milk?"

"Pull up a stool," Joe said.

He and Julie slid the cookies onto a plate, and minutes later, Julie was telling us who all the faces were—a kind of chocolate-chip-cookie mug book: guy at the grocery store, lady with a cat on a leash, me, Joe, Gloria Rose, and Martha.

"This is me," Julie said. "No one can eat this one. Not even *me*."

It was hilarious, chocolate chips arrayed across the upper curve of the cookie standing in for her curls and a chippy smile from side to side.

For an hour, I lost myself in family magic time. It was all delicious and I soaked it up. I might need to draw on the good feelings in the days to come if the horrible Burke case continued to be unsolved, devolving from horrible to cold.

CHAPTER 36

I CAME THROUGH the bullpen gate at eight on Saturday morning and headed straight into the break room.

Rich Conklin got up and followed me in, watched me vigorously clean out the coffee maker, refill the tank and the filter, tap the brew button with a vengeance.

I said, "Any word on Burke? Please tell me he came home last night."

"No such luck," said my old friend.

During the years I've been partnered with Rich, we've both grown some stress-induced gray hairs. I plucked. He didn't. A little silver looked good on him.

He took my mug down from the high shelf and we stood together watching the coffee drip into the pot. It was hypnotic and I felt myself relax.

He asked "How you doin'?" The Joey Tribbiani imitation was our shorthand way of saying "we're friends."

I replied, "How *you* doin'?"

"I asked first."

"Do I look ragged? I think I had 100 percent REM sleep. I was running all night."

"From or to?"

"After, I think. I was chasing, not catching."

We took our coffee to a table that had stood in this room since the Kennedy years, kicked the chairs out from under, and sat down.

Rich said, "Speaking of chasing, Cindy interviewed Clapper this morning."

"Good for her."

"Yep. It aired on KRON."

"What did Clapper say?"

Rich was saying "Same old bull—" when Brady appeared right beside us.

"Where's Alvarez?" he asked Conklin.

"She left her charger in her car. She'll be right back."

Brady said, "I need alla y'all in my office, PDQ."

PDQ turned out to be under five minutes.

Brady's hands were clasped on his desk. Alvarez had retrieved her charger and was inside the glass box in time for roll call. We all were. Alvarez and I sat across the desk from Brady. Conklin leaned against the doorframe. Chi stuck his head in, read the tension in the room, and backed out without speaking.

Conklin closed the door.

Brady said, "There's been another ugly-ass murder."

I was thinking, *Tara*.

"Teenage girl, throat cut in her car in the parking lot at her school."

"ID on the vic?" I said, my mouth suddenly dry.

"Yeah. Sorry, Boxer, I know you talked to her. It's Melissa Fogarty, aka Misty."

I jumped up and shouted, *"That son of a bitch!"*

Every cop in the department turned their head.

Brady said, "Down, Boxer."

"She *said* she was going to break up with him."

He said, "You go to the ME's office and take a look at the victim. Conklin, Alvarez, go to the crime scene. The car will be transported to the lab soon. Stay with the CSIs at the scene and then head out to Hunters Point and have someone there show you the car. Killer had to leave something at the scene, in the vehicle or on the girl. Y'all stay in close touch with me."

Alvarez and Conklin edged past and Brady shook his finger at me. "Get a grip, Lindsay. No mistakes."

I nodded, left Brady's office, took the stairs at a jog, exited by the lobby's back door to the breezeway that connected the Hall to the medical examiner's office.

Hitting speed dial, I left a message for Claire, saying, "I'm on my way."

CHAPTER 37

JONNY SAMUELS SAID, "He's changed in the space of a week, you notice?"

Cindy had just wrapped her interview with Chief Charles Clapper outside the Hall of Justice. The building was gray granite and a pretty good backdrop in the morning light.

Clapper had said to her and the camera, "We're still looking for Tara Burke. The *San Francisco Chronicle* is running her photo on their website and in the print edition. Our tip lines are open. If you've seen Tara or think you know where she could be...Look. This is a twenty-year-old woman. She doesn't have much money on her, if any. Her young daughter has been murdered.

"We need the eyes of the people of this city to help us find her. Ms. Thomas will give you the numbers to call. Thank you."

Clapper thanked Cindy, and Samuels turned away and walked up the steps to the Hall of Justice.

Cindy was going over her notes, figuring out her

lede, and Samuels was looking at the raw video he'd shot when Cindy looked up and shouted, "Oh, my *God*!"

Six or seven cruisers parked outside the building were suddenly backing out, tires squealing, and heading up Bryant. Sirens blasted.

"Quick," she said. "I saw Richie in one of those cars. We've gotta move."

"Give me the keys," he said.

She handed them over. They ran a long block to where they'd parked on Bryant at Sixth. Samuels opened the door for Cindy, then got behind the wheel. Cindy buckled up and grabbed the dash as the car lurched out onto Bryant, then went flat-out as Samuels headed north. They drafted behind the police cars for as long as they could see and hear them, and by then Cindy had picked up a few words through the static on the scanner.

The words were "Sunset Park Prep." Lucas Burke taught English Lit there. Cindy picked up code 10-10 for "ME needed," but nothing for "shooter at large" or "ambulance needed" or "officers in need of assistance."

By the time Cindy and Samuels reached the school, cops had taped off the parking lot and were redirecting pedestrian and vehicular traffic. Samuels pulled into a metered parking spot outside the school and grabbed his camera. Cindy fed the meter and the two of them approached the parking lot on foot.

A girl in her school uniform walked past where Cindy stood with Samuels, her head was down as she spoke into her phone, saying "I can't *believe* it. *This can't be true.*"

She was in obvious emotional distress. Other kids were running out of the main building, hugging, crying.

Cindy reached out a hand and touched the girl's shoulder.

"Pardon me. Can you tell me what happened?"

The student said into the phone, "Hold a second." Then she turned back to Cindy and said, "Someone was killed. I heard she was found in her car and that there was a lot of blood."

The student's eyes were huge with shock.

"I'm Cindy Thomas. What's your name?" Cindy asked her.

"Tina. Tina Hosier."

"Tina, this is Jonathan Samuels. We work for the *Chronicle*. Can we talk to you?"

"Can you give me a ride home? My car's in the parking lot."

"Sure can."

Cindy would have helped this distressed teen for any reason, and at this moment, she thought she had a better chance of learning something from this student than from law enforcement.

Tina spoke into her phone. "Nana. I've got a ride. I'll see you in ten minutes. Love you, too."

CHAPTER 38

"SERGEANT BOXER," I SAID, announcing myself to the ME's new receptionist. "Dr. Washburn is expecting me."

"Just a moment, please."

I stared hard at the bodybuilder behind the desk as he made the call and kept staring until he said, "Go right in."

I thanked him, waited for the buzzer, then pulled the door open and kept going down the hallway to the autopsy suite.

Bunny was waiting for me, blocking the entrance with her size 4 body.

"Here ya go, sergeant."

She held up a green surgical gown. I slid my arms obediently through the sleeves. She went behind me and tied the strings back and front. Next, she handed me matching booties and a cap, and when I was appropriately garbed, Bunny said, "Okay. You're good."

She held open the swinging door and I stepped into the chilly tiled autopsy room. Claire stood behind the draped body on the table and said, "I haven't started. She just got here."

I said, "I have to see her."

Bunny gently folded down the sheet, exposing the girl's face, neck, and upper chest. Her eyes were half open. Lipstick smeared her lips. I groaned involuntarily. Misty Fogarty, the girl I had met for tea at four o'clock yesterday afternoon, had been effervescent and then emotional. It pained me to see her dead.

The murder weapon had opened a gaping wound, cutting through the arteries and musculature of her neck. There had been a *lot* of blood. Whatever hadn't sprayed and pumped out to cover the interior of her car had stained her hair and chest.

Claire watched to make sure I was steady.

I said, "Give it to me, doctor."

She said, "Okay, sergeant. Okay. Based only on first look, unofficially, mics off, the slime who killed this young lady has the same signature as the one who killed Wendy Franks. First, we have the slashed throat from left to right. Same blade or type of blade. And the killer made some slits in her breasts, like with Ms. Franks. Serial killer gibberish. Or so it appears pending verification. As with the previous victim, that's your cause and manner of death. I estimate she died last night between eight and ten p.m. According to the head of school, the car was in the school parking lot overnight and Misty's body was discovered by security this morning."

I said, "I was with her yesterday for an hour, from four o'clock. She was asking me what to do."

"About?"

"Lucas Burke. Remember Cindy telling us they were having an affair? I wanted to shake her. I wanted to warn her. I wanted to say, 'Get the hell away from him. Transfer to another school. Destroy your phone, drop out of social media, change your email and your name. Disappear until Lucas Burke is locked up for good.'

"But instead, I had the good sense to ask, 'What do *you* think you should do?'"

My voice broke. Bunny Ellis put her arm around my waist, and my best friend looked at me with terrible sadness in her eyes. Misty had been alive, vibrant, grinning at me *yesterday*. Now she was lying on a stainless steel table, her half-open eyes clouded over, mouth slack, blood still sticky in her hair.

I struggled on.

"Misty said, 'I should break up with him, right?' and I agreed. So what'd she do? Looks like she makes a date to see him. I can hear her, crying 'I can't see you anymore,' and him going, 'Just a second, hon. I've got a surprise for you in the back seat.'"

Claire said, "Speculating."

I snuffled, wrapped my arm around my face, then used the tissue Bunny tucked into my hand. After I'd mopped up and put the Kleenex in my pocket, Claire said, "Linds, it's okay."

"No, it's not."

"I understand, but she was a potential witness against him. You had to be neutral in that diner. And *you* didn't get *her* killed. If you'd said, 'Don't see him, get out of town,' would she have listened? She didn't have to see him. She could have called him or texted him or just walked away. You're not responsible."

"I hear you. Anything else?"

"Okay. There are no bruises on her that I can see. We bagged her hands. I'll go over every finger carefully. But I haven't started an external exam, never mind internal. You're about five or six hours ahead of me, girlfriend. Any questions before I sneak you out through the ambulance bay?"

I shook my head, whispered, "No. Not now. Thanks."

"I'll tell you this right now and for free," Claire said, as she gently covered Misty's face. "Assuming this same guy killed both women. Whoever he is, whatever his motive, he's organized. Calculating. Manipulative. He kills with deliberation and precision and deceit.

"This dude doesn't feel love. He doesn't feel hate. He just likes to kill women."

CHAPTER 39

LEAVING CLAIRE'S OFFICES behind me, I went for a long walk under the overcast morning sky.

I took deep breaths, felt the pavement under my shoes and used the traffic on Bryant as a backdrop for my thoughts about Misty. I thought about being eighteen, falling in love with a seductive older man, a psychopath who specialized in English literature and teenage girls.

That made me think of Tara, who'd been even younger than Misty when she married Burke. The search for Tara seemed to have stalled, which only made the daily calls from Kathleen that much more fraught.

The Hall of Justice is cut on an angle at the corner of Bryant and Seventh. I climbed the granite steps to the glass and steel door, pulled it open, and went through security. Put my gun in the tray, my phone followed, and after clearing the metal detector I treated myself to an elevator ride to the fourth floor.

Brenda handed me some messages.

"Any bad news?"

"If so, I wouldn't tell you," she said. "This messenger hates getting shot."

"Hah. I wouldn't shoot you. I'd ask for a Kind bar."

She opened her drawer and handed me one.

"Thanks, Brenda."

I flipped through the tip line calls she'd fielded as I went to the back of the squad room. Looking into Brady's office, I saw that his elbows were on his desk and his phone was hard against his ear. I pressed my hand to his wall and he looked up, signaled me to come in.

My morning coffee was still on my desk — cold, but I didn't care. I brought it with me and sat down across from Brady and propped my feet up against the side of his desk. I unwrapped my Kind bar as Brady was saying, "Okay, Hallows, thanks."

Brady hung up. "Hallows. Letting me know they're processing the car. Have all of Misty's things. Bag. Clothes. Phone. Surveillance video from the parking lot."

"Misty told me she had a date with Burke in that car last Sunday night. More than once, I'm sure."

I told him about Misty's body, what the killer had done to her, what Claire had told me.

"She's sure it's the same doer?"

"Not yet, but she says Wendy Franks and Misty Fogarty have the same MO. Exactly."

"Ah, sheet," he said. "So we've got a serial."

Brady's intercom buzzed.

He pressed the button hard with his thumb.

"What? Who?" He stood up so he could see to the front of the squad room. Then he said to Brenda, "Tell them I'll be right out."

He sat down and pressed speed dial 1.

"Chief," he said, "Lucas Burke is in the house. Looks like he brought his alibi with him."

CHAPTER 40

LUCAS BURKE STOOD in Brady's doorway, shaking a newspaper at us, bellowing, "What in God's name is this? Bait to get me here? If this is fake, I'm going to sue this city, and whoever planted this story is going to be very sorry. Am I clear?"

I said, "May I see that?"

Burke threw the late edition of the *Chronicle* onto Brady's desk and I read the headline: "Slash-and-Gash Killer Takes Second Victim."

Misty Fogarty's picture was centered on the front page. The stark headline punched me right to my heart. I felt light-headed and had to grip the edge of the desk.

Steady, girl.

Brady pointed at Burke. "Stay right there," he said, before picking up his phone.

"Brenda, are the interview rooms vacant?"

To me, Brady said, "Sit tight. Be right back."

I sat tight as directed, but my brain was ranging. Cindy had written this story with no help from me or Richie, but still she'd gotten out the details of the murder, possibly attracting the interest of a copy-cat. Probably contaminating a future jury. If there'd ever be one.

I heard Cindy's voice in my mind; "I'm doing my *job*."

There was a tapping on the glass wall from outside Brady's office and I came back to the moment. It was the woman who'd accompanied Burke to the Hall.

"This is my ex-wife, Alexandra Conroy," Burke said. "She called me when she heard that Lorrie was murdered. Do you have any suspects, sergeant? Besides me?"

"I'm very sorry," I said, dodging the question.

Brady was halfway down the squad room aisle briefing Chi and Cappy. I collected myself. I stood up and introduced myself to Burke's ex-wife. We shook hands, and I told her to sit at my desk. "We won't be long."

I started gathering impressions.

Conroy looked to be in her forties, about Lucas's age. She was well put-together in cream-colored knit separates. She had sun-streaked hair, a sun-pinked nose, and she wore no wedding band. My take? She had free time. She didn't get messy. And despite the divorce, apparently she cared for Burke.

Burke wore a short-sleeved white shirt and khakis. His face and arms were burned to the point of peeling. Since the last time I saw him, he'd been exposed to the sun without SPF anything. Could be that he and Ms. Conroy had been lounging on a beach. Was it an alibi?

I watched Burke clutch the newspaper, shaking it as he reread Cindy's report of Misty's gruesome death. He was muttering, making hurt sounds, "Oh, God. Oh, God. Why? Why her?"

I said, "Lucas. Did you know Wendy Franks?"

He looked up at me like he'd stumbled out of a dark cave into daylight. "Who? No."

I heard Brady ask Cappy and Chi to bring Ms. Conroy to Interview 1. "Take notes. I don't want to wait for the transcript."

Brady headed back toward his office, shook hands with Conroy, and introduced her to the detectives.

Then Brady said to Burke and me, "Let's make ourselves more comfortable."

Burke said, "I demand answers."

"Same here," said Brady.

CHAPTER 41

LUCAS BURKE WOBBLED, bumped into the walls of the corridor leading to Interview 2.

I put a steadying hand on his back and he shook me off. My mind split again. I suspected Burke of these horrific murders, yet his grief and rage felt absolutely real.

But if he killed these women—and his own baby—I would devote myself to nailing Lucas Burke, for as long as it took. Right now, I was glad to be partnered with Jackson Brady. He would sort out Burke and get to the truth.

Interview 2 was the larger of the two interrogation rooms, with a water cooler and a small fridge as well as a dinged-up metal table and four matching chairs. The camera in the corner of the ceiling started rolling once we opened the door. I was sure that Clapper had been notified, and that either Parisi or an ADA was standing with him in the observation room.

Brady closed the door behind us and we took seats at the table facing Burke, who could see his own tortured expression in the mirror.

I was ready. We all were.

"Who did this to Misty?"

Brady said, "Where've you been, Mr. Burke? Let's start with the last time we saw you, driving north on Dublin Street two days ago at about noon. Don't leave anything out."

I took notes as Burke described speeding away from his house, not hiding his fury that in addition to the blow he'd taken over the death of his child and the insult of being locked up as a material witness, he'd been forced to leave his house so the cops could rummage through his belongings.

"Find anything incriminating?" he shouted across the table. "Find any evidence?"

"Where did you go after you left your house?" I said calmly.

"Alex, my ex, called me when she heard about Lorrie. We're still friends."

He told us that Conroy lived in Sacramento, so he drove up there. He spent the night. She suggested they get away from everything, go to a resort in Carmel-by-the-Sea.

It was a few hours' drive. They stayed in a suite with a balcony overlooking the pool. They drank a lot, slept by the pool, and Burke checked his phone all day and night hoping that Tara would call.

"I thought she would call, and I would answer the phone and hear her crying," said Burke. "I knew I could calm her down and get her to tell me where she was. Arrange somehow to get to her. And then, I would demand to know what the hell happened to Lorrie."

He covered his face with his hands. Tears fell but Brady wasn't moved. He pushed, jabbed, prodded, and alternated his questions and demands.

"Burke, you have very limited options. This girl that was murdered? Fogarty? She was your girlfriend, isn't that right? Boxer? Jump in."

"It was common knowledge," I said, "and she told me all about your relationship. Where you met. What you said. We have a note. You promising to marry her. She was expecting to see you the same day we released you."

"I didn't make a plan to see her."

"She was disappointed, heartsick, worried about you. She wanted to comfort you."

"Stop. *Please, stop*. What you're doing is criminal."

"She died a horrible death," I said.

"I loved Misty. Someone is killing people I love! Don't you see that? I wish I were dead, too."

Brady didn't care what Burke said. "Just the facts, man. Tara's mother calls Sergeant Boxer a half dozen times a day. She hasn't heard from Tara. Where is she? You went to Carmel while your baby was dead and your wife was missing? What kind of husband does that? I need your check-in times. Will anyone at the resort remember you? Where did y'all eat? I need all your credit card receipts. All of them. We need a cheek swab. Why? Because you want to get off the suspect list. Yours is the only name on it.

"Open your wallet and take out any receipts or reservation confirmations," Brady continued. "Give me your phone now. Don't give me reasons to arrest you for murder."

Burke said, "Alex paid for the hotel. I paid for the gas. We split the meals."

He laid out his cards, handed his phone to Brady. Brady opened the phone's photo folder and held it so I could see it, too. He scrolled, stopping at the pictures of Tara, Tara and Lorrie, both together with Burke.

"And the folder where you hide photos of Misty?" I asked.

He showed us that, too.

Brady said, "I'm keeping all of this for now." He pushed a pad and pen over to Burke. "Write down your movements since Thursday afternoon. That's what we call a statement."

Burke snorted in disbelief.

"Don't try to leave the room, Mr. Burke. I have officers outside the door who will take you down and then we'll arrest you. Boxer, I need you."

I got up and followed him out of the room.

CHAPTER 42

LIEUTENANT JACKSON BRADY and I entered the small observation room situated between the interview rooms and with windows on each.

Clapper, Yuki, and Homicide inspectors Michaels and Wang had been watching the interrogations of both Burke and Conroy.

I edged over to Yuki and asked her, "Thoughts?"

"Conroy is smooth," she said. "Unruffled by the interrogation and she gave similar or identical answers to the questions you and Brady asked Burke within a normal margin for error."

I nodded and stood with her and watched as Conroy responded to Chi's questions in an even tone of voice. The word "buttery" came to mind.

As a detective, Chi is like ground-penetrating radar. He can see things that the rest of us miss, while Cappy has a knack for blending in with his surroundings. Like a snow fox. Or a water snake. His pointed questions sound innocuous and the subjects answer willingly. He has a gift.

Chi asked, "What was your room number?"

"Three seventeen. No. Three nineteen." Same as what Burke had told us.

"Who paid?"

"I did. Lucas needed a break."

Cappy said, "Not best of circumstances for a holiday, though, was it?"

"No," said Conroy, getting out her phone to show pictures of Burke with Conroy. Beachy pictures. Selfies by the pool. Views of the ocean. Burke wasn't smiling in any of them. "Luke was grief-stricken about LuLu."

"LuLu?"

"Lorrie's nickname."

I stood at Brady's shoulder as he texted Chi, telling him to keep going and when he ran out of questions to hand Conroy off to ADA Castellano.

Chi asked Conroy, "What did Lucas tell you about Tara?"

Conroy said with some feeling that Burke was still convinced that Tara was alive. "He told me that Tara was either guilt-ridden and in hiding or with some guy."

I was no longer convinced we would find Tara Wyatt Burke alive.

"I'm going in," I said to Brady.

He nodded and I knocked on the door, then opened it.

"Chi, Cappy, Ms. Conroy. I have a couple of questions."

Chi and Cappy invited me in.

I turned to Conroy. "These are a little personal, but they won't go beyond this room," I lied.

"Sure. What do you want to know?"

"Was Lucas ever abusive during your marriage?"

"You mean did he beat me?"

"Anything that comes to you when I say 'abusive.'"

"Huh. Well. To be honest. He had a temper. That's why I divorced him three years ago. But I swear—do you have a Bible? Okay, well, on my word—the worst he'd do was, he would yell. Grab my arm once in a while, twist it. He could say mean things. He scared me. We were both pretty young when we married. I didn't understand it. My father was a gentle soul. Luke was rough. But he never broke a bone or threatened me with a weapon, if that's where you're going. He was from a neighborhood where there was fighting. Now, he says please and thank you and never lifts a hand in anger. He's matured."

I thought otherwise, but said, "Did you ever meet Tara?"

"No. But I sent them a wedding present and a baby present, too. And no, I never met LuLu, either."

"What did you get for Lorrie?"

"A bouncer. From their wish list online."

"And, normally, how often are you in contact with your ex-husband?"

"I'd say every few weeks. We email when there's big news. Good news. Disappointments. But apart from these past two days, I last saw him in person at the funeral of a mutual friend, maybe two years ago."

I asked if we had her contact info and she said she'd given it to Sergeant Chi.

I said, "Thanks for your time."

Cappy followed me out. "Take it for what it's worth," he said. "She said there weren't no dirty dancing on their trip. Burke just talked, drank, cried, passed out."

Brady and Yuki were waiting for me in the hallway. The boss asked, "What did y'all think?"

"She's an innocent bystander," I said.

Yuki said, "I'm with Lindsay. I'll get their receipts checked out, but their stories were consistent enough. Then we'll see if we're arresting Burke—or kicking him."

Belief and doubt were still trading punches in my mind.

We needed a confession. A witness. Tangible evidence.

I stopped to get coffee, and once back at my desk I saw CSI director Hallows in Brady's office. The two men were in deep conversation. When Brady saw me, he waved me in.

He said, "Hallows has the surveillance footage from Sunset Park Prep's parking lot from Fogarty's murder. He thinks he's got something."

CHAPTER 43

AROUND MIDAFTERNOON, our task force gathered at the far end of our floor in a vacant corner office that used to belong to Lieutenant Ted Swanson before he went to prison.

Brady and I tacked pictures up on the cork board—Tara and Lucas Burke, plus morgue photos of Lorrie Burke, Wendy Franks, and Melissa Fogarty.

Hallows set up his laptop on the table, the team assembled around, and Brady stood at the head.

Brady said, "I don't know if Lucas Burke is the doer, if he hired a hitter, is deeply unlucky, or if he's so psychotic and freaking smart he leaves no trace.

"But this much we do know." Brady read from his phone. "From Captain Geoffrey Brevoort, Marin PD. Quote, 'We've tossed Wendy Franks's life. Such as it was. She was an isolate. A painter. Had two friends, neither of whom had ever heard of Lucas Burke. According to the friends, Wendy liked girls and was still getting over a breakup. She took her Sea Ray out in the harbor alone, and only saw her friends occasionally.'"

I said, "Burke said he never heard of her either."

"Okay," said Brady. "Pin a red flag on it, anyway. Conklin, you're up."

Conklin checked his notes. "By the time Alvarez and I got to the scene, Fogarty's body was in the ME van, but we spent hours with her SUV. She bled out in the driver's seat. The only sign of a struggle was she'd kicked off her shoes and left some fingernail marks in the dash. Her handbag was in the passenger side foot well with her wallet intact, and the keys were in the ignition."

Alvarez stood up. "Misty's phone was far back under the driver's seat. I went through her messages from the last few days, and particularly from last night. Around seven. Melissa texts to a burner phone, 'I have to see you.' Gets a return text. 'Be there at eight, don't be late.' Why was she texting Burke on a burner? To keep their plans a secret? Or was she being tricked by someone—not Burke—who lured her in?"

Alvarez sat down.

I said, "I viewed Fogarty's body pre-autopsy. As Dr. Washburn said, her throat was slashed from behind, ear to ear. What puzzles me are the seemingly random gashes on her upper breasts, same as with Franks. I don't see a pattern in these nonfatal wounds. It's like he's doodling, or drawing out the contact with the victim."

I picked up the pointer and aimed it at the morgue shots tacked on the board, running laser circles around the gashes; ten on Franks, seven on Fogarty.

"Clue anyone?"

"He's trying to throw us off with bullshit," said Cappy.

"I'll take another run through ViCAP."

Yuki stood up and said, "I got a warrant to go through Burke's financials. This is a three-day job, but

I sucked in some volunteers in my office with free eats. We processed the last three months of Burke's credit-card statements, including his gas and supermarket cards, and found no red flags. He banks at SunTrust and B of A. No big transfers of money occurred, just car payments and mortgage and day-to-day expenses. He may have another bank or cash on hand, but his personal finances look clean."

Chi stood, shot his cuffs, lined up index cards on the table; his talking points. Then, he recapped the interview with Alex Conroy.

"Conroy's stated whereabouts have been confirmed with receipts and video and selfies and corroboration from two hotel desk managers. I sent photos. They verified that Conroy and Burke checked out per their statements. We can't find any holes in her story. I'm not going to lie. If Burke's a killer, he's neat. Too neat. This worries the hell outta me."

Clapper walked in and said to Chi, "What in particular worries you?"

"That Burke is either a high-genius psycho or that someone else, a different high-genius psycho, is manipulating this case."

"If you had to pick A or B?" said Clapper.

"I'd flip a coin," said Chi.

Clapper sighed and leaned up against the wall.

Brady said, "Boxer. Flip the coin."

I folded my hands on the table and boiled down my impressions of Burke today; his appearance, attitude, fury over Fogarty's death, and his willingness to cooperate.

"He says he's being framed. If he's acting, he's un-believable. Outraged. Crying and spitting mad. And we don't have one damned fingerprint. He's not in custody, but Red Dog is sitting on him—"

Yuki laughed and several people couldn't help but join in. Parisi weighs three hundred pounds.

But the laughter faded fast under Clapper's cold eyes.

I picked up where I'd left off.

"Say Burke did it. What's his motive? Why kill his own child? How does Wendy Franks fit in? Why bury people in his own backyard? Where's Tara? Is she behind all of this? How? Why? When I flip the coin, it comes up tails. Burke's being framed."

Clapper said, "My coin comes up tails, too. As my father used to say, 'With one arse, you can't be at two weddings.' If Burke was in Carmel, he didn't kill Fogarty. But I'm betting that Fogarty's killer, that evil shit, is on video.

"Hallows, over to you."

CHAPTER **44**

BRADY CUT THE LIGHTS and closed the blinds.

Gene Hallows said, "Here we go, pards, this is Sunset Park Prep's parking lot last night before the incident."

As expected, the quality of the video was poor; it was grainy, badly lit, and due to the long, dark distance from the camera to the closest of the buildings, unfocused.

Two cars were parked within the grid of painted yellow lines on the asphalt, the license plates barely legible. Chain-link fencing surrounded the lot. The school's field house stood in the middle distance, one large tree just outside the fence on the lot's east side.

Hallows said, "I watched seven hours of this video on fast forward. The camera is mounted on a light pole with a ninety-degree angle centered on the footpath that leads from the south end of the lot to the field house. By four o' clock, school had let out and apart from those two cars, the lot was deserted. No one got into or out of those cars. I made a clip that runs from just before Misty arrives four hours later, at five to eight, until ten minutes after.

"You'll note when Misty arrives, she had an electronic gizmo that opens the school lot's gate.

"I did find another camera aimed at the gate, but it's broken and has been for a long time.

"Now, all registered drivers at Sunset Park Prep have an electronic key to that gate behind the camera. Mostly, the key holders are teachers, but also some members of the senior class. Most people park as close as possible to the footpath entrance to the campus. The exception to that is Misty Fogarty. She parks barely within camera range on the east side, under this tree."

I said, "Misty wanted privacy. She planned to break up with Burke."

"Okay, so that was the plan, right?" said Hallows. "Okay, here she comes. She opens the gate, now she is inside and circling the lot, first going straight in the direction of the field house, turning, giving us a good look at her license plate. That is her car and her plate."

"Midnight blue Outback," said Conklin. "I know this car inside and out."

"Okay, then," said Hallows. "Here, Misty parks under the tree, turns off her lights, gets out of the car. Paces a little bit. Looks at her iPhone, and we know she sends a text at eight on the nose."

"We're about to watch her final moments. That makes me sick," I said.

"Take deep breaths," said Brady.

Hallows said, "Hold your horses, friends. It's going to get worse. Here, Misty is looking toward the main gate. The person she's waiting for is approaching on foot from that direction. There is no sign of a vehicle."

"Silver Audi would be nice," said Cappy.

Alvarez said, "Could he have jumped the fence?"

Hallows said, "Some of you could get over it, some couldn't." He paused the video and pointed at the screen.

"No car," Hallows said. "But here's the psycho killer. Looks to be a male dressed all in black, sports jacket over a black T-shirt and black jeans, black shoes. A knit cap covers his ears. He walks along the fence where we just about can see him, but no matter how I fiddled with the software, I cannot make out his face. He keeps his head down. He knows about the camera. Given the height of the chain-link fence, this guy is approximately five eleven. That's all I can glean."

Hallows restarted the video. "The killer and Misty are having a discussion, looks like," Hallows said, "but she doesn't act like she wants anything to do with him."

"Know how it looks to me? She was waiting for someone else," said Brady. "She was waiting for Burke."

I rapped the table with my knuckles twice in agreement.

Hallows said, "I just look at the tape."

"Yeah, right," said Conklin.

Next to Clapper, Hallows was the best CSI around. We were all eager to hear his take.

Hallows said, "There's Misty getting back into her car, turns on her lights, backs up, and turns the car so she's facing the exit. Too bad the light nearly blinds the camera. Looks like she'd just put the car in gear when the back door opens and this character gets in. Just slides into the back seat and closes the door. He's sitting behind her when he attacks. The evidence bears that out.

"A few seconds pass," said Hallows. "If I get to make up the script, she's telling him to get out of the car. I see shadowy movement inside that I can't make out. Looks like she's pulling away from him, but she doesn't get the door open."

Alvarez looked at me and I looked back at her. We really didn't want to see this.

Hallows said, "Now look. Headlights go out. I'm thinking the guy who just slashed her throat has reached over and turned off the engine."

"He's good," said Brady.

Clapper spoke. "For sure, this guy is organized and practiced. Cocky. And he's done this before."

Alvarez said, "It's only been a few minutes since he got in the car and now the back door is opening."

Hallows said, "Yeah. There he goes, using the tree shadow for cover, walking out of view. The rest of the video is a snooze. I fast-forwarded and watched until the security guard discovered Misty's body in the early hours of the morning and cops came quick after that. Not to mention the press.

"And that's all I've got."

We stayed in the room for another half hour, theorizing, asking questions across the table.

"To review," I said, "Burke has an out-of-town alibi and looks different from Misty's killer. So, he probably isn't Wendy's killer, either. Misty and Wendy had similar wounds on their bodies. Which means that there is potentially another killer who could have attacked Tara."

Michaels said, "Wang and I will go interview the head of school, also the guard who found the body. Interview as many students as we can. Two night shift guys from Northern want to work this with us. Burton and Krebs. Okay?"

Clapper said, "Okay. Good. Yuki, tell Red Dog we still can't hold Burke. He's been put on leave from his teaching position. We'll keep eyes on him round the clock."

"You got it," Yuki said.

Clapper said, "Hallows, I need the best still shot of this killer for distribution. Thanks all for your thoughts and hard work. There will be no holidays or weekends off for this task force until further notice."

He looked around the table, turned, and walked out the door.

CHAPTER 45

IT WAS CLAIRE'S BRILLIANT idea to meet at Susie's.

Since Wednesday morning when Lorrie Burke washed up on Baker Beach, I'd been torn up and heartsick, and that went for all four of us.

We needed to be together. We needed to hash it all out.

Maybe between us, we'd hone in on that little girl's killer.

Claire, Yuki, and I got there just after five, giving us a head start on the after-work crowd. The steel band and the barflies hadn't yet arrived and Lorraine said we could sit anywhere at all. I called Joe and told him that I was out with the girls and would be home around eight.

It was unanimous. We marched along the kitchen pass-through window and into the smaller back room, slid into banquettes flanking the table. Before shutting off my phone, as was our general rule at Susie's, I called Cindy, again.

"On my way," she said. "Order for me. Whatever's today's special."

"Ham hocks over saffron rice?"

"Sounds yum. I'm in the car."

"Hurry. Safely. Going dark now," I said and turned off my phone.

Claire ordered beer for the table, and then got right into it. No small talk or jokes. Her first week back at work had been gruesome and unrelenting.

She said, "This killer is a precision blade man. No hesitation marks, no wasted motion on the slash through the neck, and then while blood is spurting like a fire hose and draining the body, he makes these random gashes on the upper breasts."

"What do you make of those marks? Don't over-think," Yuki said. "What comes to mind?"

Claire didn't get to answer right away, however, since Lorraine came over and took our orders. We ordered two chopped salads, one fish taco entrée with beans, ham hocks on rice for Cindy, and chips for everyone.

When Lorraine moved on, Claire said, "What do I think? It's some weird signature, though if we're trying to connect the cases, there were no such marks on Lorrie's body, and Wendy Franks was naked while Misty's body was clothed. He's way too good at this. It's not sexual. This is a professional-grade killer who's pleased with himself. He likes to butcher."

Cindy came through the passageway and took the empty seat next to me. I wanted to interrogate her—*what do you know that I don't know?*—but I didn't have to. She got comfortable, greeted all of us with blown kisses and fist bumps, then held up her glass for Claire to fill 'er up.

After a couple of gulps, she said, "I'm devastated about Misty. I really liked her. My story this morning generated a lot of mail, but no one took credit, or coughed up a suspect, or called the dead girl a bitch. It was just people saying they're mad and scared."

"Forward the mail to me?" I said.

"Sure, but curb your expectations," she said. "I posted about a hundred of them on my blog. I'll send you the rest."

"Thanks, and if you don't know, your story brought Burke into our house."

"What do you mean?"

"He drove in from Carmel with a death grip on your front page and came directly to the Hall."

"He turned himself in? He confessed?"

"No, Cindy, to accuse us of planting the story. To tell us he didn't kill Misty. He came with his alibi. Ironclad. How'd you get the details on Misty's murder?"

"I can't, you know, reveal my sources."

"Well, the killer's signature is now out there for a sicko to copy. Enough warning to a perp to make him run. It doesn't help the good guys, Cindy. Please don't say 'I was doing my job.'"

"My story was truthful, and good. Burke came in. That's a big deal, right? And the public has been warned that a vicious killer is roaming around. That could save a life. People start locking their car doors. Anyway, I was doing what I'm paid to do, what I'm good at, and you know I can never win these arguments with you, Linds, so let's just call it a draw. Okay?"

I drank down half a stein of beer in one draught.

Cindy said, "I also dug around a little about Wendy Franks."

Lorraine brought our dinners, told Cindy she liked her new haircut, and asked if we wanted anything else. Cindy asked for more bread.

Yuki said, "Cindy?"

"What?"

"Please don't make us beg."

"All right, girlfriends. Wendy had a boat. A Sea Ray. Harbor master says she took it out on Monday night. She had a male passenger, but he didn't see him."

Yuki said, "I don't like what I'm thinking."

I finished my beer.

Cindy said, "I'll say it. Wendy and an unknown male—possibly Burke—could have dumped Lorrie Burke into the drink."

"You're not going to put this out?" I said to Cindy.

"Hell, no. It cannot be corroborated. But I like it as a theory."

I tried to eat but kept seeing the last minutes of Misty's life over and over again. It was a cheaply produced horror movie with bad actors and an unsatisfying ending.

Lorraine came over with a basket of bread for Cindy and a cordless phone for Yuki.

"It's your husband," said Lorraine.

Yuki thanked her and took the phone.

"Hi, baby," she said. "Oh. No. Yes, she's right here."

She passed the phone across the table to me. Brady's gravelly southern-inflected voice was loud and clear.

"Brady, I had to shut off my phone while I ate—"

"Boxer. Another body turned up in McLaren, around John F. Shelley Drive. Unidentified."

I delivered the news to my friends, leaving out any details that Cindy could exploit. We paid, hugged, and left, splitting up on the street in different directions. It was the shortest, most fraught, and laughter-free Women's Murder Club meeting on record.

I called Joe to tell him my schedule had changed, got into my car, and headed out to meet Brady.

CHAPTER 46

BRADY WAS WAITING for me in front of the Hall, looking impatient, jouncing his keys in his hand.

He barely waited for me to set my brakes before opening the passenger side door of his Tacoma for me.

I said, "Is it Tara?"

He said, "Give me a sec. Strap in."

I braced as he stepped on the gas, and went code 3 with all lights flashing, sirens wailing. He took us by a now familiar route to McLaren Park and pulled up within a half mile of Burke's gabled house.

When he turned off the engine he said, "A hand sticking out of the ground alerted a couple of joggers. That's all I know."

Had to be Tara. She hadn't been in touch with Kathleen, who called me three times a day. She hadn't called her best friend. Hadn't asked Lucas for an infusion of cash. Her car hadn't been seen. She hadn't used her phone. Tara had disappeared.

Was she a captive? A fugitive? A corpse? I knew in my gut it was the latter. We pulled up to a herd of police vehicles at the verge of the park. Brady shut off the car and we both took deep breaths before extricating ourselves from seat belts and door locks. Brady checked in with the uniforms and CSIs standing by their vehicles at the curb.

McLaren was wooded at that point in its terrain, but I could see four bright halogen lights up-lighting the trees a good trek away.

Hallows came toward us, stoop-shouldered, grave, saying to Brady, "This guy is crazy, lieutenant. We need horse patrols and cars in this park until he's caught."

I clamped down on my frustration, then asked Hallows, "What do we know about the victim?"

Hallows looked at me, the disappointment on my face. "Sorry, Boxer. It's not Tara."

Sunset had faded and night had come on.

Hallows, with his monster tactical flashlight, led the way along a trail, and ten minutes later we reached the scene. CSU had set up an evidence tent a dozen feet from a body-sized mound of dirt half obscured by shrubbery. Items had been placed on a table for photographs, later to be bagged, tagged, and transported to the lab. I saw an inexpensive pearl necklace that had been found in the grave. There were sneakers of unknown color and brand. The victim was wearing the rest of her clothes and removal would be the ME's job.

Culver was overseeing CSIs who carefully shoveled dirt from the grave onto a tarp to be screened later.

"Dale, did you find her ID?"

"Nope. But look, we could still find her handbag in here."

I stayed long enough to see the remains lifted out of the two-foot-deep grave and laid carefully on a sheet. The victim's clothes were unremarkable: jeans, a V-neck pullover, a blue windbreaker.

"Was her throat cut?" I asked Culver.

"Can't tell and I don't want to poke around there. The ME will tell us—"

"Look at her fingernails," I said.

"We're going to screen everything that comes out of this hole."

I said, "Okay, Dale. I think my job here is done."

I found Brady out on the street. He said. "I'm going to stick around. We'll pick this up tomorrow. Have a uniform give you a lift."

I got my stuff out of Brady's car and asked an officer for a ride back to the Hall. I was buckling up when there was a rap on the glass.

It was a uniform. I buzzed down the window.

"Sergeant, the victim had plastic in her back pocket. We've got a name."

CHAPTER 47

I CALLED RICH CONKLIN from the car and we agreed to meet at the Hall, ASAP.

He was at his desk when I got there at 7:15 p.m. I collected my laptop and slipped into my old swivel chair behind my old desk. Adjusted my lamp. Moved folders belonging to Alvarez over to Conklin's desk and repossessed my territory.

Felt damned good to put aside task force protocol and step back into my accustomed routine.

I said, "There has to be a connection with the other murders. This could take ten minutes or ten hours."

"Either way is okay."

I showed Conklin the photos on my phone; a few angles on the victim and the shot of her credit card.

He said, "Susan Wenthauser. How do you want to do this?"

"You start with the white pages and the DMV database. After we have her address and phone, we'll go to the credit card company, see if we can get the date of her last charge."

"Copy that."

I typed "Susan Wenthauser" into my web browser. A second later, her name came up.

"Rich?"

"Yo."

"Susan Wenthauser was reported missing last month when she was a no-show for her night flight back to Boise. She was twenty-two, visiting a cousin who lived here. The case went cold, fast. No body, no one saw her. Filed under missing persons."

Conklin was also typing her name.

"Here's a story from a Boise paper," he said and began to read out loud. "Thelma Wenthauser, mother of missing twenty-two-year-old Susan, tells this reporter, 'Susie is such a good girl. She's never been out of Boise before. She's been waitressing, you know. And making plans to get married. She wanted to visit her cousin in San Francisco. She's not a runaway. Something has happened to her. Please say, 'If anyone has any information that will help us bring Susan home, call the newspaper or the police.'"

Conklin said, "No one called."

Susan's picture was in the article, her arm around her mother's waist. Cute picture.

And then I found an article quoting Boise PD quoting the cousin saying she and Susan had had their visit, said good-bye, Susan called a cab but never made her flight. A political firestorm had blotted out news of the missing young woman, and nothing further was written in San Francisco about Susan Wenthauser.

I picked up the phone and hit number 2 on my speed dial.

"Brady, the victim. Susan Wenthauser? She was visiting from Boise. Last seen three blocks from the

Burke house waiting for a cab to the airport. Her credit card was never charged for a ride, so there is no driver to trace. I'll bet some psycho offered to give her the grand tour of San Francisco before he cut her throat."

CHAPTER 48

JOE OPENED THE front door.

"The kiddo's asleep," he said.

I fell into his arms.

He hugged me close, rubbed my back, and walked me backward to the living room, dropping me gently into his well-loved recliner. He even pulled up on the handle raising the foot platform. Then he took off my gun, my jacket, my shoes, placed my phone on the side table.

"What can I get for madam?" he said. "Wine? Ice cream? Sleep mask?"

"I'm sorry for being so late. People keep turning up dead."

"I heard."

"You did?"

"Claire. No news, she says. Just call her in the morning."

"Okay. Could we have wine and ice cream in bed?"

"Who's going to stop us?"

I was in the shower for what could have been

twenty minutes. Martha sat on the bath mat watching the spray against the shower curtain. I talked to her, telling her in detail about my shitty day. Joe reached in, turned off the water, and handed me a fluffy white towel.

"You're using all the hot water in the building."

I laughed. Didn't know I had a laugh left in me.

Joe was wearing pajamas I'd given him for his birthday, blue and white striped, bottoms only. He helped me out of the shower, bundled me up in a terry cloth robe and said, "Do you want to look in on Julie or just come to bed?"

There was a glass of wine in his hand and he handed it over.

"I didn't dish up the ice cream. Yet."

I kissed him, took the wine and sipped, then handed the glass back to him. "I think I'll take a peek. Maybe watch her sleep for a minute."

I tiptoed into Julie's dandelion-yellow bedroom. She was in her big-girl bed, "without fences, Mom." As she was turning four in another week, we'd all agreed that a bed without rails was age appropriate.

As I looked down on her, Julie opened her eyes, gave me a sleepy smile, and said, "It's past your bedtime."

I cracked up. It wasn't just that she liked to mimic me, it was that she knew exactly how and when to do it.

"I'm going to bed now, Julie Bugs. See you in the morning."

I kissed her cheek, and she held up her toy cow, Mrs. Mooey Milkington. I kissed Mooey, too, and Julie threw an arm around my neck. I tickled her until she let me go. Still smiling, I backed out of her doorway and went to my favorite room in the house.

The blue-painted bedroom at the corner of our

apartment was cloud-like with white curtains and a big bed. It was the place where we'd made Julie and where I had delivered her, on a dark and stormy night, with the help of a dozen SFFD firefighters.

Joe had missed the drama, but has made up for it in so many ways. As he was doing now. He handed me a bowl of pralines and cream ice cream in a blue earthenware bowl, the still-chilled Chardonnay, fluffed pillows behind me. Then, my gorgeous husband got into bed beside me.

"Are you taking care, Blondie?"

He was worried about my recurring condition. Pernicious anemia can be fatal and had given us a bad scare. More than once.

"I'm emotionally exhausted," I said, "but not physically."

He looked at me dubiously.

"How are *you*?" I asked him.

"All paperworked out," he said.

"Awwww. Tell me all about it before I fall asleep with a spoon in my hand."

My cell phone rang out from the living room. I knew it was on the table next to Joe's chair. I tried to sit up.

Joe said, "Nope. No way. You're off duty."

"I'm working tomorrow."

"Tomorrow is still a day away."

Right he was.

I rolled over and wrapped myself around my husband. He shifted me until my robe was on the floor. I put my arms around his neck and I looked up at his face, taking my time. He kissed me, taking his time.

His hands moved over me, stirring me up.

I said, "Mmmmm."

He took that as a yes.

I sighed happily and let him have his way with me.

CHAPTER 49

MY EYES OPENED Sunday morning to the sound of my phone ringing in the living room.

The bedside clock read just after 5 a.m. This time, I had to pick up the call. I slipped out of bed, careful not to wake Joe, and found my phone in the dark. I looked at the caller ID.

Brady.

He said, "Sorry to wake you, Boxer, but I think you'd want to know."

"What? What's happening?"

"A red car, looks like a Volvo, was spotted a hundred yards out in the low tide off China Beach."

I knew the place, a large public parking area, five minutes off the tony Sea Cliff neighborhood and just south of Baker Beach. A curved tree-lined road led to the beach. The waters here could be brutal. When the storms whip up the surf, this was one of the most dangerous beaches in California. The tide gave no warning, no second chances as water poured in under the bridge, shifting dramatically with unpredictable undercurrents and deadly riptides. Daredevil swimmers had died at China Beach, a half dozen this year alone.

I said, "Brady, you're thinking it's Tara's car?"

"Could be. I can just make out the roof. I'm on the lot overlooking the beach right now. Coast guards brought in a couple of small track cranes and tow trucks. Motorboats. CSU has a flatbed truck and—Uh-oh. The car slipped the cable. This is one tough whale to beach. They've been at it for hours.

"Could be lost sleep for nothing. But I think you'll want to see this."

I shook Joe awake very gently and told him I had to go, that I would call him later.

"What time is it?"

"Just past five."

"Be careful."

"I will be."

I kissed his face all over, picked up my shoes from under the chair, and tripped over Martha as I dashed for the door.

"Sorry, Boo. Good girl."

I geared up in the living room and, out on the street, found my car and unlocked it without setting off the alarm. The engine started up easily and I drove up Lake Street to China Beach, arriving in about eight minutes. I took the access road to the overlook and parked next to Brady's Tacoma and a coast guard van. He was standing at the edge of the lot looking at the police activity underway in the wild dark sea through his binoculars.

A stiff salty breeze whipped my hair as I walked up behind him and shouted "Hello!"

He said, "Look out there," and handed me his glasses.

The first light of dawn lit the scene as the vehicle in question surfaced and bobbed in the tide. A crane was lifting the front end, and two tow trucks had hooks into the undercarriage, ratcheting in cable, balancing the vehicle still in the surf. And now the red car was inching up the beach, getting dragged up and out of an ocean that was reluctant to give it up.

I saw CSIs taking a tarp out of their van.

"They're going to wrap up the car?" I asked.

"Let's move," said my lieutenant.

CHAPTER 50

BRADY OFFERED A MUSCULAR ARM to help me down the stairs, and our timing was such that by the time we reached the beach, our badges in hand, the car was on four wheels.

We identified ourselves to the coast guard officer, then ducked the tape and walked up on the red Volvo as water and fish and sand poured through the underside and out the open windows. Something pale caught my eye. An arm followed the flow of water and flopped out of the passenger-side window. It was a woman's arm, abraded and bloated from soaking in seawater and mauled by sea animals.

As we circled the car, I braced myself for the sight of the dead woman's ruined face. She had been in the passenger seat when the car was driven into the ocean. She was still seated with the shoulder harness firmly locking her in place. Her head was flopped to the side and the gash across her throat was swollen nearly shut, no longer a clean cut. There was a large, flat stone on the accelerator that had caused the car to take flight.

I was sure this was Tara Burke, but I couldn't make a positive ID by looking at her. Still, I recognized the denim dress Tara had been wearing, the outfit that had been captured on video when she'd left her house with Lorrie on Monday morning. She wouldn't have fingerprints any longer, but presumably dental work, if she'd had any, could identify her.

Brady called my attention to the pink diaper bag jammed under the back seat, where there was also an unbuckled infant car seat. As I studied the woman, I noticed something inked onto the inside of her wrist: a small heart-shaped tattoo that confirmed her identity.

My hand was shaking as I took a picture with my phone and walked around the car to show it to Brady.

A CSI said, "'Scuse us, lieutenant. We're going to wrap the car with the body inside. Take it all back to the lab."

"Uh-huh, uh-huh," said Brady. "Good catch, Boxer. I say we leave this to Hallows and his crew. We'll go wake up Burke and take him in. Time and tide wait for no man."

"What was that?"

"Chaucer. I took English lit, too. It means 'Let's git.'"

CHAPTER 51

I TROTTED BEHIND BRADY up the stairs to his vehicle in the parking area. He opened the door, grabbed the mic, and requested backup to Burke's address.

"Three patrol cars. Code two," he said.

Urgent, no lights or sirens.

Within minutes we'd parked on Persia Avenue, three hundred yards from Burke's front door. The house was dark. The silver Audi was in the driveway and Reg Covington, SWAT commander, had blocked the driveway with his armored car. Two unmarked cars were parked at the curb, and cops wearing Kevlar jackets quietly disembarked and crept toward the house.

Brady and I exited the Tacoma and with our BearCat backup only yards away and two teams surrounding the house, we moved in on 79 Dublin Street. Covington's team of six used the hood, roof, and doors of the BearCat as shields and gun rests. We were covered.

Brady unlatched Lucas Burke's picket gate and

we approached the dark blue front door with its fist-shaped brass knocker. I stood to the side. Brady stepped in, knocked and announced, then I got out of his way as he lifted his leg and kicked in the door.

No alarms or lights came on, either inside or outside the house. Covington and two of his team rushed in, yelling.

"SFPD! Speak out!"

No one did. The advance team cleared the downstairs rooms and thundered up the stairs to the bedrooms.

I heard Covington shout, "Hands up! Face the wall!"

Burke's voice. "What now? This is harassment."

Brady and I bounded up the staircase and found Lucas Burke standing beside the bed in a T-shirt and boxers. He showed us that his hands were empty and Brady turned him 180 and told him to put his hands on the wall. One after the other, Brady jerked Burke's arms around to his back and cuffed him, then spun him back around to face us.

I said, "Lucas, I'm sorry to tell you that we've recovered Tara's car from the ocean. Her body was inside. You're under arrest for suspicion in the murders of Tara Burke and Lorrie Burke."

He howled, "Noooooooooo!"

I read him his rights; to remain silent. Anything he said could be used against him. Right to a lawyer and the state would provide an attorney if he couldn't afford one.

"Do you understand your rights?"

He glared at me.

"I haven't killed anyone."

"Boxer, do it again, louder," said Brady.

I shouted what I'd just said, one sentence at a time, asking him after each, "Do you understand?"

Burke hissed, "Yes, yes, yes, I understand."

"Let's go," said Brady, pushing Burke to and through the bedroom doorway. Covington's team followed Brady, and Burke and I brought up the rear, helping Brady stuff the accused into the back seat of our unmarked.

Burke would be charged with reasonable suspicion of homicide. Although we hadn't caught him in the act, had no witness or physical evidence of any kind, by his own admission, Burke had fought with his wife the morning she disappeared. It would be harder or even impossible, with what we had, to prove that he'd killed Misty Fogarty, Wendy Franks, and Susan Wenthauser. So the DA would go with our strongest cases, and if we found further evidence we would charge him for those crimes, too.

But, what we had was compelling.

One, Tara strapped into the passenger seat of her car, her throat slashed; and, two, the dead baby, evidence of manual asphyxiation, her diaper bag stuffed under the same back seat, infant car seat unbuckled. Burke had seen them last. There had been a history of spousal abuse. He had been having an affair. Three strikes.

A good prosecutor would be able to convince a jury that Lucas Burke was a wolf dressed in a high school teacher's tweeds. An impartial jury would buy it.

That's what I believed.

CHAPTER 52

IT WAS FRIDAY MORNING, ten past nine.

Brady, Yuki, and I were with DA Len Parisi in his office with Lucas Burke and Newton Gardner, his publicity-grabbing hard-ass criminal defense attorney.

I was rested and focused and eager to hear what Lucas Burke would say about the recovery of his dead wife.

Lucas Burke was in jailhouse orange with flip-flops and a two-day beard. He looked bad, smelled bad, and I was guessing he hadn't slept since we booked him two days ago. Whatever thoughts had kept him awake were surely compounded by the awful accommodations offered in our sixth-floor jail. It was dirty, bright lights were on all night, and the other guests were generally foulmouthed, pissed off, and bordering on violence.

For his own safety, Burke had likely slept while leaning against the wall of his cell.

I almost felt sorry for him.

But now he had first-class representation in Newt

Gardner and was paying a thousand bucks an hour for the privilege. I'd never met Gardner before, but I'd seen him in front of the courthouse and on late-night news standing with A-list clients, mesmerizing the press with his wit and showmanship and obvious ambition for an ever bigger stage.

As morning rush traffic whooshed past the windows two stories above Bryant Street, Len Parisi sat at his super-sized desk. Above him loomed the red pit bull face of his wall clock. The rest of us, including Burke and his attorney, had pulled up chairs around the desk.

Gardner was wearing a smart gray suit, starched white shirt, and classic black oxfords buffed to a high shine. His head was shaven, making his sharp black eyes his standout feature. He'd asked for this meeting and had one thing on his agenda: to convince Leonard Parisi to drop the "ridiculous" charges against his client before another day had passed, before the world media saw this as O.J. two-point-oh, and had implied that he would put the city of San Francisco through a humiliating trial that it would lose.

Parisi said, "Mr. Gardner. It's your meeting."

Gardner said, "Thanks, Mr. Parisi. It's really very simple. Lucas Burke did not kill his wife and child, and I'm quite sure you know the SFPD has no evidence, none, not a hair or a fingerprint or a speck of DNA belonging to my client on the bodies of the victims. There's no witness, no video, no nothing. I'm asking you to drop the charges for one simple reason. Lucas didn't do it and you have zero probable cause to charge him."

"Okay. Thanks for coming in," said Parisi, looking at his watch.

Gardner got the slight as it was meant and he took

umbrage. "I promise you," he said, "I'm going to win, Mr. Parisi. I'm going to get my client out of this trap you've set for him."

"Do your worst, Mr. Gardner. That much I expect," Parisi said, unmoved and unafraid. He knew our case cold.

Gardner wasn't done. He fixed his bullet eyes on Parisi.

"About now, I should get up and say to my client, 'Don't lose any sleep over this, Luke. They have nothing. I'll see you in a couple of days.' But I want you to know that along with dismantling your circumstantial case, I'm going to introduce a few dozen character witnesses; educators and neighbors and even a man of the cloth. In short, Len, you have no case. Not a prayer of one. Do you really want to go through the wood chipper? Or would it be better for all concerned if your cops took a little more time and found the real killer?"

Parisi crossed his hands over his large belly and smiled ever so slightly. I had a good idea that he was just fine with Newton Gardner laying out his case.

"And here's the bonus round," Gardner continued. "Drop the charges and release my client, now, and we won't sue the city for police harassment and I won't get on a soapbox and mock the SFPD for their incompetence. How does that sound?"

Parisi said, "Mr. Gardner. I'll leave you to froth and wriggle alone. I'm not a stupid man. We're charging your client with two counts of murder, and that's a gift. We can prove that he killed his wife and daughter with malice aforethought. And that's what we'll be telling the judge at Mr. Burke's arraignment. The charges stand. And now, I have to prepare for a meeting."

I wanted to cheer, but exhilaration was premature.

Said Gardner, "I hate to tell you, my friend, but you can't convict a man because you need to clear a nasty case."

Parisi said, "That's enough, counselor. You've said more than enough."

Gardner didn't turn to his client and say "Let's go." Instead he said, "We have something to offer that will unsnarl this whole big ball of nothing."

"You've got three minutes, sir. I have other business to attend to," said Red Dog Parisi.

What came next was almost beyond my comprehension.

CHAPTER 53

NEWT GARDNER LEANED against the arm of his chair and whispered into his client's ear.

Burke nodded, and said, "Yes, yes. Okay."

Then, he looked up and spoke into an unfocused middle distance between Brady, Parisi, and me.

"I've been holding something back."

Burke had all of our attention. Even Red Dog, who sat in his chair like a stone Buddha, leaned forward.

What the hell was this? I tried to imagine what Burke could have kept from us, but nothing lit up. Not an idea in the world, but I was sure it was going to be bull.

Burke said, "I know full well that what I'm going to tell you is going to sound like I made it up to mislead you. It's not. I believe I know who killed Lorrie and Tara. And Misty. When I was in your office, sergeant, holding that paper with Misty's picture, I wanted to scream it. But I can't prove he did it. That's why I've kept it to myself."

Brady said, "I'm going to record this. Any objection?"

No one spoke. Brady pressed a button on his cell phone and put it down on Red Dog's desk.

He said to Burke, "Once again. From the top."

Burke sighed. But his face was full of emotion. I'd never seen him look like this. Furious, yes. Crushed by events, definitely. But this was different. He looked afraid.

He spoke toward the phone, saying, "I'm Lucas Burke and I didn't kill my wife and daughter or Misty Fogarty or the other women whose bodies you've found. But I think I know who did. I'll cooperate fully and help you catch the killer if I can, and I'm willing to testify against him."

"Talk," said Parisi. "We ran out of patience a week ago."

"Fifteen years ago, my mother, Corinne, and my sister, Jodie, disappeared. Maybe you remember the case. If not, look it up. Their bodies were never found. No one was ever arrested. I was already in my mid-twenties when they disappeared, and I wasn't living at home. But while I've done everything a human being could do to convince myself that it isn't true, I have reason to believe that my father, Evan Burke, killed them. I know my father. And you see? First my mother and sister. Then my wife and daughter, and a woman I loved. I can't ignore what I know. My father is a true psychopathic serial killer—the real deal."

Yuki scoffed. But my attention was on Lucas Burke and Brady's phone recording this frankly fantastic story. Burke asked for a tissue, for water, and Parisi asked his assistant, Katie Branch, to come in.

After a short intermission, Burke went on.

"I had twelve years of therapy working to convince myself that my father couldn't be a killer. But there's one connection I can't shake. My father has always been drawn to the water. He always had boats. I've done research and now it seems obvious. Women disappeared in Catalina where we lived. Women disappeared in Isla Vista near the campus of UC Santa Barbara. Women's bodies have been found in coastal areas.

"I can't say that he killed them all, but many of those murders were never solved and often the bodies weren't found. My father is smooth. And charming. And sly. And he likes to kill women. And maybe because he wants me to both suffer and bear witness. That's why he made sure that Tara and Lorrie died in the water."

Lucas Burke seemed parched and worn out from his speech, but Parisi was unmoved. Same for Brady.

Parisi said, "Mr. Gardner. Mr. Burke. This is your defense? 'The other dude did it? And he's my father?'"

Gardner said, "My client can provide the names of possible victims, approximate dates when they disappeared. With fresh information and good police work, I'm confident proof exists that Evan Burke, not Lucas, killed Tara and Lorrie Burke."

I adjusted my chair so that I was right in Burke's face and questioned him.

"What's your father's full name?"

"Evan William Burke."

"When did you speak with him last?"

"When Tara and I got married. Three years ago. But before that? Maybe three times after my mother and sister disappeared."

"Where does he live?"

"I got a birthday card from him on my fortieth. The return address was somewhere in Marin County. If I look at a map, I might remember. But logic tells me that he may have a place near where I live now. So that he could watch me, follow people in my life and kill other people to muddy the picture. Look. This man is a high genius. You have to be prepared—"

I interrupted, "You have a picture of him? You have anything with his DNA? That birthday card for instance. The flap of the envelope?"

"I threw it out. Took it down to the trash. But," said Burke, "talk to the police in Marin County. He was arrested when Mom and my baby sister disappeared. They'll have a mug shot, won't they?"

This was Lucas's recollection. Police records might well show otherwise.

Katie knocked on the office door, opened it, and said, "Mr. Parisi, you have a meeting with the mayor in five minutes. After you see him, you have a meeting with the victims' families."

"Thanks, Katie. Yuki, you want to add anything?"

"I do," said Yuki. "If Mr. Burke didn't kill his wife and child, he and Mr. Gardner can tell the judge at arraignment."

"Okay, then," said Parisi. "Mr. Burke, we'll investigate your claim, as far-fetched as it is. I suggest you and Mr. Gardner prepare for court. Sergeant Boxer, if you will be so kind, take Mr. Burke back to his cell."

CHAPTER 54

THE TASK FORCE GATHERED once again in Swanson's empty office at the end of our floor.

I ran the story for those who hadn't heard it.

Brady stood with his back to the whiteboard and said, "Show of hands, who believes Lucas Burke is innocent?"

No hands went up. And then, as if it had its own mind, my right hand lifted from the table.

"Boxer?"

"I've spent a lot of time with Burke. I don't like him. But I find his emotional distress, over the baby, over Misty, real. When I'm with him, I believe him. Otherwise?" I threw up my hands. "I've struggled with this, you know that, lieu. So, it's either that he's a dirty old man who has positioned himself to date underage girls, end of statement. Or all of that plus he's a gifted liar and a stealthy killer. Or all of the above and his psycho killer father is setting him up for a fall. Count me on the fence."

Brady held me in his ice-blue stare a beat too long,

and then said, "I'm going to meet with the mayor. Boxer, you're in charge. But this is how I see it. What Gardner said is true. We have only circumstantial evidence. So, if Lucas Burke is telling the truth, we need to find Evan Burke, bring him in and question the hell out of him. We do impeccable police work. Determine whether Burke Senior has a California residence. Check out his movements over the last week, down to the minute. What we *don't* want to do is send the DA into court to arraign the wrong man."

Brady left the room and I took the floor.

I divvied up the manpower, six teams and me, and assigned them to NCIC, ViCAP, and other databases we had at hand. Until we found Evan Burke, we would scrutinize every unsolved murder of every female going back fifteen years.

The state of California had produced a lot of data.

We hit the keys.

A simple search for "Evan Burke" turned up sixty men with that name in California alone. We halved the list to men in their sixties, but that wasn't enough.

I reached out to Captain Geoffrey Brevoort, Marin County PD. Although Brevoort quickly confirmed Corinne and Jodie Burke's disappearance, Lucas's memory of his father's arrest didn't match the records. Brevoort had nothing on Evan Burke; no mug shots, no prints or DNA. He'd been questioned, yes. But his alibis had held up and the man not only cooperated, he was an emotional wreck.

While I was on the phone with Brevoort, Conklin found a dozen Evan Burkes in the DMV so now we had addresses, birth dates, and best of all, photos of several dozen Evan Burkes in California. None of them resembled Lucas.

And then, Alvarez found a California boating

license for an E. W. Burke in Sausalito, six nautical miles off the coast of San Francisco. There was no photo attached to the file, no prints, but it was a place to start.

I called Brevoort again and plugged into the detectives working on the Wendy Franks case, told them what we knew. I reached the harbor master in Sausalito, the one who had seen Wendy Franks taking her Sea Ray out with an unknown male passenger.

I sent him a clip of the man in black who was captured on video in the Sunset Park Prep parking lot. Not good enough for facial recognition or any recognition, but hell, maybe the dim and grainy photo would come up as a "maybe."

It didn't.

I texted him the info Alvarez had turned up; name and numbers of the certification and vessel ID. The harbor master had no such vessel at his marina. He offered to check around and I thanked him.

We broke for pizza, and then put our eyes back on our screens. The day moved so slowly that when Brady arrived back in the task force HQ, I was surprised that it was still light outside.

Five fifteen to be exact.

I gave Brady the rundown. "We've made some progress. No man called Evan Burke has a record. One did live in Sausalito and his wife and child did disappear and it is a cold case. Ten years ago, that same Evan had a Century Boats 30 Express and a license to operate it. He sold it. The current owner lives in the Caribbean. We do not have a current address for that Evan Burke, but it's still more than we had."

"Good work, Boxer. Time to quit for the day."

"Really?"

"Yeah. And everyone try to go to bed early tonight."

CHAPTER 55

OUR TASK FORCE of eight put place marks between pages, saved files, made notes for the next day, and we did it quick. Then we filed down the hallway to our bullpen.

I phoned Joe from my desk and he said Julie had just had her dinner.

"Want to meet us at the park?" he said.

This was a question that made Martha act like a pup, and I was having a similar reaction. Park. Grass. Lake. Daughter, husband, and dog all together.

"You don't have to ask twice," I said. "I'll be home in fifteen minutes, traffic permitting."

Traffic permitted.

My family was waiting on the front steps of the apartment building when I cruised to a stop at the curb. Joe opened my car door, and while Julie hung on to our old doggie's leash, Joe gave me a big smooch.

I locked the car, then picked Julie up and carried her for a full block, glad to stretch my legs and hear my daughter's breathy voice in my ear.

"We had chicken wings."

"Oh, good."

"Dad saved you some pie."

"What kind?"

"Dad, what kind?"

"Peach, right?"

"Good. I love peach pie."

"Put me down now, Mommy."

The park was full of dogs and families when we got there, and Julie found her friend Chrissy. While they counted, named, and fed the ducks, Joe and I took a bench with a view of the children at lake's edge and the surrounding park.

My husband and I sat close together on a wooden bench in the twilight and I squeezed his hand.

"Bad day?" he asked me.

"Not the worst ever, but knotty."

"Well my day hasn't been knotty or even tangled. So lay it on me."

"I'd hoped I could co-opt your brain for a bit."

"Ready and eager," he said.

I let it all out. Since I had free access to the former director of Homeland Security with years of experience with the CIA and the FBI, I thought maybe he could help me with my tricky damned case. I told him about the meeting this morning with Red Dog and Lucas Burke and his shark, Newt Gardner.

Joe said, "Burke either has more money than we know, or Gardner is seeing a lot of cameras in this case."

"Wouldn't be surprised," I said. "Man killing his wife and baby isn't just tabloid news. It's *60 Minutes*. We're holding back the other victims."

"So holding back on Misty and the sea-loving artist who'd lived in Sausalito?"

"Wendy Franks. And that young girl from Boise,

Susan Wenthauser. We can't prove anything, not even motive. Maybe before the trial, if there is one, we'll get some evidence. We can always hope someone comes forward on Franks or Fogarty."

"Could be very afraid."

"Yeah. But. Right now, we have a potential turn in the case you're not going to believe. Picture this, Joe. Burke is in the hot seat, all of us sitting around Parisi's desk. The meeting is over. We're two seconds from leaving the room. Then Gardner whispers to Burke and then Burke said this, Joe——"

I had to pause to get up and grab Julie before she waded into the lake. She and I had a very agreeable chat about the ducks, I said hello to Chrissy's mom, then went back to Joe, who was smiling fondly as he watched this little scene.

"You cliff-hung me," he said.

"Sorry. Where was I?"

"Lucas Burke said something."

"Right. Right. Then he says with his lawyer's encouragement, 'I think my father killed my mom and sister and maybe others. I think my father is a serial killer and I think *he* killed Lorrie and Tara.'"

"His *father*?" said Joe. "Burke says his father killed his wife and daughter?"

"That's what he said. His own wife and daughter *and* Burke's, yes." I let him in on the day's work. Evan Burke had an old boat license and no known address; I had a verified police report that Evan Burke's wife and daughter had in fact disappeared and been investigated as a homicide.

"It's a cold case now."

Joe said, "So I'd look for patterns of several women disappearing in various places. See if Evan Burke lived in the vicinity."

"Yeah, yeah, sure. Might be able to find something like that if we had a computer wiz on staff or three of them who could just hunt for that."

We were both silent for several minutes, watching the kids, having thoughts of serial murder.

Then Joe said, "I have a thought. Did I ever mention a guy named Berney?"

"Don't think so. Who is he?"

"He was with the FBI, DC office, back in the day. We used to think of him as a magician of the dark side. He had contacts, informants, a network here and overseas. And a special kind of mind for detail. I think I still have his number."

Joe pulled his phone out of his jacket, swiped a few buttons, and a few seconds later, his call was answered.

The two did some catching up. *Where are you? What are you doing? How long has it been?* Then Joe said, "Berney, here's why I called. You remember my wife, Lindsay, an SFPD Homicide sergeant? She's working on a case that resembles a black hole."

I didn't have my ear to the phone, but from what Joe said, I got the impression that Berney's network remained intact. He knew of the Burke-related killings. He also knew that Lucas Burke was on the hook for them.

Joe said, "Could you run a check on the father? Name's Evan Burke. And before you ask, I don't have a location beyond our general vicinity."

Joe listened. Berney was doing the talking, punctuated by Joe saying, "Okay, I understand," "Got it," and finally, "Well thanks. I'll tell her. You, too."

Joe disconnected the line.

"Berney knows who they are. He said words to the effect that this is a dangerous situation—for you.

I can't swear but I think Burke and son might be an active case with the FBI. Or, maybe Berney has been aware of them for a while on an earlier crime. Lucas Burke's mother and sister, say. Either way, Lindsay, be very careful when you're around Lucas, and if you find Evan, that goes for him, too. Berney will call me if he gets anything solid."

"That's it?"

"That's a lot."

With her usual impeccable timing, Julie ran toward us and climbed over Martha and into my lap.

"Home now," she said.

"Home, now, pleassssse."

She laughed at me. So did Joe.

Fine. We gathered our belongings, including Martha's leash, and making a family chain with our held hands, walked slowly home.

PART TWO

CHAPTER 56

WHEN YUKI'S EYES OPENED Monday morning, the sky was black outside her window.

She checked her sleep tracker, and by that slight green glow she learned that it was just after four. *No, no, no.* Too early. Her head was swimming with thoughts and images, and the sound of Lucas Burke's pathetic voice. She thought about the autopsy pictures Claire had shown her of Tara Burke, and before that, the heartbreaking images of Lorrie. She pictured Newton Gardner, Burke's showboat attorney. Yuki knew that if anyone could get Burke off, it was Gardner.

She fluffed up her pillow and closed her eyes, tried counting backward by sevens, but it was hopeless. Ninety-three, eighty-six, and then she was flashing on Gardner's TV appearances and recalling a time she'd watched him in court. She'd both despised and learned from his attack-dog methods and his ability to captivate juries. They loved him. During recesses, he'd go out to the hallway outside the courtroom and manage the press. They loved him, too.

Gardner would turn this Burke case into a billboard for himself.

Yuki lay quietly under the bedcovers, thinking, dozing off, thinking some more, listening to her husband breathing beside her, dozing again.

Next thing she knew, Brady was standing next to the bed, towel around his waist, saying, "Your turn, darlin'."

"Okay. Can you make the coffee?"

She got out of bed, showered, washed her hair, blew it out, twisted the blond streak around her finger. All the while, she was organizing her thoughts, wondering if things would go much better for her if she just ignored Newt Gardner. *Yeah, yeah, he'd hate that.*

Besides, this was arraignment court. *Guilty or not guilty, how do you plead?* And she thought about the judge, Vivian Kahn, a no-nonsense litigator, originally from LA, appointed to the bench in San Francisco three years ago. Yuki thought Kahn was the perfect judge for the job. She had personality. She could be acerbic, but she also had a sense of the absurd. And if Burke told the judge that his father did it, Yuki thought there was no way Kahn would take it seriously.

But there was no way to know until she was standing before her, presenting the charges against Burke.

Yuki slipped on her robe, checked the time. Only seven fifteen. She would have time to get to the office, meet with Red Dog, check her mail, and obsess a little more. Yuki found Brady in the kitchen dumping the dregs of his coffee into the sink.

"A little high-test goes a long way," he said. He scrutinized her expression and said, "You've got this in the bag, darlin'. I'll try and git there to see you running over the defense counsel."

"Yeah. You always say that."

"Let me put it this way, then. I'll do my best. But I can already see it. You're gonna leave the courtroom glowin'. The press is gonna be all over you. Newt Gardner is gonna think he lost his mojo. That might give him a breakdown."

"You're awfully cheerful," she said.

"I want Burke behind bars and I'm going to get my wish, that's why."

"You're going to jinx me if you don't stop."

He grabbed her and kissed her.

"Wear your blue Armani," he said.

"That's why I hung it on the back of the door."

"Need anything before I go?"

"I'm good. Keep your phone on."

Brady kissed her again and left the apartment.

CHAPTER 57

YUKI SLIPPED INTO her sharp blue suit and heels, then drove to the Hall, where she took the elevator to the second floor.

Walking through the reception area, she took a hard left and saw down at the end of the corridor that Len Parisi's door was open. When she got to his office, she tapped lightly on the door. Parisi looked up and waved her in.

He was in shirtsleeves, tie loosened, a stack of paper in front of him.

"Do you want to do a run-through?" he asked.

"I've got it, Len."

"Clapper's likely to show up. He'll be standing in the back row near the door."

"Not a problem. What about you? Gonna come and watch?"

"You've done a thousand of these, Yuki. You don't need any help from me."

She smiled, thanked him, and walked down the hall, her shoes clicking on the linoleum flooring. She

entered her office to check her interoffice mail. She
closed the door, checked her makeup, her teeth, the
blond streak just dipping over her eyebrow. All as it
should be.

Yuki wondered if she wasn't a touch overdressed,
but Newt Gardner would be, too. *Showtime.* They
might have to wait hours for the case to be called,
but when it was, the entire process might take five
minutes. But in those five minutes she wanted to
run right the hell over the defendant and get him
remanded, no bail.

Yuki opened her door again, and exchanged greetings with her intern assistant, Deirdre Glass. Deirdre
was also wearing a suit, had put on some pearls with
matching earrings. She told Yuki that the charge file
was in order and looked eager and ready to go.

"You want your briefcase or a folder?"

"Briefcase. Let's get this bastard arraigned," she said.

Arraignment court was on the same floor as the
DA's office. Deirdre carried the briefcase with the
charge document and the two walked to the courtroom. A guard opened the door for them and Yuki
and Deirdre took two seats behind the bar in the large
and teeming courtroom. Yuki saw Gardner across the
aisle with Burke. The attorney was doing the talking
and Burke looked utterly confident.

Not for the first time today, Yuki felt doubt.

Defendants, court officers, and attorneys came
through the room and took seats in the gallery. The
press was visible crowding the seats at the back, and
every time the door opened, Yuki saw the men and
women with cameras and mics who were all here
today for this one thing: the arraignment of Lucas
Burke.

What stunt would Gardner pull?

Would Lucas Burke be remanded, or would Gardner ask for a continuance? If so, would Burke immediately flee?

He'd done it before.

She could only do her best, as she always did.

Deirdre patted Yuki's sleeve.

"You totally rock, Yuki. No worries. At all."

CHAPTER 58

THE CLERK STOOD in front of the bench and announced, "The Honorable Vivian Kahn, judge, presiding. Please be seated and come to order."

Judge Kahn was in her fifties but looked younger. She had straight, dark, chin-length hair, red-framed glasses, and was looking through them at the charges in front of her.

She looked up at the attorneys and the defendant before her and said, "Good afternoon, ladies and gentlemen. In the matter of the people of the state of California versus Lucas William Burke. Counsel, your appearances please."

"Yuki Castellano for the people," she introduced herself to the court.

"Your Honor, good afternoon. Newton Gardner, attorney on behalf of Lucas William Burke, who's present in custody before the court."

"Very good. Ms. Castellano, are you ready to proceed?"

"Yes, Your Honor. At this time the people would file

with this court a two-count complaint against Lucas Burke, this defendant. Both charges are murder in the first degree as well as special circumstances pursuant to penal code regarding the willful death of a tender age child. That child is the defendant's daughter. A baby just over sixteen months in age."

Judge Kahn asked Yuki, "Have you advised the defendant of his constitutional rights?"

Yuki said, "Yes, Your Honor, and the arresting police officers, Lieutenant Jackson Brady and Sergeant Lindsay Boxer of the SFPD Southern Station, also advised Mr. Lucas Burke of his constitutional rights when he was arrested."

"Mr. Gardner, has your client signed and produced the form to that effect?"

Gardner said, "Your Honor, we received the copy of the complaint late yesterday afternoon. It is about fifteen pages. My office would like to look at it more closely to make a decision regarding if the defense would like to request a continuance."

"Ms. Castellano, do you wish to respond?"

"Yes, Your Honor. The people would certainly object to the request for a continuance. The defendant put forth an opposing theory of the crimes, and our police department, in conjunction with other police departments, have spent the last three days investigating the defendant's theory and finding no evidence to support it whatsoever."

"The theory being?" the judge asked Yuki.

"The defendant said that he didn't commit the crime, that someone else did. The prosecution would suggest that this alternate theory of the crimes be presented in court to a jury, and furthermore, Your Honor, this is a mandatory filing. It's mandated by the code."

Judge Kahn agreed with the prosecution and asked, "Are there any other issues that need to be addressed at this time, counsel?"

Yuki said, "For the record, Your Honor, we should address the issue of bail."

"All right," Kahn said, removing her glasses, letting them fall to the length of the chain she wore around her neck. "As I understand penal code section 1270.5, the defendant is not entitled to bail because of the nature of the charges, most specifically the 'special circumstances' regarding the baby. Do you wish to be heard on the matter of bail, Mr. Gardner?"

Gardner seemed utterly confident that he would win his point.

"Yes, Your Honor. Mr. Burke is an outstanding citizen, and even counsel for the People would admit that they have no direct evidence against him. They have a theory that this man killed his wife and child. In fact, nothing could be farther from the truth. He is a minute away from a nervous breakdown over the loss of his family."

Kahn said, "Okay, that's enough, Mr. Gardner."

"Ms. Castellano, you have something to add?"

"Yes, Your Honor. Mr. Burke is a flight risk. When the police searched his house, Mr. Burke took the opportunity to leave town. The people cannot take a chance that he will do so again."

The judge said, "Mr. Burke, how do you plead?"

"Not guilty, Your Honor. May I speak?"

"Save it for your trial, Mr. Burke."

"Your Honor, I didn't do it."

"Okeydoke," said Kahn. "Based on the language of the referenced section of the penal code and the allegations as to the special circumstances, the court finds that the defendant is not entitled to bail and will be remanded to the Men's Jail at the Hall of Justice for trial. To be held, let's see, in three months. The precise date will be forthcoming."

The clerk called the next case and Yuki headed toward the doors at the rear of the courtroom. Chief Charlie Clapper was standing in the aisle as Yuki and Deirdre headed to the door. Clapper touched her shoulder and said, "Well done."

Yuki thanked him before she was carried along by the force of the crowd behind her.

As her husband—and her intern—had predicted, Yuki rocked.

And she glowed.

CHAPTER 59

CINDY HAD BEEN STANDING in the narrow space behind the last row of seats in Courtroom 2C, with a view over the heads of the spectators in the gallery.

As soon as Judge Kahn denied bail for Burke, Cindy left the courtroom and stationed herself in the corridor so that she faced the double door. Her pal and cameraman, Jonathan Samuels, stood right behind her and was already shooting video to capture the flow of people in the corridor.

Cindy fluffed her hair, straightened her collar, pressed her lips together.

In seconds Yuki would be there. In Cindy's opinion, Yuki had handled her part like the pro she was. In the process she had steamrolled Newt Gardner and had walked away with the win.

Now the courtroom doors opened and the fresh tide of people coming out blocked Cindy's view. She looked up at Samuels, who was a head taller than she.

"Jonny."

"Shove your way in. I got you."

Cindy cut through the crowd, spotted Yuki, and called her name.

Yuki turned to Cindy and grinned. They put up their right hands and slapped them together. Samuels held up his fingers, folding them in one at a time. Five, four, three . . .

Then Cindy said, "We have with us Assistant District Attorney Yuki Castellano, who has just presented charges against Lucas Burke, English teacher at Sunset Park Prep, and accused murderer of his wife and child. Mr. Burke's request for bail was denied by Judge Vivian Kahn. Mr. Burke has been bound over until his trial. Ms. Castellano, a comment please for our readers."

"Sure, Cindy. In brief, it was a good day for the people of—" She didn't get to finish. Kathleen Wyatt came through the courtroom doors, manic, wild-eyed, wearing a cap over her hair, a red tunic over her tights. She threw her arms around Yuki, saying, "Ms. Castellano, thank you, thank you!"

She collapsed against Yuki and was crying on her shoulder.

Cindy stepped in and said, "Kathleen, it's me, Cindy Thomas. Do you wish to make a statement on camera?"

Kathleen nodded her head vigorously, mopped her eyes with the back of her hands as Yuki slipped away through the crowd.

Cindy said, "I have with me Kathleen Wyatt, mother of Tara Burke, and grandmother of Lorrie Burke. Kathleen?"

Cindy put the mic up to the distraught woman's face.

"I want to say that though Tara will never see her twenty-first birthday, and Lorrie will never reach her second, I'm happy to see Lucas Burke has been locked up. That's all. And to thank the SFPD and the district attorney's office for everything they did."

Samuels shut down the camera as Cindy ended her conversation with the woman in red.

Once Kathleen walked out, Cindy said, "Wow. I couldn't have planned that. Do we have something we can use? I know. I'll call Yuki if needed and we can do a solo shot out on the street."

She saw Newt Gardner leaving the courtroom, winning attitude on display, reporters bunching up around him.

He stopped walking and addressed the press.

"Folks, what you've just seen is a classic example of lazy police work, a rush to judgment. My client has suffered an unspeakable loss, and he has pleaded 'not guilty' to the charges. Mr. Burke has been falsely accused and we will prove this in court. Like all citizens, my client will have a trial and be judged by his peers.

"That's all. Thank you."

Samuels said to Cindy, "Now, *that's* a wrap."

CHAPTER 60

I LEFT THE COURTROOM, taking the fire stairs to escape the mobbed corridor and caught up with Yuki on the second-floor landing.

My hug caught her by surprise and almost threw us both down the staircase. I grabbed a bannister to stop our fall, then we both started laughing.

"High heels are no joking matter," she said, shaking her finger at me.

"Sor-*ry*," I said. "Yuki, you were great. You made that newt look like a worm."

"Hah! Well either way, he didn't get Burke bonded out. Did you see Brady in the gallery?" she asked.

"I didn't, but let's go see him now."

Yuki looked at her watch. "Sure. Okay."

She took off her shoes and—holding them in one hand, other hand on the bannister—we climbed to the fourth floor. I could see from the entrance to the squad room that Brady was in the house and he wasn't alone.

"There's Cindy," Yuki said, "and her photographer.

I'm gonna duck out. Best if she interviews Brady without me. What if we meet at MacBain's after work and talk over bottomless beer?"

"Brilliant," I said.

MacBain's, the after-work beer-and-burger joint, couldn't be more convenient for me, Yuki, and Claire, and a short cab ride away for Cindy.

By six, Claire, Yuki, and I had taken the table against the wall between the front window and the old-timey juke box. Claire had pulled up Cindy's front page story on her phone and was reading it aloud for Yuki's enjoyment. I remarked that Cindy was late as always, which was her cue to blow in through the front door.

She swung her eyes around ninety degrees before spotting us waving to her. She was loaded down with bags: purse, laptop, police scanner, and a video camera. Took her a couple minutes to settle down.

Sydney MacBain brought Cindy a Sam Adams and refilled the bowl of chips.

"Yuki," said Syd. "I just heard. Congrats."

"Thanks. It's just step one, but at least Burke's locked up."

We toasted Yuki, then my friends toasted me. We drank long and deep, and after putting down my mug, I said, "Remember when life was normal?" I put air quotes around "normal," but I was feeling it. "Weekends off. Actual time to read a book, take a run. Play the guitar."

The girls looked at me like I was out of my mind.

"What'd I say?"

Claire said, "When was the last time you played the guitar, sweetie?"

"Well. I may be rusty, but I still know *how*."

The girls laughed, but Claire laughed the loudest because she *knows* how long—years and years.

I think Yuki was laugh-coughing into her beer when a shadow fell across the table. I looked up and did a double take. It was my husband, Joe. He never comes to MacBain's, and yet here he was.

"Is Julie okay?" I said, immediately concerned.

"She's fine. She's in the car with Mrs. Rose," he said. He greeted my friends, then said, "Hon, I've been trying to reach you."

"Joe. Our phones off rule."

He seemed amused, but there was something else in his expression I couldn't quite read. Like he had something big by the tail.

He said, "Got a second? I need to talk to you. Outside."

"Uh-oh. Okay." I looked around the table and said, "I guess I'll be going." I put ten bucks on the table and followed Joe out. He held the door open, and when we were on the sidewalk said, "I just heard from Berney."

CHAPTER 61

JOE HAD PARKED his car at the far corner of the block.

He unlocked the doors with his remote and I saw Julie and Mrs. Rose in the back seat. Mrs. Mooey Milkington was lying across Julie's knees, and she was wearing headphones, her attention fixed on her tablet and a game in progress. She looked up when I opened the door and reached for her.

"Mom. Don't. I'm countin' chick'ns."

This video game had become an obsession, but, I thought, a harmless one. I said, "Okay, okay."

I kissed my hand, tapped the top of Julie's head, and waggled my fingers in greeting at Mrs. Rose.

"Thanks, Gloria."

She winked at me and said, "Happy to do it."

"Joe," I said softly. "What did Berney say?"

"Quite a lot, Linds. Almost too much."

"I'm braced. Now, talk."

"Don't rush me. I'm speaking from memory."

"Sor-*ry*."

"Okay. First thing. Berney said that Evan Burke changed his name to Jake Winslow about fifteen years ago, after his wife and daughter disappeared. The three of them had been living in Marin County. Lucas had already left home."

"Gone to college, you mean."

"And grad school."

"So, after the wife and daughter go missing, presumed dead, Lucas's father sells the four-bedroom house with an ocean view and moves to parts unknown. He's just been located in the Mount Tam area where, Berney says, he's created a life for himself off the grid. Damned few records of him using either name. He's a cash-only kind of guy."

I thought if Burke didn't want to be found, living off the grid was the way to go. Mill Valley is upscale but if you keep driving north, you reach the smaller communities in the woods surrounding Mount Tamalpais. A lot of free thinkers from the sixties and seventies live there so as not to leave establishment footprints.

Joe said, "Google Earth has never recorded his place, but from drone shots on file, Berney ID'd Burke's house in the woods. Look here," he said, showing me his phone. "Cabin at the end of a deer track leading to the front door."

"Hunh. Not much to it."

"Right. There are several of these hunting-type cabins in the area. No addresses. If Burke gets mail, it goes to the Mill Valley PO. And get this: The former Evan Burke had some work done on his face."

I said, "Why would he do that *and* move to a remote place like this? Sure sounds like he's on the run to me. There a picture of Evan Burke's new face?"

"I sent it to you, Blondie," my husband said. "You'll get it when you turn on your phone."

"Thanks," I said, punching him lightly in the shoulder. I took my phone out of my breast pocket.

"Hmmm," I said, staring at a candid shot of a man crossing a street under slanting sunlight—somewhere. He was good-looking but unremarkable.

I said, "No distinguishing features that I can see. Around six feet. Full head of dark hair. He looks younger than—what? He's got to be sixty."

"That's right. Might color his hair to go with his unlined new face."

"What kind of vehicle does he have?"

"He had a cabin cruiser at one time," Joe said. "The type you could live on. He might still have it."

I said, "Gotta give the guy an 'A' for getting away from it all. What do you think, Joe? Is he escaping his grief, reinventing himself? Or is he a killer in hiding?"

Joe said, "But, here's why this couldn't wait, Lindsay. Berney says Burke usually makes a move after a kill. He could be getting ready to take off about now, or may already be gone. That's all Berney's got."

I said, "So, a career killer in hiding and now on the move."

"All we know or think we know is that he's breathing free air. Right now you might get the jump on him. He won't be expecting the SFPD."

"Gotcha. I'll share with the boss. Thanks for doing this, Joe."

"Happy to do it. Maybe one day you can thank Berney."

With the comforting sound of electronic chickens clucking in the back seat, I slid closer to Joe, put my arms around his neck, and kissed his cheek.

I asked the little chicken counter in the back seat for a kiss and said thanks and good-bye to Mrs. Rose.

"You're too farrrrr."

I got out of the car, opened the back door, said, "I'm leaving now, Bugs."

She threw her little arms around my neck and gave me a kiss.

"Be careful," Joe said. "Assume he's a psychopath with a vengeance."

"I'm just going to see Brady." I patted my holster. "See you in a bit."

I walked back into the Hall and up to our department. Brady was on the phone when I slipped into the seat across from his desk.

He said into the mouthpiece, "Love you, too."

After he hung up with Yuki, I spent ten minutes briefing him on the news from Joe's mysterious CI.

Brady said, "We have to check it out. Tell all of this to Conklin. I need to make some calls."

CHAPTER 62

RICH CONKLIN WAS working alone at his desk.

I dropped into the swivel chair that had molded itself to my weight and shape over the years. Then, I stuck out my arm and swept all of Sonia Alvarez's things aside; sunglasses, thermos, stack of papers, glass paperweight, a number of pens. Then I folded my arms over the space I'd made for myself.

I looked up to see Conklin grinning.

"What?"

"I think you'd like her if you gave her a chance."

"You're talking crazy, Richie. I like her fine. She's been here for what? A week? I'll take her to lunch, okay? I just need room to spread out."

"She's so excited about our everyday—"

"Our everyday is about to get more intense." I looked at my watch, then back to Richie. "Soon."

"Tell me."

I told him everything that Joe had told me, except the name of his source. I told him about Evan Burke changing his name and face, the warning from Joe's

CI that Burke was on the move, that we had nothing on him except Lucas Burke's untested and self-serving theory that his father was a mass murderer.

I told him we were going to make a move.

Conklin wasn't grinning anymore, and I wasn't thinking about singing along with Sheryl Crow on my guitar, either.

I said, "Call Alvarez. Tell her we need her now. Is she ready for this . . . baptism by fire?"

"I have no doubt."

By 8 p.m., the Burke task force met on the street in front of the Hall of Justice.

Brady briefed us under a streetlight, laying out our objective: to bring him in to get his comments on his son on the record. "We want to bring him in without a shot fired or a door kicked in. But if it goes that way, we're ready."

And then Brady got into a van with Cappy and Alvarez and two other cops with tac team experience.

Conklin and I were assigned an unmarked car with a dedicated channel, high-tech navigation, and vest mics. Conklin wanted the wheel, so I willingly agreed to navigate us to a place I'd never been. Captain Brevoort had assigned the Wendy Franks investigators to join our caravan while Chi stayed back at the Hall and used Brady's office as command center.

As the mission clarified and became real, my emotions bounced between excitement and something resembling stark fear.

The task force was acting on my secondhand intel. If Berney was wrong, I'd hold myself responsible for sending this crew on a road trip to nowhere, and God forbid resulting injuries or death.

If Berney was right, we were about to confront a crafty killer without probable cause to arrest him. If

Evan Burke, aka Jake Winslow, was that killer, he was remarkable for his cold-blooded brutality. He'd murdered his wife, daughter, his son's wife, child, and lover as well as a few victims who matched his preferred victim profile. Lucas had thought there were more bodies than he knew.

If all of that was true, tonight might be our best chance of capturing a mass murderer of the psychopathic kind. In doing so, we might save untold lives, close cold cases, and overall, feel the deep satisfaction of being a cop.

But it could go wrong and tonight could end in tragedy.

CHAPTER 63

WE STARTED OUR ENGINES and rolled out at 8:15 p.m.

Conklin knew the way, leaving my mind free to picture a dead baby with pale red hair and the bloated, gnawed body of her mother strapped into a red Volvo. I felt Misty Fogarty clinging to me as we'd left the Comfy Corner Diner, four hours before a monster slashed her throat.

I willed Conklin to drive faster. I projected into the near future and saw myself standing with my partner at Evan Burke's door, hoping he'd put up a fight so we could arrest him for assaulting a police officer. Cuff him. Throw him into the back of the car and then treat him to a marathon interrogation in the box.

"Linds?" Conklin said.

"Hmmm?"

"I asked if you wanted to stop for coffee."

"No thanks, Rich. Let's just get there."

I needed to find out for myself whether Lucas Burke, the man awaiting trial on the sixth floor of the Hall of Justice, had been framed by his name-changing, face-changing father who lived in a cabin too remote for even Google Earth to have recorded.

It only took our caravan fifteen minutes to cross the Golden Gate Bridge into Sausalito. Once within the Marin County lines, Brady patched us into his call to Captain Geoffrey Brevoort to let him know that we were in his territory.

"Captain. We have to question a suspect on other homicides. As soon as we have him, we'll bring you into the loop."

We exited the highway at 445B, passing the Commodore Dock and a small marina on our right-hand side. About a dozen houseboats were tied up to finger slips and a couple of seaplanes bobbing gently on the water. I didn't see a cabin cruiser, but I made a mental note. *Maybe he's on it.*

For the next several miles, we drove through the pretty, upscale towns of Mill Valley. Our wheels hugged the road as it curved upward, taking us away from genteel civilization toward the deep woods of Mount Tamalpais.

At one point I called Brady and we pulled up on the verge of the paved road, the police van sliding in behind us. We climbed out and leaned against our cars, examined the maps on our phones, and reviewed again the unlit twisting roads and trails that curled around rocky outcroppings and doubled back under the shadow of Mount Tam.

Brady had a collection of drone shots of a cabin presumed to belong to Burke/Winslow. It sat alone in a clearing the size of my fingertip, and in the darkness we would have good cover. There were no other cabins within a quarter mile of Burke's. We surely would surprise him, and he would agree to come back with us to the Hall. Please, God, without bloodshed. And since I was reaching out to God, I put in another request.

That Evan Burke would say, "You got me. I did it all."

Brady asked us to run mic checks again. Afterward, we all tightened our vest straps and got back into our vehicles, the van right behind us. As the road climbed, it narrowed, changed from macadam to rutted clay. Tree roots encroached on the dirt roads. It quickly became clear that the van would be unable to negotiate the tree-bound trails. Brady found a better road for the van, but it was a good five minutes from the Burke cabin.

It was the best we could do.

Conklin took a narrow trail on our right, keeping only the parking lights on. Unmarked vehicles were not meant for off-road travel, but surprisingly our tires made good contact with the ruts we were riding. There was one moment of unplanned confusion when our downlights showed our trail diverging into two.

I grabbed the mic and talked to Brady and we decided that Conklin and I would take the right fork; the van would still be within jogging distance of the cabin.

Even with low visibility and little knowledge of the terrain, our plan looked good. We kept driving, startling flapping, scurrying, and leaping creatures as we drove. Conklin made a turn onto a driveway of sorts and we parked there.

We radioed the van, and while waiting for confirmation that they were in place, Conklin and I sized up Burke/Winslow's house and grounds.

CHAPTER 64

THE CABIN WAS CENTERED in a weedy clearing encircled by a half dozen trees of various types and heights. A toolshed stood off to one side.

Small, approximately four hundred square feet, the cabin was too makeshift to be a prefab "tiny house" but could have been built from scratch in a few days by a reasonably handy worker or two.

That might explain why there was no record of this house in the tax rolls, no transfer of title. One day this area had been a clearing, part of state protected lands, a few days later a small corner had been confiscated, unnoticed.

I hoped to see a car with a license plate, but there was none such. But I did see the blue light of a screen, and firelight flickering through the windows.

Someone was home.

I radioed Brady, summarized what we knew and that we were about to make our approach.

I said to Conklin, "Ready?"

"Let's go."

We drew our guns and proceeded toward the front door, but when we were twenty feet from the porch, floodlights snapped on and blazed from under the eaves.

The light was blinding. I could no longer see the cabin.

A man's voice rang out. *"Drop your weapons. Now."*

He stepped out onto his porch, a silhouette, but I saw the AK in his hands. A light pull on the trigger and he could cut me and Conklin down.

This was on me. All of it was on me. My idea. I was the senior officer on scene. I had no time flat to figure out how to get us out.

The voice called out, again. "Trespassers. Toss your guns toward me."

"Can't do that," I said. "We're SFPD. I'm holstering my weapon and backing away."

The speaker said, "Police? Why didn't you say so? Show me your hands. Believe me," said the man standing behind the floodlights. "I'm not kidding around."

CHAPTER 65

I HOLSTERED MY GUN.

I showed the SOB on the porch my hands and Conklin did the same. In the process, I thumbed my mic into the open position so that Brady could hear us.

"We're not going to shoot," I called out to the man with the assault rifle. "You're in no danger. We came here to talk. How about you cut the lights so we can do that?"

He stepped inside his cabin, and pulled a plug or threw a switch. All but one of the security lights went out. We were twenty yards away from the porch, close enough to recognize the man from the photo Berney had passed on to Joe. His gun was still aimed at us.

"Talk fast," he said.

I identified myself and asked him to do the same.

"Winslow," he said. "Jake. You're here about my son?"

"Right," I said.

My heart pounded right about where Burke was aiming his weapon.

He said, "Then this is what you need to know. You won't prove a thing against Lucas. He's a strategic genius with a gift for the dramatic. He has no conscience. None at all. But I'll tell you this—he did it. He killed his mother and sister. Now he's gone and killed his wife and baby girl."

"You have any proof he did any of these murders?" I called out. "A witness? A letter? A taped conversation?"

"Do you?" he shouted back. "Take my word for it, or don't. Lucas has been a killer since he was a kid. Animals, of course. But my wife and daughter were his first human kills—that I know about."

His voice broke. He coughed. Then he spoke again.

"I do not know what he did with their bodies. Maybe he'll tell you if you make him a deal. He wouldn't tell me. Lucas is a sick human being. And he's a liar. He's the one who sent you here, isn't he?"

"Your name came up," Conklin said.

Burke snorted.

"We'd like your comments about your son for the record," Conklin continued. "We can give you a lift to our station, get this on tape, and drive you back. Door-to-door service and that will be the end of it. Check off, 'did my civic duty.'"

"That's not happening. You've got your man and I'm done with you two and him. Now get off my property and stay off it.

"You know the drill. 'All trespassers will be shot on sight.'"

CHAPTER 66

BRADY WAS STANDING on the road when our headlights hit him.

Conklin pulled in next to the van and Brady opened my door. "Tell me every detail," Brady said. "Start with when the guy called you out."

I told him about the floodlights, the AK, the man who looked like the picture we'd seen of Evan Burke.

"His features were smooth and ordinary," I said, "what we could see of him. He said his son, Lucas, has killed a lot of people, starting with his own mother and sister, and including Tara and Lorrie Burke. But he, Evan, doesn't have any evidence whatsoever."

Brady said, "He was too far from you for me to hear what he said about Lucas."

Conklin said, "He said that his son is a psychopath and a genius and that we'll never catch him in the act of anything. But sure as shootin', Luke did it."

"Starting to sound like both of them are psycho," said Brady. "Suggest we keep our vehicles so we can see the roads leading to Burke's place tonight. Maybe he'll bolt and we can follow him."

Cappy and Alvarez got out of the van, stretched their legs, and Brady brought out a cooler from the back. There was enough water and sandwiches to take the edge off our hunger, but I still felt the sting of being run off by Burke.

We returned to our vehicles and prepared for an all-night stakeout. As the adrenaline I'd been mainlining burned off, I felt deflated, bordering on depressed.

One good thing.

I was in a car with Conklin.

It felt good. Like old times.

Sometime later, when Rich shook me awake, I said, "What?"

"Motorcycle. Alvarez saw it coming down from Burke's house. Buckle up."

Brady's voice came over the radio. "Boxer. Conklin. Follow the bike. No flashers. No sirens. Do not lose him."

The bike had a head start and we pulled out, followed it at a distance of thirty yards. There were no other cars on the road. I looked in the rearview and saw our van behind us.

We were keeping up when the bike took a hard turn, uphill. It wasn't going to Burke's cabin, so where? I was on the comms with Brady when another motorcycle came down the mountain from a different mountain trail. One of these bikes was a decoy, the other could be Burke. The second bike was on Route 1 heading south toward the bridge. Conklin sped up and passed the bike and as we passed him, the biker made the motion of pulling the chain that blows a trucker's horn.

His helmet and goggles covered most of his face, but not his mouth and I saw that he was grinning.

When the bike took Morton Road I knew that in

fact our chain had been yanked. Brady made a U-turn back to where we'd come from. He must have used the force of his will to get that van up the mountain or maybe they pulled over and ran.

Brady's voice came over the receiver.

"House is empty. I threw a rock through the window to see what would happen, but nothing did. No lights, horns, or explosives. I pushed in the door and had a look around. No one was home.

"The bastard's playing with us."

Didn't surprise me. At all.

Brady went on. "Where're you at?"

"Coming up on the marina, this side of the bridge," I told Brady. "We're going to stop there and look around."

The harbor master was in his small multi-windowed office on the pier. He was a windblown but upbeat and talkative man in his sixties who introduced himself as Monty McAllister. Sure, he said, he knew Jake Winslow, said he did keep a boat at the marina, but no, he hadn't seen him in weeks.

"No motorcycles came in tonight, nope. Not a one."

Conklin asked to see Winslow's boat. McAllister said, "Follow me."

The boat, in good repair, was a Century Boats 30 Express named *Lucky Strike*. Definitely not occupied.

We went back to our car and reported in. Brady said, "Stay there. He could show up at any time."

"Any time" came and went. The sun was rising in the east, lighting the upper architecture of the famous bridge. McAllister brought us mugs of coffee and we sat in the car until eight in the morning.

Brady called to ask, "Anything?"

"No, boss."

"Me, neither. Burke didn't go back to his house, either. Fucking guy is just fucking gone."

CHAPTER 67

CINDY THOMAS WAS driving over the Golden Gate Bridge while Jonny Samuels dozed in the seat beside her.

They were on a field trip to Mount Tam with one objective: to interview Evan Burke or people who knew him, get a verifiable story, an unshakable quote, and if feasible, a good photo of Burke talking with her.

Cindy felt lucky to be the one reporter with an actual smoking-hot lead. She had reliable sources at the Hall, four of whom had told and then confirmed that Lucas Burke claimed that his father, Evan, had killed Tara and Lorrie Burke. Lucas implied that there was a strong likelihood that Evan had also killed Wendy Franks, Misty Fogarty, and Susan Wenthauser, and even Evan's own wife and child. Lucas was telling everyone in the sixth-floor jail that his father was a serial killer, out to frame his son.

That was his story, Lucas Burke's defense, but as far as Cindy had been told, he had no evidence to prove it.

That said, if true, this story of familial murder was stunning, a bombshell with staying power and ripe for movie interest. *If true*.

Lucas Burke's claim had leaked like fuel from a broken gas line and caught fire. Cindy's crime blog had been flooded with questions and accusations against Evan and against Luke. People had taken sides. Cindy had published a few logical and well-written posts from readers and with the disclaimer that posts from the readers did not represent the opinion of the *Chronicle*.

Cindy had done her own after-hours research, phoning friends who did administrative grunt work throughout the Hall, and she had learned something that she could possibly verify. That Evan Burke might be living in Sausalito in the foothills of Mount Tamalpais.

She hadn't been able to confirm this location with anyone who would actually *know*. For instance, her lover, Rich Conklin, or close friends, Lindsay Boxer, Yuki Castellano, and Jackson Brady—but at least she had a lead. And she'd been working that lead all morning, driving from hill to dale around and up Mount Tam, knocking on doors, asking whomever answered if he, she, or they happened to know Evan Burke.

She had worn a dress. Yes, a dress. A somber print that hung below her knees and a navy blue blazer. In her opinion, she looked fetching, not slick.

But she'd gotten the door-to-door salesman treatment.

Once she said she worked for the *San Francisco Chronicle,* the door was slammed in her face.

This had been going on all day.

It was a terrible feeling. She knew that the old-timers around Mount Tam hated the "fake" press more than almost any other institution. This was disturbing, and at the same time motivating. She was sure she could get someone to talk to her, and she had good company in Samuels, who would back her up, physically, if needed.

Samuels was six two and 220 with a black belt in karate. He was an intimidating force, for sure.

But for now, Cindy let Samuels sleep.

She'd studied the map while at home, and as soon as she'd brought it to Richie, he'd started shaking his head no, saying, "You know I can't help you with your story. But you are so nosy—"

"Inquisitive."

"—and I know to lock my phone. Which I forgot to do."

He went on to say, "If any of this Evan Burke story is true, you could be poking a serial killer, and if so, Cindy, you're inviting very big trouble. You look like the kind of victim this killer likes best."

"What kind is that?"

"Cute. Female. Small. With a nice-looking neck. Don't quote me."

"And what's *your* type?"

"Same. Come here so I can bite you."

Cindy was glad for Richie's warning, and she wasn't careless or stupid. If she could locate Evan Burke, she was sure he would talk to her.

*   *   *

Cindy was driving while casing the area. From the density of the woodland and the narrow bike trail to her right, she felt as if she was finally homing in on the location that she'd gathered from her quick peek at Richie's phone. She signaled for a turn, pulled onto the verge off Morton Road, and took in her surroundings.

Cindy looked up the trail on her right, a wider rut than most of them. She put her Acura into third gear, and let the car do the work, the tires wobbling and righting themselves as the trail climbed. At one point, the road forked. *Left or right? Eenie, meenie, miney, mo.*

She took the right-hand road.

Samuels woke up.

"Where are we?"

"Damned if I know. This trail is unmarked."

A half mile up, the road came to a clearing and in the center was a small, odd, asymmetrical house, without a window curtain or flowerpot or even a clothesline.

Her take? A man lived here alone.

Cindy braked, said to Samuels, "Please stay here, but keep your eyes on me. I'm not going in, but just in case."

"I got you," said Samuels. He rubbed his hands together, buzzed down the window.

Cindy got out of the car and crossed the dirt and gravel car park, then climbed the two narrow steps to the porch. She heard nothing. No dog. No music. No car or bike in the drive or around the house. She was pretty sure no one was home.

Still, she knocked and waited.

She knocked again, and called out, "Hello? Anyone home?"

When her tapping went unanswered, she slipped her business card into the crack between the door and doorframe and hoped that whoever lived there would call her.

Back in her car, she drove down the rutted trail,

taking the left-hand turn this time, and a few minutes later, arrived at a very different kind of woodland house.

Also hemmed in by forest trees, this house was cedar shingled and had a proper flower garden in front, a wheelbarrow planter, and a shiny late-model SUV in the driveway.

These homeowners were a definite possibility for an interview. They might want to help her.

Cindy heard jazz coming from inside the house. A red tabby cat sat on the back of a sofa watching her through the living room window.

A neat-looking woman with silver-blond hair came to the door and opened it.

She smiled. "Hello. May I help you?"

"Hi, I'm Cindy Thomas from the *Chronicle*. I'm writing a story about the killings in San Francisco and a resident of this community was one of the victims—"

The woman in the doorway said, "Fuck off" and slammed the door in Cindy's face.

Cindy yelled, "Hey!"

Samuels was getting out of the car. Cindy waved him back and knocked on the door again.

Inside, the music was turned up loud. The cat continued to watch Cindy until she left the doorway, got into her car, and started the engine.

"Nasty," said Samuels, when Cindy told him what had happened. "Want me to punch some holes in her tires?"

"Jonny, don't you know that journalism is a glamour job?"

He laughed. "Absolutely. Where to, now?"

"Down the mountain, over the bridge, and back to work. We live to fight another day."

CHAPTER 68

IT WAS STILL THE DARK before dawn and Joe and I were in bed, awake, and talking.

He said, "No, yeah, wear it. I love the red."

I had to laugh. I still looked hot in my red floor-length silk gown, even after my pregnancy. In the ten years since I'd bought that dress, I'd worn it maybe four times.

Today wasn't going to be the fifth.

The individual known as Berney was in San Francisco. He had some information for Joe, but it had to be strictly confidential, untraceable. When they talked over the phone last night about where to meet, I'd been sitting next to Joe on the couch with my ear close enough to hear Berney's voice.

I'd said, "I want to meet him."

Joe shook his head no.

I'd nodded emphatically yes, and Joe said to the magician of the dark side, "Lindsay wants to meet you."

To our surprise, Berney said, "I can come to your place."

Joe said, "Excellent. Six thirty tomorrow morning?"

Now, Joe's projection clock flashed five fifteen on the ceiling.

"Do you want to shower first, or me?"

"Me," I said. "I'm quicker."

After my shower, I opened Julie's door and brought Martha into her room, to keep the elderly dog out of our way. Julie's eyelids flew open.

She asked, "Did you have a bad dream?"

"No, I wanted to check on you, straighten your blankets. Go back to sleep," I told her. "It's very early."

She yawned and then said, "Why are you up?"

"Daddy and I are having a meeting with an old friend. You and Martha go back to sleep."

When Martha jumped into bed, Julie hugged our old dog. Conversation over.

I left her room quietly, put the coffee on, and found a bag of muffins in the freezer. I turned on the oven and the TV to hear what the morning anchors had to report, and of course the unsolved murders of Tara and Lorrie Burke, Misty, Wendy, and Susan, were still top of the news even now, a month later. There was a close-up of Brady and me talking to Cindy outside the Hall. Yuki was saying that Lucas Burke was going on trial for the murders of his wife and daughter. Pictures came on the screen of mother and child.

It was painful to see.

If only we were sure that we had the right guy.

Maybe Berney would give us something Yuki could use in the trial. Anything.

Joe emerged from the bathroom, freshly shaven, wearing a nearly identical outfit to mine, jeans and a white cotton shirt. He lined up the muffins on a cookie pan, and slid them into the preheated oven.

I've gotten over Joe being more domestic than I am. I'm glad he is. I'm glad about everything Joe.

I asked, "Is Berney his first name or last?"

"I don't know if it even is his name. It's what he goes by and it's all I need to know."

At precisely 6:30, the intercom buzzer sounded. Joe told his friend to take the elevator, and, a few minutes later, opened the door to the mystery spy, one-name Berney.

He looked nothing, but nothing, like what I was expecting.

CHAPTER 69

I GUESS I WAS EXPECTING a scruffy World War II–type spy. Berney was five eight, mid-forties, with thinning blond hair, wire metal-rimmed glasses, khakis, and a pink sweater hiding the pudge around his midsection.

In short, he looked like a modern-day middle-aged Protestant minister.

When we were seated at the kitchen table, he said, "Lindsay. Don't take this wrong, but since we've just met, I must advise you. I'm a terrible conversationalist. Can't tell you where I work or live or what I do for fun. Nothing I tell you now can be tied back to me in any way. I won't testify. I won't talk to the DA. I don't exist."

"Got it," I said. "And thanks for your help."

"Joe," said Berney. "Okay?"

"*A-OK.*"

"Good," said Berney. "So." He took a muffin but passed up the sugar and cream for his coffee.

"This is what you'd call a postcard from the field.

Overheard by a friend of the company, Evan Burke told a friend of his that his rotten son, Lucas, put the cops on him for the recent murders. Then he says, 'Luke's smart. But not as smart as he thinks.'"

I said, "He said almost the same thing to me outside his cabin on Mount Tam. He said that Lucas killed his mother and sister and was psychotic. I gotta say, Evan was convincing."

"Evan *is* convincing," Berney said. "It's one of the secrets of his success. And he was trained in special forces."

I looked across the table at Joe. Special forces was big news.

"We've been watching him for decades," Berney continued. "We call him the Ghost of Catalina, or Quicksilver, because he never slips up and he never gets caught. We've never had evidence we could link to him. Now all of a sudden, fresh bodies appear. Burke likes to mix it up. Sometimes a strangling. He's used a gun. What is consistent is the absence of evidence. No sexual assault, no trace we can pin on him."

I nodded, thinking about the morgue photos of Misty Fogarty.

"On those bodies you attribute to Evan. Were there ever any nonfatal wounds on the upper chest? Little gashes about the size of pocket change?"

"Nope. That's new. He might've had a new idea. Seems possible. He has the blade in his hand."

I thought back to what Claire had said after performing the autopsies on Wendy Franks and Misty Fogarty, terming this kind of knife work "serial killer gibberish."

"What's your theory on Lucas?"

Berney shrugged. "I know more about Evan than I want to and I still don't have anything to go on.

I'm not watching Lucas. But the reason I'm here is because I brought you something, Lindsay." Berney took a small brown envelope from inside his shirt pocket under the pullover. "You got this on your own, right, Joe? When you were on the job."

He passed it to Joe, who said, "Do I want this?"

"Someone you love may find it comes in handy. If not, burn it and scatter the ashes.

"I got this item from Pentagon files," Berney explained, "after Burke's wife, Corinne, and daughter, Jodie, went missing fifteen years ago. There were no digital copies and it wasn't on any known database."

I was holding a ten card, ten inked fingerprints with a photo of Evan Burke when he'd joined the Green Berets at age eighteen.

"We couldn't use the prints officially without jamming you up," I said to Berney, "but we could run the prints against suspicious unidentified prints. For instance, there may have been assorted prints on Misty Fogarty's car."

Berney nodded in agreement.

I continued to spin the theory out. "If Forensics got a match to Evan Burke's prints, that could prove that senior had been in proximity to Misty before she was killed."

That ten card with photo gave me hope.

CHAPTER 70

JOE WALKED BERNEY OUT, and when he returned minutes later, I had to ask, "So whodunit? Lucas or Evan?"

"Uh. There's only one guy, a changeling space alien posing as both father and son."

In other words, Joe didn't know, either.

As I started up my car, I thought again about what Evan Burke in his Jake Winslow persona had stated while holding Conklin and me under the cold black eye of his gun. He'd said that Lucas has been killing since he was a child psycho, had killed his mother and sister, that he'd never been caught.

I didn't like father or son at all, and yet I couldn't shake the feeling I had that Burke senior was telling the truth.

When I was only a few blocks from the Hall my phone buzzed. I took a quick peek at the caller ID. It was Yuki.

"Could we meet in my office?"

"You bet," I said. "Okay if Richie joins us?"

"Sure. I'll call him."

My fifteen-minute drive to the Hall was through the normal Friday morning stop-and-go. I watched traffic without seeing it while I thought about Yuki, readying herself to try Lucas Burke for a double homicide while Lucas's star defense attorney mocked her case built on circumstantial evidence. It was strong evidence. The dead were Lucas Burke's pretty young wife and adorable daughter. He had the means and the opportunity—that case could be made.

But one juror insisting on a smoking gun could tip the prosecution's case.

I left my car in the day lot across from the Hall, and as I crossed with the green I saw that Cindy and a few dozen other reporters had set up on the sidewalk.

Cindy was with her photographer, Jonny Samuels, and the grieving Kathleen Wyatt.

As Kathleen had told Cindy the day she'd barged into the *Chronicle* offices demanding to know why her post on Cindy's crime blog accusing Lucas had been removed, Tara and Lorrie were at the center of her life. Tara called her mother every morning, and when she didn't call or answer her phone the day of Tara and Lucas's fight, Kathleen knew something was wrong. Why? Because she'd been afraid Lucas might harm her daughter.

I waved to Girl Reporter and she waved back, made a move toward me, but I kept walking. Took the front steps two at a time, cleared security, and jogged up two flights of the back stairs to the second floor.

Yuki was waiting for me at the entrance to the DA's offices, which took up half a floor. She buzzed me in and I told her that Conklin was coming directly.

"He's in my office already," Yuki said.

She looked like she'd slept on a bed of nails. Jacket

misbuttoned, hair sticking up in back, lipstick on her teeth.

I wanted to say, "Everything's going to be fine," but this was Yuki and she ran on her own instincts. I knew she had big moments of doubt, asking herself why she kept running, wondering if she should have babies and devote herself to keeping her family and home. Sometimes she'd blame herself for the pothole that had suddenly opened just before the finish line. And sometimes, she'd be the first through the tape and the crowd went wild.

I always told her she was living her passion. How many people get to do that?

I followed her into her hard-won office. And there he was. My good-looking-good-doing partner of many years, the brother I never had, and a friend I entrusted with my life as he entrusted his with me.

He was lounging on the two-seat sofa, his long legs stretched out in front of him, brown hair falling over his eyes. Today, Conklin looked calm, like it was a day at the beach. Which it was not.

Yuki did not look calm. She didn't sit; rather, she paced her small office, speaking in her trademark rapid-fire delivery. Her ability to tell a story with confidence and in so doing engage her juries was one of her strengths.

She summed up her situation for her audience of two.

Today was Friday. The trial started on Monday. She knew the material cold. Her opening statement was killer. But the weakness in her argument was that all she had against Lucas Burke was his association with the victims, and that he had no documented alibi.

If she did her job well, that would be enough to convict him. Yuki cited several major cases of this size and interest that had been won with circumstantial evidence. Scott Peterson came immediately to my mind. On the other hand, O. J. Simpson had been famously acquitted.

"Look at this," Yuki said.

She held up the front section of the *Bay Area Herald,* a quality paper that ran straight-up mainstream news. She turned it this way and that way so that Rich and I could both read the headline, see the picture of her leaving the building last night with her computer bag, her blond streak of hair falling over her eye, looking up the street for her car.

The headline read, "Parisi subs out Burke trial to an ADA with spotty track record."

Yuki's voice quavered as she read the lede: *"Accused of double homicide, defendant Lucas Burke's chances of acquittal just improved by facing off against prosecutor Yuki Castellano, an ADA with an iffy conviction track record in criminal court."*

Conklin said, "Don't let that a-hole throw you, Yuki," and I said something much the same. I believed it. Yuki was terrific; through no fault of hers, she'd had some stinkers tossed her way. She'd lost a couple of big cases, not because she was unprepared or overmatched but because of circumstances such as key witnesses changing their stories—or dying—during trial.

Even so, Yuki had won more cases than she'd lost, and she was an attractive woman, now married to a top cop. The camera liked her and sometimes reporters found her an easy target.

Yuki said, "The jury is going to love Burke's showboat defense counsel. Newt Gardner has a made-for-TV personality and believable charm. He can spin arguments seamlessly, and the jurors buy it. I've seen him do it. He even makes me think, Jesus, do I have the wrong guy?"

I had nothing for her. Certainly not the thing she wanted most: bulletproof, direct evidence that Lucas Burke had killed his wife and baby.

Yuki said, "I know you all have been working non-stop, but I can tell you that Newton Gardner's opening and closing statements are going to be one and the same. 'Lucas didn't do it. The prosecution can't and didn't prove that he did.'

"And then all of us—you, you, me, Brady, Red Dog, Clapper, and the whole of the SFPD—are going to take hard indelible hits to our careers, and the psycho is going to go free."

CHAPTER 71

AN HOUR HAD PASSED since the meeting with Yuki.

Rich Conklin was at his desk, facing Inspector Sonia Alvarez in Lindsay's old seat at the front of the bullpen.

They had coffee containers at hand while their computers continued their daily searches for pattern murders of young females across the country over the previous thirty years. So far, the neck-slashing pattern accompanied by a constellation of gashes across the top of the women's chests seemed unique.

The personal line on Richie's desk phone lit up. He punched it, said "Conklin," and put Claire on speaker.

"Hi, Claire," Rich said. "I'm putting you on speaker so Sonia can hear this, too."

She said, "I've been on the medical examiner's chat line for a couple of hours so I could get the East Coast into it."

"What's the consensus?" Rich asked.

"That the murder weapon was likely the same or

similar used on Tara Burke, Wendy Franks, and Melissa Fogarty. As you know, the baby was smothered. The earliest victim, Wenthauser, last seen blocks from Lucas Burke's residence, was skeletal. We couldn't get a good cause of death off her. But back to your other victims. A straight-edged blade—a razor or a well-honed knife—was used, but I can only say 'similar' weapon because the length and width of Misty and Wendy's slashes were consistent."

"And Tara?"

"Her mortal wound was distorted by soaking in the water. As for the chest gashes, six of the MEs and I agree. Those little stab wounds are serial killer gibberish."

Sonia said, "A game he's playing? He's just horsing around?"

"Right," said Claire. "The stabs or gashes or puncture wounds were applied both ante and post mortem. Killer didn't care if the victims were alive or dead. He's just screwing with the cops and the Forensics crew or playing mumblety-peg."

"Any thoughts on why?" asked Alvarez.

"Nothing consistent. Three negatives all different. One hypothesized that the victim got a stab wound for each emotional wound she inflicted on the killer. Nothing to back that up. Another thought was that the killer was marking how many seconds it took the victim to die once her throat was slashed. Possible. Uh. The third opposing thought was that the killer was stabbing to the beat of a favorite song.

"To me," Claire said, "that falls under the heading of 'pathological gibberish.'"

After the call ended, Alvarez tipped her chair back so that she was looking at the ceiling with her large, black, unblinking eyes.

"What you thinking, Alvarez?"

"Long version or short?"

"You choose."

"Okay," she said, "my thoughts on Lucas are that this man is not a cool customer. He's volatile. Highly emotional. Agree?"

"Agreed."

"If he's a psychopath, maybe he could fake it, but no matter what, he couldn't have been in Sacramento and in Sunset Park Prep's parking lot at the same time."

"His alibi and corroboration by his ex-wife that he left his house and drove to Sacramento, arriving by nine, are why we didn't charge him with Fogarty."

Alvarez said, "Maybe the ex stretched the time of his arrival, but still, I don't think Lucas killed Misty. He loves this girl and he's carving on her chest? I've seen sicker stuff that I will never ever unsee. But mutilating Misty's chest does not compute."

"Gotcha. But since we're not charging him with the Fogarty murder, how does this help us?"

"I don't know yet," said Alvarez. "But we have to make sure that it doesn't hurt us. If the same person killed Tara, Misty, and Wendy, and Lucas *didn't* kill Misty, there's a chance he didn't kill Tara or Lorrie, either. That's why I chose the long version."

Sonia Alvarez smiled with her mouth but not with her eyes.

She looked sad and Conklin didn't know why. She hadn't gotten emotional even when they'd gone through Misty's car, bagging all of her little personal items they'd pulled from the glove box, her scarf smelling of flowers, her life's blood drained onto the car seat.

Alvarez had handled it like the pro he recognized she was.

So what was getting to her? She took a sip of her cold coffee to give herself pause.

"Sonia?"

"Okay. So, I'm driving home last night listening to the car radio. Clearing my brain. And this old song comes on from I think the seventies. I only know it from riding with my parents and they're tuning into the oldies but goodies station and singing along."

He smiled. "Gotcha. What song?"

"'Cat's in the Cradle.'"

"Harry Chapin," Rich said, singing, "'Cat's in the cradle and the silver spoon.'"

"That's it," said Alvarez. "'Little boy blue and the man in the moon.'"

She rocked Lindsay's desk chair forward so that the feet hit the floor and said, "So, you know. This is a sad song about a little boy wanting to be like his dad. But dad's got work and he's away all the time, making promises to his kid about being together soon, then breaking the promises. And the little boy who loves his father wants to be like his father when he grows up. That's what he says. He wants to be like his dad."

"Oh, my God," said Richie leaping ahead.

"The kid grows up, gets married, has kids. Dad is retired and wants to be with his son. And son has no time to be with his father. And father says—"

Conklin said, "His son grew up just like him."

Alvarez said, "I just started crying. Me! Vice. Narcotics. I've seen it all. No real problems with my parents. So was my tearing up from empathy? Or sentimentality, remembering my father singing that song in the car? Then I started really listening to the lyrics."

"I'm wondering where Evan was when Lucas was growing up. Did Lucas want to be like his father—who probably killed his wife and child? Was Luke the little boy blue? Evan, the man in the moon? According to a source of Joe's, he's been under investigation for decades for multiple murders across the country. What did Lucas know consciously or in a very guarded place, deep in his brain?"

"It's a powerful thought, Sonia."

Alvarez nodded, then said, "But wait. There's more."

"Keep going. I'm your captive audience."

CHAPTER 72

THE SQUAD ROOM was in typical morning activity mode.

Cops were working the phones, escorting subjects through to Interviews 1 and 2, guys shouting to each other across the aisle, Brenda answering all of her phones. Traffic to and from the break room kept up a pretty constant stream past Conklin and Alvarez's desk.

But Conklin and Alvarez were in their own bubble.

Alvarez said, "I turned the car around and came back here."

"Hunh?"

"Night shift didn't know me, but I said I was working with you. Then, I sat down and pulled up the video."

"Which one?"

"This one."

She cued up the Sunset Park Prep parking lot tape on her desktop computer, turned the monitor so Rich could see it, too. This was a copy of the ten minutes of

Misty waiting. She was there, standing in front of her car, looking in the camera's direction.

"Here we go, Rich. A guy shows up all in black who may have been Lucas or may have been stranger danger."

The two watched the image of the man in black stick to the side of the lot where it was darkest. A chain-link fence divided the parking lot from the rough-mown field behind a gas station on the other side of the fence. A tree with its roots in the field lowered its many branches over the fence, throwing moon shadow into the parking lot at about eight o'clock that night.

Alvarez said, "I still believe what I did when Director Hallows showed us this footage. As the suspect comes closer, we see in Misty's body language that she knows it isn't Lucas. So then—"

"She gets in the car and turns on the headlights," said Conklin. "She's ready to pull out of the lot when this psycho gets into the back seat, reaches over, and slaughters her like a pig."

"Yup," said Alvarez. "Now watch this. It's dark, but the headlights and floodlight affixed over the camera are on, and that's both good and bad for us. We can see the lot, but the dude in dull black clothing looks even darker by contrast as he exits the car and leaves."

"Yes. I see that."

"Watch this closely, Rich. The unidentified subject stays close to the fence, passes under the tree branches—more cover, right? And then he does *this* with his hand."

She pointed to the computer monitor.

Rich said, "Pushed back some leaves or something? Or maybe touched his hat. Making sure he still has it on?"

"Could be. But let me roll this back. Look at it again."

Alvarez backed up the video, hit Forward again, and then hit Pause.

Rich said, "Is that the best picture we can get?"

"Unfortunately, this is enhanced. Now, look here," she said. "Could that motion when the killer lifts his hand, could that be him whipping something over the fence?"

"Oh, Christ," said Conklin. "The murder weapon? You could be right. Call Brady. Number one on speed dial."

CHAPTER 73

CINDY AND JONNY SAMUELS stood in the street outside the yellow tape still roping off Sunset Park Prep.

Adjacent to the parking lot where Misty Fogarty was killed was a vacant lot behind an old gas station. The field was overgrown with tall weeds reaching up through stacks of old tires and rusted-out chassis.

In the last few hours, the field had been transformed. Tall stakes had been planted every four feet in a grid. CSU was covering the area, ten CSIs and techs in a line, arm's length apart, passed metal detectors across the ground. They also concentrated their attention along the chain-link fence dividing the two properties.

Cindy scanned the school parking lot. Clapper was in center field giving Hallows the business. Brady stood with his enormous arms crossed, watching through the fence, clearly perturbed. And she saw Richie, talking to a woman she assumed was his new partner, Sonia Alvarez, whom she hadn't yet met. She admired the horseshoe charm Alvarez wore around her neck. Everyone working this case could use a bit of luck.

Rich was on speed dial so she handed off her police scanner to Samuels and phoned her boyfriend.

"Pick up, Richie. Pick up."

She watched him pull his phone from his back pocket, see who was calling, and answer.

"Yeah, hi, Cin. I'm working right now."

"I can see you."

"Where are you?"

"Turn your face sixty degrees and look for the tall guy out on the street. I'm standing next to him."

"Oh. Okay. I see you."

"Rich, I got the bulletin off the scanner. So I'm here, but you didn't tip me off. Okay to interview you? Just tell me what's going on? Wait. Let's do it this way."

"What way?"

"I'm going to make a guess. If I'm right, say, " 'Love you, too.' If I'm wrong, say something else and I'll take another guess."

"I love you, too."

"Wait, damn it. Let me guess."

She heard Rich say to Alvarez, "Cindy."

Cindy said, "CSU is doing a search for the murder weapon."

Rich was looking toward the fence, seeing the grid breaking up, techs in hazmat suits converging on a perimeter about twenty feet in circumference around an old oak tree.

One of the searchers was holding up something that seemed to have a little shine on it, calling out, "Got it!"

Cindy disengaged the call before Rich could say, "I love you, too," but she knew she was right.

She heard Brady call Rich and Alvarez over, and Samuels aimed his long lens toward the CSU.

Cindy asked Samuels, "Did you get it?"

Samuels showed her the small viewfinder at the back of his camera and enlarged the image. She saw it. A gloved hand was holding what looked to be a closed straight-edge razor.

It looked like every straight razor Cindy had ever seen. The blade was four inches long; the hand holding it in the air provided scale.

"You like?" Samuels said to Cindy.

"Do I? Oh my God. Pulitzer," she said. "Send the photo to Tyler. I'll start writing in the car."

CHAPTER 74

YUKI CASTELLANO AND NEWT GARDNER sat in the waiting area outside Judge John Passarelli's chambers.

Gardner said, "Your nerves getting to you?"

"My nerves are fine," said Yuki. "But, you're sweating, Newt." She swiped her index finger under her nose. He pulled out a handkerchief and dabbed at his face. She'd gotten to him.

He said, "Really. So, calling a meeting with the judge a half hour before the trial starts means 'No problemo,' huh? I can't wait to hear what you've pulled out of your, uh, hat."

Gardner shot his right cuff and looked at his watch. "This is nuts, even for you. Jurors are assembled. I'm ready. Why aren't you?"

"Because we're going to charge Burke with an additional count of murder one."

"Give me a break. You have nothing on Burke but guesswork. Pin the tail on the donkey. This case should have been thrown out and you know it. Parisi's having a fit about bad press. Okay with me. This is what I call a dream case."

Yuki smiled. "Dream on, counselor."

Gardner scoffed, and the door to Passarelli's chambers opened. Judge Passarelli invited the two attorneys into his office and they grouped around the table near the window. Greetings were exchanged. Yuki put her briefcase on the floor next to her chair, extracted a folder, and placed it in front of her.

Judge Passarelli said, "Ms. Castellano, it's your meeting."

"Your Honor. Mr. Gardner. Evidence came to light on Friday afternoon that appears to be the murder weapon used in the killing of Melissa Fogarty, Lucas Burke's girlfriend. This item, a straight razor, was processed at our crime lab immediately. Last night at nine, I received this report."

Yuki passed copies of the report to Judge Passarelli and Gardner.

Gardner said, "Judge, this is all news to me."

Yuki said, "The report goes into this in depth. But the bottom line is that a straight razor was found with Melissa Fogarty's blood on the blade and Lucas Burke's fingerprints on the handle. It was found in the weeds fifty feet and over a chain-link fence from the crime scene. Your Honor, we didn't charge Mr. Burke with Ms. Fogarty's murder earlier because we had no evidence until now."

"Wait, wait," said Gardner. "The evidence just showed up on Friday. Prints and blood? A little convenient isn't it, Ms. Castellano? By chance could this razor have been planted by the police?"

"Under close re-examination of the video shot by the parking lot surveillance camera," Yuki said, "the killer was seen disposing of this evidence."

Judge Passarelli said, "You're adding Fogarty's murder to the charges?"

"That's right, Your Honor. I'm asking for a continuance so that Mr. Gardner and I can gather our witnesses and recast our cases, taking the new evidence into consideration."

"Mr. Gardner?" said the judge.

"My client continues to be held without bail, Your Honor. I'm not opposed to a continuance, but I ask you to consider bail at this time."

"Your Honor, we're going to charge Lucas Burke with another charge of capital murder. The people maintain that Burke's a danger to the public and a flight risk, now more than ever."

"Agreed. As for the continuance, will two months from now work for the both of you?"

"Yes, judge," Yuki said.

Gardner said, "I want to meet with Ms. Castellano to view the video she cited. You available this afternoon, Yuki?"

"I have time between two and four."

The appointment was agreed upon, the judge was thanked, and the prosecutor and defense attorney left chambers together, peeling off in different directions as soon as their feet touched the marble-floored corridor. "I'll see you later, Newt," Yuki said to Gardner over her shoulder.

Gardner said, "I'll be there at two and I'll bring my skepticism with me."

Yuki said, "Hah. Good one."

She took the elevator to the fourth floor, walked into the Homicide squad room, waved at Brenda as she passed, and took the center aisle to her husband's office.

Brady said, "All good?"

"Yes. Give me a hug."

He squeezed her until, laughing, she begged him to stop.

"See you later," she said.

She left Brady, gave Lindsay a high five as she passed her desk, then went downstairs to brief Red Dog on her meeting with the judge.

TWO MONTHS LATER

CHAPTER 75

COURT HAD BEEN CALLED into session.

Judge Passarelli had instructed the jury, *"Don't read the paper or watch TV, I mean it. Don't discuss the case with anyone, not spouses nor blood relatives, nor strangers on a train. That goes for comparing notes with your fellow jurors or talking to yourself out loud when you're washing your hands or in your sleep or under any circumstance whatsoever until you're in the jury room to deliberate. Then you can and should talk to your fellow jurors until you've arrived at a verdict. Okay? Very good."*

All but one of the jurors had smiled. They liked the judge as much as Yuki did.

The gallery was packed and it murmured like a beehive. Press was allowed, but not cameras. Yuki turned her head to face the rear and saw Cindy in the last row, on the aisle. Since Cindy had rung the bell on this case since before baby Lorrie Burke had even been found on the beach, Yuki hoped her friend would get the story she'd earned. A guard opened the door and Brady slipped inside the courtroom and stood next to Cindy. He gave Yuki a thumbs-up.

She nodded and turned back to the courtroom and her cocounsel, Nick Gaines, sitting to her left.

Gaines was Yuki's second chair. He had just returned to the DA after several years in a start-up law firm. He was a great number two. Organized, supportive, and funny, and Yuki was very happy to have him back. It worked both ways. Nick liked being on the prosecution side and was excited to have accidentally timed his return with a chance to work with his former mentor on the case of the decade.

The high and low points of this trial would be reported not only in the United States; the Lucas Burke case had also attracted the avid attention of the international press. The outcome of this trial would stick to the San Francisco DA for years, win or lose.

Adrenaline shock waves were coming more frequently as the business of the court was concluded and the moment was coming when the judge would say "Ms. Castellano, you're up."

Yuki turned her head forty-five degrees to the right to check out the defense table. At that precise moment, Newt Gardner turned his face to hers. He was ready for his close-up: head freshly shaven, shirt as stiff as marble, and his suit was fine and smart. Handmade, a classic navy blue.

Gardner smiled and tipped his head in greeting. Yuki nodded back. There was no point in taking anything Gardner said or did personally. Yuki's phrase for the day was "Steady, girl. You've got this."

Nicky Gaines wrote on his tablet. *What a creep.*

She nodded, added to the note, *Yeah and he's not even the killer.*

That said, Lucas Burke, the accused, looked the part of the villain. He had shaved badly, like he wasn't used to plastic razors after the sharp steel he formerly used. He was allowed a suit, shirt, and tie, rather than the orange jumpsuit that could unfairly prejudice the jurors. Still, his rumpled tweed jacket and dingy dress shirt didn't support a look of innocence.

Yuki also observed that he had aged since the murders. He had more wattle under his chin probably because of the weight he'd lost. His hair had gone from auburn to gray. His attorney leaned toward him and whispered in his ear. Burke then sat up straighter, as if good posture would acquit him of triple homicide.

Yuki took some deep breaths, released them silently, and with eyes closed visualized this blond-wood-paneled courtroom as Baker Beach. She'd seen photos of the baby at the shoreline, and that was the image that she would implant in the jurors' minds.

Nick nudged her with a knee under the table.

The gallery that had been buzzing softly went quiet.

Judge Passarelli said, "Okay everyone. Settle down. No talking to each other or anyone on pain of removal from the courtroom. There will be a lunch break at around noon. Anyone who thinks they will need a bathroom break should leave now and come back at one. Any questions? Good.

"ADA Castellano. Ready with your opening statement?"

CHAPTER 76

CINDY THOMAS HAD BEEN WAITING for this day since Kathleen Wyatt had crashed into her office, wild-eyed and shrill, demanding attention for her missing daughter—who had only been missing for a few hours.

Kathleen's instincts were sharp.

Cindy had done the right thing by getting Lindsay involved.

And the whole rotten story had unspooled from there: Lorrie, Misty, Wendy, Susan, and last, Tara with her throat slashed and still strapped into the passenger seat of her Volvo.

Starting today, Cindy's job was to report this trial daily. She knew her column would be lifted and reprinted elsewhere or rewritten and rerun in all forms of media around the globe. If Yuki's argument won over the jury, Lucas Burke would be convicted on three counts of murder.

He would never be free again.

The judge called on Yuki to make her opening

statement, and Cindy had a pretty good view of her dear friend walking over to the jury box.

Yuki said good morning and introduced herself to the twelve jurors and three alternates, a total of eight women and seven men. Cindy thought the more women the better, and in this case the foreman was also a woman.

Yuki stood in front of the jury box, her hands at her sides and said, "I want to bring you to a Monday morning in Lucas and Tara Burke's small house on Dublin Street. According to the defendant, he and his wife have a fight. Lucas is angry that Tara is spending too much money on clothes and trifles. Afterward, he describes this altercation to the police as a shouting, door-slamming kind of fight. Nothing physical.

"There's a security camera mounted above the front door of the Burke house, and when we show you the footage you will see that on the morning of this fight, Mr. Burke gets into his silver Audi and drives north on Dublin Street at high speed. Twenty minutes later, Tara Burke, age twenty, leaves the house with their sixteen-month-old baby girl, Lorrie Annette Burke. She also has three bags: computer, diaper, and an overnight-sized bag. The tape shows Tara getting into her red Volvo, and after she secures the baby into the car seat and buckles herself into the driver's seat, she drives south on Dublin Street, in the opposite direction her husband has taken.

"Once Tara drives out of sight of the camera, she and Lorrie are never seen alive again."

Cindy watched as Yuki paused to take in the jurors' expressions, and then she continued her gripping narrative.

"Records and witnesses tell us that Lucas Burke arrives at Sunset Park Prep before eight that morning.

He remains at the school, teaching his classes, meeting with students. Records also show that at ten after eleven, he calls his wife from his cell phone and she answers. Their call lasts just under three minutes.

"What was said? Were apologies exchanged? Were they accepted? Did Mr. Burke arrange to meet his wife after school, and did they in fact meet? Mr. Burke has told the police that he apologized to Tara and said he would see her at the end of the day, but that Tara and Lorrie did not come home."

A bout of coughing came from the gallery, reverberating around the room. Yuki used the moment to return to the counsel table, where she sipped from a glass of water and let the last sentence hang.

Cindy wrote down, "Tara and Lorrie were not seen alive again." She was recording the entire proceedings on her phone, but that last known communication was a standout subhead. And it bracketed Tara and Lorrie's last living moments that morning.

The coughing had stopped and Yuki again addressed the jury. "Tara and Lorrie did not come home that night or ever again. At six fifteen on Wednesday morning, Lorrie's small body was found washed up on Baker Beach."

CHAPTER 77

YUKI'S EYES WERE DRAWN to the female juror in the second-row left side of the jury box.

Five minutes into the opening, the pretty young woman had a wad of tissues in her hands and tears in her eyes. Yuki knew from questioning her during *voir dire* that juror number three had a baby at home.

Colossal overconfidence on Newt's part not to exclude her.

Yuki dropped her eyes to the front row and, having summarized the last known sighting of Tara and Lorrie Burke, said, "The same day, after the discovery of Lorrie's body, Mr. Burke tells the SFPD that the house was empty when he came home the night before, that he watched TV and turned off the lights at ten.

"So, I ask a question that has not been satisfactorily answered. Where was Mr. Burke after three thirty on Monday when he left school? He says he took a long drive down the coast so he could think about his marriage and his life.

"Tara and Lorrie Burke died that night and their

bodies later washed up from the ocean. The water washed away most of the evidence, so we will never know exactly what happened. But this we know for sure...

"When Lucas Burke comes home Monday night, Tara and Lorrie are not there and they are absent all night and the following day. Yet we know that Mr. Burke does not call his wife beyond the one three-minute call I've cited. He does not call the police to report Tara and Lorrie missing. Wednesday morning, he goes to work and is interrupted in class by the head of school, who has to deliver terrible news. A baby girl, about sixteen months old, has washed up on Baker Beach.

"Burke leaves Sunset Park Prep and arrives at the crime scene by nine o'clock. The public parking area is already packed with bystanders, reporters, and police and a cordon has been strung up separating the lot from the road. Police are shooing the bystanders away, getting drivers to remove their cars.

"A distraught Lucas Burke identifies the deceased as his daughter. But when he was interviewed by SFPD investigators the day before, on Tuesday, he'd told them that he was unconcerned that Tara and Lorrie hadn't come home. He described Tara as manic, impulsive, 'crazy,' and claims that she's run away before.

"He says he assumed that Tara went shopping and was still angry with him, and despite his sincere and ardent apology for the fight, he guessed that she checked into a motel or bunked with a friend. He had canceled her credit and debit cards prior to the fight, and Tara doesn't have much cash, so he figures she'll run out of money soon and come home.

"But, ladies and gentlemen, Tara doesn't come

home, not even after her daughter is discovered dead. Her car hasn't been sighted. She hasn't called her mother or any of her friends, and she hasn't called her husband.

"So, Mr. Burke is held as a material witness and questioned. He is enraged during questioning. He is sure that his wife has done something 'crazy.' That the police should keep looking for her. Twenty-four hours later, after Mr. Burke is released, a warrant has been signed to search his house for evidence of foul play. While his house is being searched by police and the Forensics team, Mr. Burke takes off in his car and is not seen or heard from for the next two days.

"Where does he go?

"He drives to Sacramento, where his ex-wife, Alexandra Conroy, lives, and the two of them go to a resort in Carmel-by-the-Sea. According to Mr. Burke, what brings him back to San Francisco is a newspaper with a headline reporting the murder of his teenage student and mistress, Melissa Fogarty, known as 'Misty.'

"How can the People charge Mr. Burke with Ms. Fogarty's murder when he was out of town?

"Because although he cannot be in two places at once, we believe his alibi was either intentionally or unintentionally falsified. We believe that Mr. Burke's ex-wife is incorrect about Mr. Burke being with her the whole time they were in Carmel, and that he returned to San Francisco to kill Ms. Fogarty on Friday evening.

"We will show video of Ms. Fogarty waiting for Mr. Burke in the parking lot of Sunset Park Prep at about eight that Friday night. Misty attends this school. It is where Mr. Burke teaches and where they met and began their affair. That night, as she waits for him, you will see Mr. Burke get into the back seat of Ms.

Fogarty's car. You will see the movement of his arm as he draws the blade across this teenager's throat. It was quick, done from behind, from left to right.

"Moments later, as Ms. Fogarty bleeds out, Mr. Burke leaves the car. He disposes of the murder weapon by tossing it over the fence that separates the school parking lot from a field of unmown weeds and car parts. Still, due to diligent police work and additional reviews of the video taken of the murder, crime scene investigators find the weapon, a straight razor belonging to Mr. Burke.

"The Forensics lab has determined that Lucas Burke's fingerprints and Ms. Fogarty's blood are both on the razor that was used to slash her throat.

"Circumstantial evidence combined with the physical evidence all points to one person only.

"The defendant, Lucas Burke."

CHAPTER **78**

YUKI WAITED OUT the crying in the gallery; Misty's parents and friends were sobbing uncontrollably.

The gavel came down hard and several people got up from their seats in the gallery and, without being asked, left the courtroom. Some spectators used the opportunity to move from the rear of the room to the front.

At the defense table, Newt Gardner was whispering to his client, who looked as though his brain was in park. No wheels appeared to be turning at all.

Judge Passarelli asked Yuki to continue.

Yuki said, "That Sunday, four days after Lorrie's body washes up on the beach and two days after Misty Fogarty is murdered, Tara's red Volvo surfaces at low tide off China Beach. Her body is strapped into the *passenger* seat. Her throat has been slashed. A rock the size of a loaf of bread, weighing eight and a half pounds, has been placed on the car's accelerator to keep pressure on the gas. The baby's diaper bag is wedged under the driver's seat, and Tara is wearing the same clothes she was wearing the morning she left her house for the last time. No sign of her computer, her handbag, or her overnight bag.

"So what has happened?

"Mr. Burke denies any knowledge.

"According to San Francisco's chief medical examiner, Dr. Claire Washburn, Lorrie was smothered, but Tara's cause of death was a clean cut by a sharp blade across her throat, and Dr. Washburn will also testify that Melissa was killed the same way.

"We will show you the murder weapon, Mr. Burke's razor with his fingerprints on the handle, and Melissa Fogarty's blood on the blade.

"It's direct evidence, ladies and gentlemen, and the murders of these three completely innocent victims will be proven to you beyond reasonable doubt.

"Thank you for your attention and your service."

Yuki returned to her seat. The gallery began to buzz. She glanced at Cindy and saw that Brady had vacated his spot. Nick Gaines's tablet was in front of her with a note.

Great damned job, Yuki. Flawless.

She thought so, too.

The defense was called to make its opening statement, and Yuki's sense of a job well done was about to come undone.

CHAPTER 79

CINDY STRUGGLED WITH her phone charger, trying to insert it into the electric socket on the baseboard behind her seat, eventually completing the task.

The judge had asked if defense counsel was ready with his opening statement, and he said he was. This would be a bad time for her phone to run out of juice. Cindy watched as the battery icon showed the phone charging. She picked her notebook off the floor and—along with all 140 people in the courtroom—focused her gaze on Newt Gardner. He was known for his showmanship, and although Cindy was with Yuki all the way, she *was* a working reporter, and where there was Newt Gardner, there was news.

Gardner stood and moved his chair back so that it rested against the bar. He put his hand on his client's shoulder familiarly, showing what a good guy Lucas Burke really was. He stood behind his table for a moment, letting the suspense build. Then Gardner walked across the well to the lectern in the center of the floor, where he could speak not only to the jurors but all of the spectators as well.

He introduced himself, casually stating that he had been a defense attorney for thirty years. It was the definition of false modesty, Cindy thought. He might as well have said, "I know I need no introduction," but he said his name and that he was representing an innocent man.

"I'm glad to be representing Lucas Burke, who has never committed a crime or a misdemeanor; not parking in a no-parking zone, never arrested for vandalism or disorderly conduct, and certainly not murder. The prosecution is asking you to connect dots.

"Anyone see any dots?

"There are no dots. Terrible events happened and Lucas is one of the victims. His daughter, his wife, and yes, his girlfriend, have all been killed in the space of a week.

"But the killer is not on trial.

"The murderer is a serial killer who is still at large. If Ms. Castellano had him in the dock she'd be telling a different story. She would say that this killer has been sought by the FBI for decades. That he is a psychopathic killer. That he was the subject of a manhunt for killing his own wife and daughter, as well as many other innocent young women.

"And the person he hates most in the world is my client.

"His vanity is at stake. His narcissism is in a fury. He may have other reasons for his actions, but we can't begin to understand a man like this. Top law enforcement have sought him for decades, always missed catching him by a hair that he has never left behind. He has military training. He's adept at killing by hand."

Gardner paused to look around at the spectators and swung back to face the jurors.

"In the last twenty years or so, this murderer has been known by many names: the Ghost of Catalina. Quicksilver, for the liquid metal we call mercury. You can't grab mercury. It slips out of your hands. The killer has had other names but the most powerful one, the one that will grab your heart and squeeze it, is the name my client has called him his whole life.

"Lucas has called him 'Dad.'"

There was a lengthy rolling gasp throughout the courtroom. Cindy took it all in, the shock on the judge's face, the way the defendant collapsed onto the counsel table as Yuki sat stone-faced.

Time went by until Judge Passarelli said, "Mr. Gardner?"

"Sorry, Your Honor."

Gardner walked to his table, lowered his mouth to his client's ear. Lucas Burke nodded, wiped his face with a pocket handkerchief, and, gripping the arms of his chair, sat more or less erect. Cindy wrote, "Lucas Burke seems broken."

Newt Gardner went back to the podium and said, "Ladies and gentlemen of the jury, I'm not making up this shadow individual. He is real in every way, and according to my contacts with government investigators we don't know a fraction of the women this man has killed.

"But for the purposes of this trial, we are concerned with three individuals. Tara Burke, Lorrie Burke, and Melissa Fogarty, an eighteen-year-old high school girl who loved Lucas, who loved her, too.

"I swear to you. Lucas didn't kill any of them. He'd rather have killed himself."

CHAPTER 80

YUKI WAS BOTH shocked and awed by Gardner's presentation.

He made sure when he looked around the small courtroom, to look directly at her, to unnerve her, to loosen her grip.

He was asking the jury to believe that Evan Burke, who did not even appear on the witness list because he was in the wind, was guilty of murdering three actual people.

Yuki knew where Gardner was going with his theory, but she was counting on the jurors to see through the flash of smoke and mirrors to the real flesh-and-blood killer sitting only yards from them and to find him guilty, guilty, guilty.

Tara. Lorrie. Melissa.

Means, motive, opportunity, and a murder weapon with his prints on the handle.

Gardner went on.

"The prosecution has, of course, provided the defense with the same videos they will show you.

"First, you'll see the images of Lucas leaving his house one Monday morning after a fight with his wife. Thirty-two minutes later, his wife, Tara, leaves with the baby. As ADA Castellano told you, she is carrying some belongings and likely plans to spend the night away from home.

"Later, past dark on that same day, the camera will record Lucas coming home around eight thirty and leaving again the next morning at seven. Tara's car is not in the driveway. On Tuesday, he is questioned by SFPD in his office and cooperates fully. The next morning, he gets the horrifying news that his baby daughter is lying dead in the surf of Baker Beach.

"A police sergeant drives him to this very building, where he is questioned and held as a material witness, released the next day. He goes home, and several hours later police cars pull up, several inspectors come to the front door and hand Lucas a search warrant. He is asked to stay outside while they search his premises and Lucas, nearly deranged with grief, gets into his car and drives clear to Sacramento.

"After the police and CSI enter Dublin Street, there is no more video from the Burke house surveillance camera. CSI disconnects the receiver and takes it back to the lab.

"But the most important piece of information in this case is on the video. We see Tara Burke leaving the house and *she does not lock the door.* My client has told me that his wife *never* locked the doors, front, back, or side. And so if you were planning to kill her, you would be aware of this, and you would have had access to the Burke house from the rear, where there was no camera.

"This fact will come up again. *Tara never locked the doors.*

"The prosecution will show you video of Ms. Melissa Fogarty, known as Misty, Lucas Burke's girlfriend. The video was taken on Friday, two days after Lorrie Burke's body was found at Baker Beach. This video was taken at 8 p.m. in the parking lot of the school where Luke taught English, and Misty was in the senior class. These two often met at this time in the empty parking lot, but on this night, Lucas Burke was not coming to meet Misty. He had left town, driven from his house to Sacramento, where Alexandra Conroy, his ex-wife, suggested they both travel to Carmel-by-the-Sea for his health.

"The two of them drive to Carmel the next morning. Only a day later, on Saturday, while Lucas and ex-wife are having breakfast in the hotel, Lucas sees a newspaper with a headline he cannot believe."

Gardner said, "This is the paper."

He held up the *Chronicle* Yuki had seen enough times to memorize the headline. "Slash-and-Gash Killer Takes Second Victim." Misty's sweet face filled the rest of the front page.

Gardner went on.

"Ms. Conroy will testify that she and Lucas were together from the time he arrived in Sacramento until a day and a half later, when they returned to San Francisco. So how can the prosecution have a video of my client killing Melissa Fogarty, flinging the murder weapon into the weeds, and—voilà—it has Melissa's blood on the blade and Lucas Burke's fingerprints on the handle?

"I call bull on the prosecution's theory. It is a theory full of holes because Lucas wasn't there. They have a possible murder weapon, and it *may* have belonged to Lucas. But they don't have proof it was in his hand when Melissa Fogarty was killed.

"I will prove to you that someone else committed these unspeakable murders. He had access to my client's house. He had access to his razor blade.

"As for Tara's body. By the time that poor woman's car floated up near China Beach she had been in the ocean for nearly a week. She was bloated, and ocean animals—fish, crabs, seals, whatever—had been rough on her. But it was still clear that she had been killed with a straight-edge razor sliced across her throat from left to right. When she was dead or dying, her killer weighed down the accelerator and sent her car into the ocean, with mother and baby daughter inside.

"My client, Lucas Burke didn't do this. And the prosecution can say what they want, but they have no witness, no trace evidence, no clear video of the person who killed Tara Burke.

"My client didn't do it.

"Lucas killed none of these people.

"He's never killed anyone in his life. But as his attorney, I don't have to prove his innocence.

"The prosecution has to prove his guilt beyond reasonable doubt."

Yuki watched Gardner thank the jury and return to his seat. He put his arm around Burke's shoulders, and his client put his head down on the table and sobbed loudly and authentically.

The judge called Yuki and Gardner to the bench and said, "I feel strongly we should recess now and pick up again after lunch."

Gardner said, "Yes, yes, for the love of God, yes."

Yuki said, "I agree, Your Honor."

Court was adjourned until one o'clock.

CHAPTER 81

I WAS IN BRADY'S OFFICE when he got the call.

After a moment, he said, "Hold on, hon. I need you to tell Lindsay, too."

Brady stabbed a button on his console and I went out to my desk and said, "Yuki? What's wrong?"

Her voice was strained.

"Linds, I asked Brady if you can take another stab at finding Evan Burke. I want to talk to him."

"We've kept a camera on his house on Mount Tam. He hasn't been back. His cabin cruiser is still in its slip at Richardson Bay Marina."

"So, you're saying this is a dead end?"

It was ten thirty Monday morning.

Yuki asking us to take another run at Evan Burke meant she was having doubts about her case, and if she was feeling that way, jurors would surely feel the same.

I asked, "What happened this morning?"

"I was on fire, but Gardner brought a bomb to the firefight."

"Say a few more words, please."

She sighed, "Okay. Gardner made a strong case that Evan did it, killed them all. Lucas broke down. Judge called the game on account of crying. Reconvening after a long lunch break."

"I'll call you later," I said. "Buy you a drink."

"Or two," she said.

"Chin up, girlfriend," I said.

I hung up, left my desk, tapped Cappy and Chi, Alvarez and Conklin, and we went down the hall to our task force office in the corner. We'd gone on to other homicides once the Lucas Burke trial had been scheduled.

As the five of us dragged chairs up to the table, I told the team we had to go over everything again with fresh eyes.

"Look for one unturned stone. Don't worry if it's not the holy grail. We need a lead."

Evan Burke's ID photo from his military days was centered on the whiteboard. He'd been a kid when the photo was taken, and while Lucas resembled him, Evan was better looking. If he was the killer, I could see how he could put a spell on young females and kill them before they had a hint of the danger.

We had piles of data in both hard copies and digits, and since Paul Chi was super organized, he knew all of it.

He took charge now, calling up files, slapping maps on the whiteboard. There were now cold cases across the West Coast that had fallen into geographical patterns of five to seven victims centering on but not exclusive to California. Oregon, Nevada had a few clusters as well.

The victimology was vague and at the same time told a lot about the killer. Bodies had turned up both fresh killed and long buried. They were all women under thirty, and they'd all been killed by a sharp blade across the throat.

Chi said, "He sticks to the coastline and interior waterways when he can. If you draw lines from the victim locations, you can see that the nexus is San Francisco."

We looked at the compiled data on the possible victims and found only one case of a woman who had stab marks on her chest like those we'd found on Misty and Wendy Franks. Possibly the killer was only now trying on a style.

Alvarez had told us her theory that Luke had been attached to his father when he was young, but that his father was never there, which caused him to have a longing for his father and to hate him at the same time.

Where was Daddy? On a killing spree out of town before he brought it back home to murder his own wife and daughter.

Alvarez said, "I did some research on this sick on-and-off parental disconnect," she said. "In France and Switzerland in particular, they refer to hardly home dads as 'eclipse fathers.'

If that was true of Evan, then Lucas longed for his attention. And then his mother and sister disappeared. Their bodies were never found. Maybe Luke knew. Maybe he had a bad feeling he didn't bring out into the sunshine. Or. Maybe *he* did the killings to get his father's love."

I asked if anyone else had a theory. No one did. If dozens of Homicide divisions hadn't landed him, how could we do it in this dreary room with the clock ticking toward the afternoon court session?

I went outside to the noise of Bryant Street and called Joe.

"Can you reach out to Berney? Please. Couldn't be a more important time than now."

CHAPTER 82

JOE PHONED ME BACK before I reached the squad room.

"I reached Berney," he said. "He's tracking Evan Burke toward Nevada. Burke's haunted Vegas in the past."

And then Joe said, "Berney added the kicker: *Tell Lindsay to meet me at the Bellagio Hotel this evening.*"

"That's all he said?"

"He's a man of few words. Sometimes no words. Linds, I suggest you bring backup."

I was pretty sure the bosses were going to spike this request, but hell. I had to try. Clapper was making a rare visit to the squad room and was meeting with Brady. I rapped on the glass and barged in. Both men looked up at me, said nothing until I finished my short, sharp presentation.

"Yuki needs to depose Evan Burke. A confidential contact of Joe's is tailing Burke and has advised me to go to Vegas ASAP. If you agree, I want to bring Alvarez. She knows Vegas, knows cops and security at the casinos. I'm going to need clearance from LVPD."

Brady said, "Fine with me. Chief?"

Clapper said, "Good choice of Alvarez."

He snatched up Brady's phone and called LVPD's Chief Alexander Belinky, saying that Alvarez and I were "dogging a witness" and that we had a subpoena.

"We do?" I said, after he hung up.

"You will."

An hour and a half later, Alvarez and I were at SFO in Terminal 3.

Our flight was scheduled to depart in forty-five minutes. Alvarez brought Cinnabons and coffee to our seating area, where I was FaceTiming with Joe and Julie.

I showed Julie the herd of metallic sculptures hanging from the ceiling above our seats. They were shiny bronze lights reflecting our surroundings from twenty feet up, showing curvy views of the concourse, the moving crowds of people, and storefronts. Mood music was playing and the temperature was optimal.

I tried to sound like I was having fun, but of course I was faking it. I said good-bye to my family and said I'd call from Vegas.

Then I called Richie.

"You okay?" Rich asked.

"I'm having flashbacks."

The last time we'd been inside Terminal 3, there'd been a ticking time bomb somewhere inside the airport. Shots were fired by cop impersonators and a foot chase took us up through the airport layer cake to the Loop trains. There'd been a shoot-out with fatalities. And we could have easily joined the departed. I could still see it as clearly as if I were wearing a virtual reality headset.

I wasn't ready to share my posttraumatic flashbacks with Alvarez, so I sipped coffee and watched the escalators and the airport shops. Even with one leg in the past, I was anxious about the immediate future. We were going after Evan Burke and our spirit guide was the mysterious spook called Berney.

Joe admitted that Berney had been vague.

"It's how he is," Joe had said. "I trust him."

I had no basis to trust or mistrust the man. I had no doubt that Joe had great experience with Berney, but to me he was a question mark, and Evan Burke was in my own experience armed and very dangerous.

Alvarez brought me into the present.

"Boxer," she said.

"Hmm?"

"Our flight's been called."

We headed to the gate, with no information about our mission beyond "Tell Lindsay to meet me at the Bellagio."

CHAPTER 83

THE FLIGHT TO VEGAS was short and smooth and our Uber was waiting outside McCarran's main terminal when we exited the airport at two o'clock.

We quickly reached the Bellagio; we passed the design wonder of the Bellagio's fountain, which was synced to over thirty different songs. Alvarez and I checked into the hotel, and the desk clerk handed me two envelopes; one was white, marked "Business Center." My name had been typed on a label. The other was a Bellagio hotel envelope, my name printed in blue ballpoint ink.

I waited until Alvarez and I were ensconced in our two-bedroom suite—thanks to Clapper's decision to put us up at the same location as Joe's CI. We had a dazzling panoramic view of the neon city. But this was a business trip. I tore open the end of the larger envelope and slid out the contents. There were two stiff papers, each folded in thirds.

Document one was a faxed subpoena for Evan Burke's appearance signed by the trial judge and DA

Leonard Parisi. Document two was an extradition order to be forwarded to the Nevada supreme court if needed.

Alvarez said, "Clapper is tremendous, isn't he?"

I agreed and peeled open the flap of the smaller envelope. Inside was a page torn from a notepad. It said, "Meet me at Lago at eight. B."

I showed it to my roommate.

"Lago is here in the hotel."

I said, "Sonia, can I go to dinner like this?"

I was wearing my usual: slacks, man-tailored shirt, blue blazer, holstered Glock, flat-soled shoes. She nodded, shrugged, then said, "You're fine, but I'm going down to the lobby boutiques to get a dress from the sale rack. Otherwise, we're going to look like a couple of cops. You're a size ten?"

"Ten to twelve," I said.

"Let me see what I can do. I'm good at costuming."

"Maybe I'll take a quick nap."

"Keep your phone on."

"Copy that."

I put my phone on the nightstand in the closest bedroom and dropped onto the bed. When my head hit the pillow, I was already asleep. I dreamed about Berney. In this fantasy, I was interrogating him in the box.

What's your name? Your real name? What's your interest in Evan Burke? Am I bait? Or free labor so you can nab Burke and take him back to Washington?

In my dream, the spy who looked like a preacher man just smiled but didn't answer.

I was awoken by the sound of crinkling paper. Alvarez was back from her shopping excursion to the lobby, and she had a couple of shiny bags with her.

"What'd you get?"

Sonia opened one bag and took out something black and slinky with sprays of sequins from shoulder to hip.

"Try this on," she said.

"Me?"

"I've got a backup for you in case…"

I stripped off my shirt and trousers and stepped into the sparkly black cocktail dress. Alvarez said, "So far, excellent. Shoe size nine?"

She took a pair of black shoes with a short heel out of a bag and handed them over. I wiggled them on.

They looked good.

While I was admiring my legs, Alvarez had put on a cream-colored pantsuit. We were transformed.

"Cagney and Lacey," I said.

"Rizzoli and Isles."

I told Alvarez we could always try to expense the undercover outfits. We laughed, then Alvarez said, "We're not done yet."

CHAPTER 84

NICK GAINES HAD POSITIONED the whiteboard so that the judge, jurors, and witnesses could see the photos of Lorrie and Tara Burke and Melissa Fogarty, along with their names and dates of birth and death.

Yuki felt good. She was stacking her points brick by brick as she built her case against Lucas Burke.

She'd put on a series of cops and coast guard officers, all of whom were experienced at testifying in court.

Patrolman Jay Whitcomb had been first on the scene when the body of a red-haired female child was found on Baker Beach. Coast guard lieutenant Samuel Waverly directed the recovery of Tara Burke's vehicle. School security guard Mike Cassidy was the unsuspecting soul who'd found Misty Fogarty sitting in her own blood in her car parked in the Sunset Park Prep student lot. And Misty's best friend, Johanna Weber, testified that Burke told Melissa that he loved her and wanted to marry her.

Yuki also had a copy of the note from Lucas to Misty saying so. It was entered into evidence and shown to the jury.

It was about three thirty when Yuki called Dr. Claire Washburn to the stand.

Claire was both authoritative and accessible, and her testimony was in spoken English, not medical jargon.

She explained that the baby had been asphyxiated and, judging from the bruises on her face, most probably smothered by hand.

And she described to the jury what she could tell from the autopsy of the baby's mother.

"Tara Burke's body was bloated and, no other way to say this, chewed on by sea life. Her eyes, fingers, parts of her cheeks were gone, and the fatal injury was also swollen and disturbed. That said, only a sharp blade across the throat could have made that mortal wound. Force had been used, and Mrs. Burke was nearly decapitated. Both Tara and Lorrie were dead before the car went into the ocean."

With Yuki guiding her witness, Claire described Melissa Fogarty's slashed throat, the seemingly gratuitous stab marks on her chest.

Yuki walked to the whiteboard and indicated Fogarty's photo.

"Is this Melissa Fogarty?" Yuki asked her witness.

"Yes."

The jurors turned to look at the picture of Misty. From her expression, she had good feelings toward the person behind the lens. Her eyes smiled. Her grin was verging on laughter. She had been a beautiful eighteen-year-old.

At Yuki's questioning, Claire described the slash across the girl's throat, detailing the "serial killer gibberish" of the gashes in her upper chest.

Yuki entered the morgue photos with close-ups of the injuries into evidence and then passed them to the jurors.

Yuki thanked the witness and turned her over to defense counsel.

Newt Gardner had had no questions for the law-enforcement witnesses, but he wanted to cross-examine Claire. Gardner stood, and this time he spoke from his position at the counsel table.

"Dr. Washburn, is it your professional conclusion that all three of these victims were killed by the same person?"

"I see a pattern in the manner of death of the two adult women."

"Please just answer the question, doctor. Can you tell us if the victims were all killed by the same person?"

"Not definitively, but the evidence points to one killer."

"How so?"

"Tara and Melissa both died from similar slashes across their throats."

"So, if I understand you correctly, you have no evidence leading to Lorrie Burke's killer."

"No scientific evidence."

"So, that's a 'no.' During your postmortem examinations of Tara Burke and Melissa Fogarty, did you obtain evidence that they were killed by my client?"

"As I said, Mr. Gardner, Mrs. Burke's throat was slashed. She was in the ocean for days. What we could tell from that waterlogged fatal wound was that it was inflicted with a sharp blade. Same type of wound Melissa Fogarty suffered."

"Same or similar?"

"Due to the condition of Mrs. Burke's body, I can only say 'similar.'"

"So you can't even be sure that the throats were slashed by the same weapon or the same individual, can you?"

When Claire didn't answer, Gardner said, "You found nothing in or on any of the deceased that would lead you to believe that my client killed them, isn't that right?"

Claire didn't speak.

"Yes or no, Dr. Washburn?"

"I have no direct evidence that your client killed those people, correct."

"I have no further questions for the witness."

Yuki stood and said, "Redirect, Your Honor."

She walked over to Claire.

"The shallow gashes on Melissa Fogarty's chest that you called 'serial killer gibberish' could be the killer's signature, his way of marking the victim, is that right?"

"Yes."

"Were there any similar gashes on Tara Burke's body?"

"The condition of the soft tissue indicated random blade-induced injuries of the chest with force. So, I see a pattern there, the killer's signature on both women."

"Thank you, Dr. Washburn. You may stand down."

CHAPTER 85

YUKI HAD PREPARED Kathleen Wyatt for what would be an ordeal for anyone, and grueling for Kathleen.

Together they had talked across Kathleen's kitchen table. Yuki had played the role of defense counsel and questioned Kathleen, gotten a little rough to show her what Gardner could do. As Kathleen teared up, Yuki had gripped her hand and said, "He may try to discredit you, but he has to be careful not to make the jury see *him* as a villain. Just tell the jury what you know. Answer Gardner's questions and don't go off script or call Lucas names. It's okay to be mad or sad, just—"

"Don't go crazy."

"Because?"

"Because if I go off, it'll hurt my credibility."

"Exactly right. I'll object if he leads or badgers you or misstates what you say. If you feel overwhelmed, tell the judge you need to take a break."

They'd had that conversation two days ago.

Now, Yuki called her witness.

A security guard opened one of the courtroom's rear doors and Kathleen came through and headed up the aisle.

She was wearing a slim gray pantsuit and had put some gel in her unruly hair. Nick held the gate open for her and she approached the witness box. It seemed to Yuki that Kathleen was moving very steadily and she wondered if she had taken something to calm her nerves. It would be good if she wasn't manic, but things could go wrong if she came across as sedated.

The forty-six-year-old woman reached the base of the witness stand, put her hand on the Bible, and swore to tell the whole truth.

Yuki approached her and said, "Good morning, Ms. Wyatt. Was Tara your only child?"

"Yes, and a very good girl she was."

"Are you married?"

"My husband died of cancer about five years ago."

"Very sorry, Kathleen. Are you employed?"

"I teach yoga three days a week at a gym on Hyde and I do mailings for the SPCA."

"Thank you. And now I want to take you through the recent events as regards your late daughter and granddaughter."

Kathleen said, "Okay. Yes."

"Good. Now thinking back over the last year of Tara's life, did you have occasion to call the police?"

"Yes, several times. Three or four."

"Why did you call them?"

"Once because Tara called me, screaming that Lucas was trying to kill her. Another time, I was washing my hands when she got out of the shower. I saw bruising on her shoulder and thigh. This big," she said, putting out her hands, holding them five or six inches apart. "Another time, I saw bruises on Lorrie's arm. Looked like fingerprints."

Yuki pivoted toward the bar so that she could see Lucas, who as before, was hunched over the table, looking like a balled-up paper bag. His eyes appeared to be focused between his folded hands.

"Did the police come when you called them?"

"Yes. But each time, Tara said I was overreacting, and made up some story. Luke hadn't been trying to kill her, he'd caught her as she was stumbling down the stairs. Another time she fell off her bike. And about the baby, that was, let me remember. Oh. Tara told the police that Lorrie had put her arm through the bars of her crib and struggled."

"Did you have any private talks with Tara about abuse?"

"She denied it. Sometimes her eyes were bloodshot from crying, but still she denied it. She said Lucas was a good husband and showed me the new red Volvo he had bought her after Lorrie was born."

"Kathleen, did you tell anyone else about your suspicion that Tara was being abused?"

"Yes. I told friends, and the second Tara went missing, I posted a message on Cindy Thomas's crime blog at the *Chronicle*."

"And how did that work out?"

"The paper deleted my post, telling me that it was an unproven accusation and using real names was libel."

"When you wrote to the paper, what result were you hoping for?"

"I hoped that the police would arrest Lucas and find Tara and Lorrie."

"After your post was taken down, did you go to the *San Francisco Chronicle* to see Cindy Thomas?"

"Yes. I couldn't reach Tara, even though we always checked in on each other for about ten minutes. I called her every fifteen minutes and she still didn't pick up or call me."

"That was highly unusual?"

"It was the only time since she got married that we didn't speak. More than three years."

"Can you tell the jury what happened when you went to the *Chronicle*?"

"Cindy Thomas said she couldn't publish my post accusing Luke since it was only my word against his. So, she called the police for me."

"What happened then?"

"I spoke to police Sergeant Boxer."

Yuki asked, "And Tara? Did you hear from her?"

"No. Two days later, I learned that Lorrie, my angel, my dear little grandchild, was dead."

Silence in the courtroom became sighs and murmurs. The judge slammed his gavel once and silence returned.

"I think it was four days later, Tara's car floated up in the ocean. She was in it. Dead. Her neck had been slashed. Her death was pronounced a murder."

"Kathleen, do you see the man you accused sitting in this courtroom?"

"Him," she said, pointing her finger at Lucas Burke. "My son-in-law, Lucas Burke, my daughter's husband, or should I say widower, my deceased granddaughter's horrible, evil father."

Yuki said, "Thank you for your testimony, Kathleen. Mr. Gardner, your witness."

CHAPTER 86

KATHLEEN CLASPED HER HANDS on her lap as Newt Gardner stepped up to the lectern.

Gardner ran a palm over his shaven head, his handsome face looking thoughtful when he said, "Ms. Wyatt, we're all very sorry about the loss of your daughter and your granddaughter. Terrible tragedies."

"Thank you and yes, they are."

She lifted her eyes to look at Lucas Burke but he stayed focused on the counsel table.

Gardner said, "You said just now that you contacted the police three or four times to report that Mr. Burke had abused your daughter."

"Yes, I did."

"Was he ever arrested?"

"No. Tara did not press charges. She told them that she had hurt herself."

"Did Tara ever complain to you about abuse?"

"She didn't have to. I saw the bruises. Her eyes were red from crying."

"So, that would be 'no.' No, she didn't tell you that Lucas abused her."

"She made excuses for him."

Gardner said, "I see. Some people take pictures of their injuries from spousal abuse and they tell their friends."

Yuki said, "Objection, Your Honor. Leading the witness."

"Let me rephrase," said Gardner. "Is there any proof of this abuse?"

"Is her murder proof, Mr. Gardner? What about Lorrie's death? Is that proof?"

"It's proof they were murdered, Ms. Wyatt. Not that *Lucas Burke* murdered them. Thank you. I have nothing further. Again, sorry for your loss."

Kathleen shouted after Gardner, "A mother knows things. I know he put the baby in the closet if she was crying—"

Gardner said, "I'm done with this witness, Your Honor."

"Lucas. Look at me, you," Kathleen shouted across the room to Burke. "You killed them. Tell me why. Why did you do it?"

The judge signaled to the court officers, who were already on their way to the witness box.

"I don't need an escort, Your Honor," Kathleen said to the judge. She was on her feet, walking past Burke when the guards each took one of her elbows and steered her toward the doors.

"You're not getting away with this," Kathleen shouted over her shoulder as she was marched to the door.

Yuki couldn't tell how the jury felt about Kathleen's outburst. Would they see her as a maniac, or as a woman inside the same room with the man who had chopped out her heart and left her bleeding at the side of the road?

CHAPTER 87

I WORE A NYLON stocking cap to flatten my hair, and Sonia Alvarez pulled a brown, chin-length wig over my scalp.

"Owwwww," I said. "Take it easy."

"Sor-*ry*. Now, we're done. What do you think?"

"Who is that girl in the mirror there?"

"That's the idea, right?"

The doorbell on the suite rang.

I went to the door and looked through the peephole. I was thinking maybe it was Berney, but it was *Joe*.

I opened the door, saying "My God, Joe. What's wrong?"

He said, "Hell of a greeting, uh, Blondie."

"Is everything okay? What are you doing here?" I searched his face as I let him into the suite. I didn't see tragedy in his eyes. Didn't see that something had happened to Julie. He smiled.

"Figured I'd have dinner with you and Berney. I'm flying home later."

Alvarez said, "Hello, Joe? I'm Sonia Alvarez. I've

been partnering with Conklin," she said. "Vegas is my native land."

Joe shook her hand, both saying "Nice to meet you." And to me he said, "I brought you a change of clothes, and Julie sent you a toy and a book."

I didn't know whether to laugh or cry. Nothing was wrong. Joe was wonderful and my kiddo had sent me a toy.

"Your friend is meeting us at eight," Alvarez said.

"My friend's not expecting you," Joe said to her. "I'll give him a heads-up."

"We've got time to kill. Anyone feel like having a late lunch? I recommend Lago, here in the hotel."

Soon we were seated at a table at Lago, an elegant "small plate" restaurant with a cinematic view of the lake beyond the iconic Bellagio fountain. Someone in accounting was going to have a stroke when they saw our expenses.

Joe and Sonia were getting along like college friends at their twenty-fifth reunion, only it was more that they'd both worked undercover. I divided my attention between watching my phone for a text from Berney and munching bread. Which was delicious.

Joe was the foody at the table, and he was going over the menu as our proxy when the chair next to me was pulled out and Joe introduced Alvarez to "my old friend who goes by the name Berney."

Berney reached across the table, shook hands with Alvarez. The waiter came over and Berney ordered Scotch on the rocks. He looked cheerful.

"The eagle has landed," he said.

"Evan Burke?" Alvarez asked.

"I meant me. Just kidding. Burke is close by and I am tracking him via GPS." Berney took his cell phone out of his jacket pocket and waggled it. "I can feed information to you. But you cannot mention me or the agency. That's the deal. If you burn me, I can't help you now or ever. My career will be over."

Alvarez and I crossed our hearts, exchanged numbers with Berney, and then chose Joe's recommendations: a yummy, hot seafood salad for me, a mini Margherita pizza for Alvarez. Joe went for the shrimp-stuffed squid, and Berney was all in for grilled lamb chops. Joe and I shared a few bites, and when the plates were cleared I ordered a platter of mixed sweets for the table.

And coffee, of course.

Berney said, "So, here's how it goes. I'm the cheese in the trap and the spring is set. After you're done with him, we're going to take him off your hands."

Until that moment, I'd been stuck between fear of Evan Burke and excitement. It would be tremendous to bring him in. Quicksilver, the Ghost of Catalina, an unexposed criminal who'd aimed his AK at Conklin and me from his narrow front porch—and then vanished.

The fear had burned off, leaving only the thrill of cuffing the bastard and interrogating him back at the Hall.

I had a subpoena in my pocket and many questions to ask the man in the moon.

CHAPTER 88

CINDY WAS IN HER SEAT in the back row of the courtroom, flipping to a clean page in her notebook when Kathleen Wyatt freaked out.

Guards had half dragged, half pulled her out of the courtroom. It was awful. Cindy was about to go after her, comfort her, get her a ride home, but at that moment Yuki called her next witness: Inspector Richard Conklin.

Cindy sat back down. Richie put his hand on her shoulder as he entered the room. She touched his fingers. He winked at her and proceeded up the aisle to the witness stand.

After he'd been sworn in and seated, Yuki asked preliminary questions meant to establish his role both within the SFPD and the task force assigned to this series of murders. Rich testified that he had been a witness to every step of the investigation.

In answer to Yuki's questions, Rich gave a timeline of the multiple cases that he characterized as having a connection to the defendant.

Cindy knew all of this by heart. She and Rich had

talked, but she, too, had been present at the crime scene on Baker Beach, watching from the parking lot as Chief Clapper lifted the baby out of the receding surf. She hadn't been inside Burke's house, but she'd been parked across the street beyond the tape with her cameraman. She easily visualized the scene from Rich's description of where Burke had gotten into his car and accelerated into the distance as CSU and Homicide went through the little house on Dublin Street.

Yuki asked, "Did you find anything of note inside the Burke house?"

"We found what appeared to be feces, loosely wrapped in a baby blanket on the floor of an upstairs closet. And we located the receiver for the security camera. We watched video of both Lucas Burke and Tara Burke, who was holding Lorrie, leave the house, separately. We viewed the video after we had obtained search warrants for the house and everything inside, including electronics."

"Can you tell the court what was on the video?"

"A whole lot of not much until the morning in question, when the Burkes left the house I made a general observation that they were having a disagreement, but nothing that would indicate imminent homicide."

Yuki said, "Your Honor, we'd like to enter this video into evidence and show it to the jury."

Gardner stood, shouting, "Objection, Your Honor. Showing this video is purely intended to traumatize my client. It has nothing to do with any alleged crime. Prosecution simply wants to bring the dead to life in order to get the jurors' sympathies."

"Ms. Castellano?"

"The video is clearly relevant. The jury needs to judge for themselves the last known sighting of two victims."

"Overruled, Mr. Gardner," said Judge Passarelli. "I'd like to see it myself."

CHAPTER 89

YUKI ASKED THE GUARDS to shut off the lights, and Nick Gaines lined up the laptop and hit the Play button on the video file.

The video rolled against the whiteboard.

It was as Conklin had described it; Lucas Burke leaving the house like a thunderbolt. Face dark, getting into his silver sports car, speeding up the street.

As Gardner had said, the sight of Tara Burke in her denim dress, the straps of her various bags crossing her chest, the baby on her hip, one small fist gripping a hank of her mother's hair, was enough to humanize them for the jurors. Those images could shatter a heart made of marble.

When it was over, as the overhead lights came on, Yuki glanced over to Gardner. But the defense counsel was leaning back in his chair, his face bare of expression as if to show her his contempt. *Is that all you've got?*

He knew it wasn't.

Yuki walked to the whiteboard and, after wheeling it around, pointed to the photo of Misty.

"Inspector Conklin, you were at the scene of Melissa Fogarty's murder."

"Yes, I was. Correct."

"Can you tell us about that?"

Conklin removed a couple of sheets of stapled and folded pages from his inside jacket pocket, flattened them, skimmed them, and said, "This is my report for the task force and our lieutenant three days after Lorrie Burke's body surfaced at Baker Beach. Tara Burke was still missing and Ms. Fogarty's body had just been found in her car that morning by school security."

Yuki said, "Please go on."

"Well, Ms. Fogarty was killed on Friday night, discovered on Saturday morning. Like I said, we searched the Burke house the next day. Because of this rash of murders, our squad was working round the clock. On Saturday, Mr. Burke and his ex-wife, Alexandra Conroy, showed up in our squad room. He was in a rage, waving a newspaper with the picture of Ms. Fogarty on the front page."

Richie rested his arms on the railing surrounding the witness chair, and spoke directly to Yuki.

He said, "Okay. So, we know Melissa Fogarty is—was—Lucas Burke's girlfriend. Sergeant Lindsay Boxer and I separated Mr. Burke and Ms. Conroy so we could interview them individually.

"Burke tells us that he and Ms. Conroy had been in Carmel until early that morning. Now, they've returned back to confront the police and to find out the truth about Ms. Fogarty's murder, instead of getting it off a tabloid."

"Were you able to confirm Mr. Burke's whereabouts at the time of Fogarty's murder?"

"Much of it," Conklin said. "The drive to Carmel-by-the-Sea is confirmed. That the two shared a room in the resort is also confirmed. The missing piece is a big one. We cannot confirm whether Mr. Burke left Carmel and returned to San Francisco on Friday evening.

"These are critical hours.

"Ms. Fogarty was murdered at eight o'clock. Mr. Burke and Ms. Conroy state that this is when Ms. Conroy was occupied at the spa."

Yuki said, "Inspector, at the time Mr. Burke and Ms. Conroy came to the Homicide squad, did you have reason to doubt Mr. Burke's timeline?"

"Well, that Ms. Conroy was otherwise occupied at the precise time Ms. Fogarty was killed is a little pat as an alibi. This was a conflict we could not resolve. We checked out all the information we had, and I couldn't prove Mr. Burke's whereabouts when Ms. Fogarty was killed.

"That Saturday morning when Burke appeared in our squad room, he was a suspect in more than one murder, and the victims all had close association to him.

"Still, we had held him for twenty-four hours, we had searched his premises, and CSU had gone through his devices. We had reasonable suspicion that he had killed at least two people. At that time we had no direct evidence against Lucas Burke for anything."

Newt Gardner stood to cross-examine Inspector Conklin.

He made it short.

"So you're still prepared to swear that the man on the parking lot video, the man who presumably killed Melissa Fogarty, is in fact, Mr. Lucas Burke?"

"I am, now," said Conklin.

"Well," said Gardner, "I'm equally sure that he is not. Ms. Castellano, let's go to the tape."

CHAPTER 90

YUKI TURNED THE whiteboard around so that it was again a plain white screen. Behind her, Nick Gaines pulled up the parking lot video on the laptop. And then there was the sea-spray sound of static as the tape rolled.

Yuki said, "Inspector Conklin, will you please describe what you see on the screen."

"I'll do my best," Conklin said. "It's the typical low-quality video we often see from retail-type cameras. It was dark in a virtually unlighted lot. There's Ms. Fogarty getting out of her car. She's standing, then pacing, unmistakable because she's in the one beam of the one light in the lot.

"Now, if we can fast-forward..."

Nick skipped to the part where a man entered the lot on foot.

Conklin said, "There. That's Burke. He's in black, keeping to the shadows as he comes toward Ms. Fogarty. She says something to him, but there's no audio on this security camera. But we can see that

Ms. Fogarty's last living acts were to turn her back on the defendant and get into her car. She starts up the engine and turns on the headlights," Conklin said, "but her assailant opens the back door of her SUV and gets inside. A minute later, out he goes. Watch as he sticks to the shadows as he leaves camera range. The car remains in place until the next morning when Ms. Fogarty's body is discovered. I witnessed her slashed throat and evidence that she bled out in the front seat of her car."

Yuki asked, "How did you determine that the killer was Mr. Burke from watching this video?"

"As I said, it was dark. The man in the parking lot was wearing dark clothes and a hat. That big tree, right there, is growing on the adjacent property, leaning over the fence, throwing shadows over everything. But on the eighth viewing of this video, a member of our task force pointed out an odd movement on the part of the assailant."

Yuki asked, "Can you demonstrate that movement?"

"Like this," Conklin said, brushing at his forelock of hair, moving it a little off his forehead.

He said, "I couldn't quite make out if he was touching his hat or brushing leaves away, but when it was suggested that this individual may have been flicking something over the fence and that it was perhaps the murder weapon, we asked for those particular frames to be enlarged. Our facial rec couldn't match the man in the lot to Mr. Burke because the video quality sucked. Sorry. So CSU brought in a forensic photographic analyst to examine and compare this enlargement with Mr. Burke's photo. There was a 90 percent match even with the crappy quality of the video.

Yuki said, "Mr. Gaines, could you back up the video to the point where the man in the frame makes a motion with his hand?"

Nick did it and Yuki said, "Pause it right there. Thanks."

Conklin said, "See, the fence divides the school parking lot and an overgrown, largely vacant lot behind an old gas station. Weeds are four feet tall and old car parts hidden by weeds are a hazard. Well, it isn't school property. We didn't have a warrant for that field of weeds. We searched every inch of the school parking lot, took the Subaru down to the tires at the crime lab, but it didn't occur to anyone to search the lot earlier."

"And why was that?"

"Because we had a new body."

Yuki said, "Please tell the court about that."

"Sure," Conklin said. "It was a Sunday, and at Chief Clapper's request we were working through the weekend. Tara Burke's car and body rose up in the ocean around China Beach, and we were all over that."

"Was the weedy vacant lot eventually searched?"

"Yes. Not until a couple of months later, but the murder weapon was waiting for us, four feet deep in weeds about an arm's length from the base of the tree."

Yuki showed him an array of photos taken during the search of the field: ten men in white hazmat suits, and last, the photo of a gloved hand holding up a razor.

Yuki asked, "Is this the murder weapon?"

"Yes, a hundred percent."

Yuki looked at the faces of the jury. She had every bit of their attention. The picture of the razor was entered into evidence and then shown to the jury.

Yuki also entered Rich Conklin's report on the meetings with Lucas Burke and his ex-wife.

She thanked Rich and told Gardner that the witness was his. Yuki would bet her IRA that Gardner wasn't going to ask Conklin how the razor could be linked to his client.

Lucas Burke was innocent until proven guilty.

Yuki had every intention of doing just that.

CHAPTER 91

OUR MEAL AT LAGO was wrapping up.

The dessert plates had been cleared and our waiter brought Berney the check.

I said, "Let us expense this, Berney."

He declined the offer and read the tab carefully, almost as if he was decoding a message. For all I knew, he may have been.

His plan, as I understood it, was to leave Burke's capture to Alvarez and me. He'd help us transport the SOB to San Francisco for questioning. After thanking us for our assistance, he'd fly Burke to Quantico, all softened up and ready to admit to innumerable crimes he was suspected of committing.

Alvarez looked very comfortable on her old turf. I was uneasy. The plan was mostly "make it up as you go." Alvarez and I didn't have much history together, and Berney and I had none.

I wished he'd said there were a few dozen under-cover FBI agents disguised as porters and housekeepers ready to grab the presumed killer, chopper him back to the Hall, and leave him with us for a few night interrogations that would result either in a bulletproof confession or believable deniability.

Berney glanced at his phone while reaching for his wallet. The mild, satisfied look on his face was gone.

Joe asked what was wrong and Berney said, "My signal from Burke's GPS is down."

So, Berney was in the dark with the rest of us.

Was Burke's signal down temporarily?

Or had he deliberately pulled off the road, turned off the engine, and let his GPS signal go dark.

He could be right here.

Right now.

Berney said, "You all have my number. Emergency calls only. Thanks."

He put a stack of bills on top of the check, and as quickly as he'd arrived he was gone.

Joe said, "I should be going. Got a message for the Bugster?"

A Neil Diamond classic was playing, "Cracklin' Rosie." I walked Joe to the escalator, and asked him to bring Julie a few bars of the song if he could sing it.

"I can sing it, Blondie, but I'm not sure how to explain, 'Cracklin' Rose, you're a store-bought woman.'"

I laughed. "Can you hum it?"

"May-bee. How do you feel?"

"Mixed. I want to get Burke, badly. Berney has said, 'Be very careful,' but I'm not really getting the plan."

"You've got this, Linds. You backed Burke down on Mount Tam, and Berney respects that. Alvarez is a great asset. Berney will have eyes on you. And bringing down bad guys is what you do. Get Burke in your sights, throw him down. Call Berney to help you get Burke to Clapper. That's the plan."

Hunh. I didn't love it.

Joe asked, "Where's your piece?"

I patted my handbag.

He kissed me, told me he loved me and to call him when I could. He waved as he went down the escalator. I think he was singing along with Neil Diamond.

CHAPTER 92

ALVAREZ AND I WERE in our fancy duds and had loaded guns in our handbags.

It was still early in the evening so Alvarez took me for a tour of the Bellagio's cavernous main room.

We started with a peek in at the baccarat table in an alcove off the casino. It was quieter by far than the dinging, ringing of the slots and the ten-decibel excitement of the players popping the lids off their everyday lives to sounds of Sinatra's greatest hits.

Alvarez explained to me how baccarat was played as we strolled through the marble-floored playground with its convex glass ceiling over the huge ground floor, the conservatory, the lobby with forty tons of Chihuly's glass flowers clustered at the ceiling dome. We window-shopped the high-end boutiques; Dior, Prada, Chanel, where Alvarez was connected enough to get big discounts on last season's evening clothes.

That was very cool.

But I never stopped thinking about Evan Burke.

At nine, we stood around the baccarat table with

our backs to the wall and watched Berney clean up. Either he was in his wheelhouse or the dealer was in his pocket because all eyes were on Berney. The other players were in jackets, but Berney was wearing his pink sweater. If Burke was looking for Berney, he really couldn't miss him. When the spectators were two or three deep behind the players, I signaled to Alvarez that I was going to step outside the room and have a look around.

Berney flicked his eyes toward me as I was leaving and then shot the dice. I didn't wait to see how his throw landed. I was already in the main casino, checking out the rows of slots, the poker tables, the chandeliers and swag pendant lights above it all.

And then I saw Evan Burke. At least I thought so.

He'd scrubbed up since I'd seen him on his porch staring down his barrel, aiming at *me*. Now, Quicksilver was sitting at a tall stool around an oblong table, with five other players stacking their chips, watching the dealer. The man was dressed for a night of fun, wearing a gray dinner jacket over an expensive-looking open-collar shirt, also gray.

He watched the cards, but there was a cute young girl with long curly blond hair standing behind him, touching his shoulder, murmuring into his ear. After each winning hand, they hugged like it was true love. He had winnings and a girly girl less than half his age pressing her young body to his. Looked to me like the highly trained former Green Beret, the Ghost of Catalina, had plenty to keep him busy in Vegas.

Best thing about the tableau in front of me was that Burke hadn't made me. I retraced my steps to the baccarat room and gave Alvarez and Berney a quick nod to say, *He's here.*

Alvarez moved quickly to my side and we went

back out to the casino proper, blending in with the shifting good-tempered crowd. As we watched, a loud celebratory shout came up from Burke's spot at the card table. He raked in a small mountain of chips and relinquished his stool.

Before I could say, "Mr. Burke. We'd like to have a word," the pretty young blonde opened her bag and Evan Burke dropped his chips inside. Together they headed toward the casino's front doors.

Alvarez and I followed at a distance while never losing sight of our man and his girl. I saw through the open doors that an empty cab, orange-colored and plastered with casino ads, had pulled around to the entrance and stopped. The valet opened the rear door for Burke plus one. They got in, and their tangerine ride looped around and merged into the Strip.

I pushed ahead of the waiting crowd and flashed my badge. "Police business. Excuse us. Police."

Another cab pulled up and I also badged the driver.

I hated to use the timeworn phrase, but after Alvarez and I were seated and belted in the back seat, I said it:

"Follow that cab. And step on it."

CHAPTER 93

THE STRIP WAS fully jammed with vehicular traffic even on a Monday at 9:30 p.m., and Evan Burke's tangerine-colored cab was locked in place three cars ahead of us.

Hotels came and went on both sides of the road, their hyper-bright icons leaving lingering images behind my eyes. The median planting between the north and southbound lanes of the Strip was a mesmerizing stretch of tall sabal palm trees. I processed it all peripherally, but kept my eyes glued to the orange cab.

A logjam in the intersection up ahead broke apart and cars sped up, then bumped to stops at the next light.

"Where's Burke going?" I asked myself, but Alvarez answered as our cab turned left onto Fremont.

She said, "Looks like he's heading for the Golden Eagle Hotel. Used to be a big-time movie-star hangout, but now it's mainly down-and-outers who stay there. It's due for a renovation it will never get."

I saw the massive rectangular brick building three

blocks away. It took up a whole block and was topped with a big gold eagle sculpture with its smaller twin perched over the marquis. Looked more like a wartime munitions factory than any of the other hotels on the Strip.

I said, "Sonia. You know this place?"

"Sure do. I know the layout, personnel, where to find the ladies' rooms. Spent a good part of the last ten years undercover here."

Up ahead, the traffic light turned red. The glowing orange taxi zoomed through. Horns honked, but there was no sound of crunching metal. Cars between us and Burke's cab were at a standstill.

I spoke to the driver through the partition, "The orange cab? Did you see him drop off passengers at the Eagle?"

The driver said, "Looks like he stopped at the curb and, yeah. There he goes taking a turn at the next street over."

I would have asked him to run the light, but it was impossible. We were hemmed in by traffic on four sides.

The driver turned to face me. "Want to get out here?"

I calculated time and distance, found a twenty plus tip in my handbag, stuffed it into the Lucite cash drawer.

"Let's go," I said to Alvarez.

She was already half out of the cab.

I followed her, wiggled around the lane of cars, reaching the sidewalk, and hit my stride with the Golden Eagle still a long block away.

Every second counted. If we lost Burke, we might not see him again.

Liveried bouncers opened the front doors for us.

Sonia had Burke's forty-year-old army enlistment photo now updated with facial-aging software. She showed it to the bouncer, whose name tag read "Reynolds" and asked him, "Jamie. Is he here?"

"He had a girl with him." Jamie Reynolds made a twirling motion with a finger near his head, indicating "curls" or "crazy."

"Bet they'll be in the casino."

We entered the air-cooled darkness and into a lobby straight out of the 1940s. There was an eagle motif in the mile of carpet and gold striped wallpaper throughout. The casino was to the right, the front desk just ahead. I swept both spaces with my own eagle eyes but did not see the young woman with golden ringlets. And I didn't see Evan Burke.

I said, "I'll check out the casino."

Alvarez approached the front desk, where an elderly woman was counting out cash, filing the large bills under the drawer.

I kept my eyes hidden with my fake hair and my phone as I traversed the rows of slots, looking for the man in gray, the girl with the curls.

I heard my name and turned.

Alvarez said, "He checked in under the name 'William Marsh,' identifying his companion as his wife."

"Room number?"

"I'll go you one better, Boxer. I've got the key."

CHAPTER 94

THE "KEY" WAS Christopher Johns, one of the desk managers at the Golden Eagle.

Johns was in his thirties and had worked with Alvarez as an unofficial CI for the fun of it, and a little cash.

"Detective, don't get me fired over this."

"For doing what?" she said.

"He's in room B16."

She tucked a bill into his hand.

As we peeled off, Alvarez said, "B16 is basement level. Probably costing Burke about twenty-nine dollars a night."

As we headed down a long alley of slots, Alvarez dug her phone out of her bag and made a call.

"Chief Belinky," she said. "Sergeant Boxer and I need two squad cars at the Golden Eagle. Code 2. God willing, we'll need transportation to the station house for our person of interest. Yes, that's the one. Thanks, chief."

Picturing Berney still at the Bellagio's baccarat

table, I pulled up his contact on my phone and used a maps app to share our location. I hung up and said to Alvarez, "Let's go wreck Burke's party."

We continued down the slot machine alley, alive with flash and din, whoops and curses, bells ringing and coins clattering into the trays. There was more whoop-de-doo on the margins: to our right, a darkly lit bar; left, a brightly lit, deep-fried all-night buffet; and down a little farther, a party room spilling over with wedding guests, dozens of youngsters dancing to something like music that I'd never heard before.

The open service elevator at the very end of the lobby was the size of a boxcar. Adrenaline gave me a small jolt to the heart as I pressed "B" and the car took us down one floor to the basement. *What were we walking into? Would we sleep in our beds tonight?*

I stood for a second, getting my bearings.

Opposite the elevator doors was the hotel's laundry room, dryers churning with full loads. There were sixteen guest rooms on this level, eight on each side of the corridor. An emergency exit was at the far end. Between the last of the guest rooms and the emergency exit was a vending machine alcove to the left and the subterranean kitchen to the right, workers calling out orders and sending food up to the buffet. Dance music vibrated against the ceiling and walls.

Alvarez whispered, "You think that girl would really come here with him willingly?"

"He dumped a lot of chips into her bag."

The room marked B16 was adjacent to the exit. We sidestepped a room service cart and approached Burke's door.

I trusted Alvarez and we knew the drill.

She took a position to the left. I knocked and stepped to the opposite side.

I called out, "Front desk, Mr. Marsh. Smoke was reported in the room next door. Need to check on yours, real quick."

I was expecting him to either ignore me or shout out "Get lost." Instead, a girl's high-pitched scream raised goose bumps along the backs of my arms.

"*Hellllllllp!*" she screamed. "*Help meeeeeee!*"

CHAPTER 95

I TOOK A BREATH and kicked the door open.

It only took one kick, and along with the door, half the doorframe separated from the wall. The only light in the room came from the hallway. I felt along the wall and found the bathroom on our right, just inside the wrecked entrance.

I touched the light switch and flipped on the one dull forty-watt bulb over the sink. Gunshots cracked and a bullet ripped into the open door.

Alvarez hit the floor and I used the bathroom wall as a shield.

I called out, "Evan Burke, this is the SFPD. Toss your gun toward me. Do it now or SWAT is going to take you out on my command!"

Alvarez was on her phone.

"The Eagle. Basement level. Shots fired at police officers. Be advised, two female plainclothes detectives on the scene."

The girl was crying out, "*Help me, please. He's crazy. Help meeeee.*" And then her voice was muffled. He'd put a hand over her mouth.

I wanted to help her, but the darkness cloaked everything and the weak bathroom and hallway light backlit me. The girl's situation was putting the good guys in the line of fire. Alvarez and I weren't wearing vests. My options were limited and more shooting was imminent.

Burke yelled in pain. "*Damn you, bitch.*"

I figured the girl had bitten him and had gotten free of Burke's hand over her mouth. But he still had her in his grip. She screamed loud and long.

Burke shouted, "*Shut up, shut up, shut up!*"

He sounded like he was reaching the end of the line.

"*Burke.* Let her go. Toss the gun toward me and stand up. Hands in the air. Do that and we all walk out of here. You will not live through 'Or else.'"

"That you, Sergeant Boxer? I almost didn't recognize you."

Where in this gloomy hole was he?

The room was a bear trap and I couldn't shut out the distracting sounds; the screaming, the washers and dryers and clanking from the kitchen. Any minute now, hotel workers would venture innocently into harm's way.

Finally, as my eyes began to adjust to the darkness, I saw him.

Burke was across the room, sitting on the floor, his back braced against the back wall, his knees folded up against the side of the mattress. The girl appeared to be topless, sitting between his legs.

He said, "Sergeant, you two ladies drop your guns or I'll kill her."

"We've done this before, Burke. You know I'm not going to put down my weapon."

I heard chatter in the hallway and shouts in Spanish. As I'd feared, the hallway was filling with hotel workers.

Alvarez shouted to them, "Vamanos! *Get away from the door!*"

The tableau froze.

And then it all happened too fast.

The girl let loose with a long whooping scream of pure wordless fear.

Gunshots cracked and the girl's voice stopped in mid-breath. I couldn't see blood spray, but the air smelled of it. The dim light put a glint on Burke's gun that was aimed at me.

We're trained to shoot to kill; a double tap to center mass. But I couldn't get a bead on Burke's chest, so my double tap hit the shoulder of his shooting arm.

Damn it. At the same time, the hallway was filling with civilians, screaming, running, until the first runner hit the exit door lock bar, setting off an alarm.

I could just make out Burke trying to grip his gun with both hands. But he couldn't aim.

Alvarez and I moved in. She disarmed Burke while I pulled the girl off the floor and got her onto the bed. She was bleeding profusely from the back of her head. I begged her to hang on, please. Her eyelids fluttered in the gloom. I said, "Help is coming," but I knew she wasn't going to make it.

By then, Alvarez had Burke's good hand on the wall and he was yelping when I called Chief Belinky.

"What's happening, sergeant?"

"Suspect fired on us, chief. He put a slug through his date's head. We've disabled him. We need an ambulance and the ME. Also, patrolmen are needed on the basement level to tape off a perimeter. Alvarez and I are in plain clothes and are holding down the scene."

CHAPTER 96

EVAN BURKE YOWLED as Inspector Sonia Alvarez wrenched his arms behind his back and cuffed him.

She arrested him for murder and read him his rights. He grunted, "Yes, I understand, damn you," as I switched on the overhead lights.

The blond girl stared up, seeing nothing. Blood was everywhere; on her, on the bed, on Burke, who was pressed up against the wall, grimacing out of the side of his face that I could see.

I got my phone out and punched in Brady's number. He picked up. The wireless reception was two bars, but I told him everything in twenty-five words or less.

"I'll call you back once Burke is in lockup."

Burke's actions tonight put terrible pictures in my mind along with doubt. Was Yuki trying the wrong Burke for the triple homicide? I couldn't shake the feeling, but I had a live killer right in front of me and work to do.

Turning back to Burke, I said, "Alvarez and I

watched you kill your companion. We'll make statements and testify to that. You want any help from us, this would be the time to talk."

He made a laugh-like sound.

I said, "You're looking at murder one for this. Feds get next bite at you. The DA in San Francisco might intercede on your behalf for a confession to the murder of Tara and Lorrie Burke, Melissa Fogarty, and anyone else you'd care to name."

"You're a riot, lady. Those hits belong to Lucas. I know Luke better than anyone and I'm telling you, sarge, he's a killer."

"Like you."

"He's worse. He's been killing since he was a little shit. Baby birds, puppies, cutting them, stabbing them, putting a hole in the chest every second until they died. Don't waste any sympathy on him, Boxer, is it? Lindsay. He's a savage. A monster. What kind of man kills his own child?"

Two officers were at the doorway. I gave them the short version. "He killed his date. He's under arrest. We called for an ambulance. Keep eyes on him at all times."

Cops were taping off the hallway when forensics arrived.

"Time's running out," I said to Burke.

"You look cute in a dress."

I ignored what he said and asked, "What's your date's name?"

"Candy? Tammy? Sugar?"

I snapped a shot of Burke, sent that to Berney as the room filled with paramedics and CSU. Before Jane Doe was wrapped in a sheet and carried out on a stretcher, Alvarez took a close-up of her face, the bullet hole through her forehead.

I kept thinking of her as a girl because she looked

so young. Was she twenty? A teen wearing big-girl clothes? How had she hooked up with Evan Burke?

Someone who actually loved her was going to be devastated. I felt bad, myself. She'd fought hard, screamed for help, and I hadn't been able to save her.

The EMTs uncuffed Burke, lifted him onto a stretcher, and flex-tied his wrists to the rails. Before they could carry him out, Burke called me.

"Sergeant."

Was he going to talk?

"I'm here."

"You shoot like a girl," he said. "Lucky me." He laughed and flipped me the bird.

An EMT wrapped another flex tie around Burke's upper right arm and fastened it to the stretcher rail, pulling it tight. Burke was cursing as he was carried out through the emergency exit.

I called Clapper.

"We got him, chief."

"Good work, Boxer. You two okay?"

"Perfect. Burke needs surgery. We'll have a talk with him in the morning."

It was close to 11 p.m.

I said, "We should be in the squad room by noon."

Out in the hallway, Alvarez and I high-fived each other, and then...hell. We hugged.

She said, "Oh, man."

I said, "That goes for me, too."

We were both traumatized by how close we'd come to dying in this place. I ripped off the wig and stocking cap and shook out my hair. Then, we followed the paramedics out the emergency exit, leaving the Golden Eagle's dungeon behind. Forever.

The patrolmen opened the squad car doors for us, and then drove us to the Bellagio.

CHAPTER 97

YUKI NOTICED THAT, this morning, defense counsel was wearing a baby-blue shirt with his fine gray suit.

His five-o'clock shadow at 9 a.m. made him look vulnerable, sympathetic, as though he'd been up all night working out of concern for his innocent client.

Newt Gardner even sounded caring when he said, "Good morning, Inspector Conklin."

Yuki found it a credible act, but an act it was.

Conklin was Gardner's target. Conklin's stated belief, under oath, was that Lucas Burke had lied about the time he had left San Francisco for Sacramento. Conklin had also testified that Lucas Burke was the shadow figure who'd slit Melissa Fogarty's throat in the school parking lot.

Gardner couldn't let Conklin's testimony stand, and that worried Yuki. Conklin was strong, but he was facing Newt Gardner, who was determined to win.

"Inspector, Mr. Burke told you that he was at a resort with his ex-wife in Carmel at about eight o'clock on Friday, isn't that right?"

"Yes."

"Did Ms. Conroy corroborate that time?"

"Yes, we have his word and her corroboration. But I no longer believe that the timeline—"

"Thanks, you answered the question."

Conklin said, "As I was saying, I no longer believe Mr. Burke's stated timeline because the murder weapon puts Melissa Fogarty's killing squarely on Mr. Burke."

A juror gasped, then clapped her hand over her mouth. The judge gave the juror a hard gray-eyed stare, then said, "Mr. Gardner, please continue."

"So to your mind, this murder weapon nullifies Mr. Burke's stated whereabouts at eight o'clock the night of Ms. Fogarty's murder."

"I believe the evidence, sir."

At that, Lucas Burke rose from his seat at the counsel table and bellowed, *"I didn't do it. I never killed anyone. It was my father. It had to be. My father is the most evil man that ever lived. He set me up!"*

The judge pounded his gavel until the emotions in the room abated.

Yuki calculated that took at least three minutes. She held her breath as the judge asked Gardner if he had anything else for the witness.

Gardner said, "I reserve the right to question Inspector Conklin again after the prosecution introduces their so-called evidence."

Yuki shot to her feet. "Objection to defense counsel's characterization of the evidence. Move to strike."

Judge John Passarelli sighed deeply. "Sustained. Mrs. Clemons," he said to the court reporter, "Strike 'so-called.' Jurors will ignore that characterization, and now let's move on. Yes, Mr. Gardner, you may recall this witness at a later time."

Yuki understood that Gardner was both baiting her and attempting to raise reasonable doubt in the jurors' minds. Had it worked? Had Burke's plaintive bleating moved someone in the box?

Yuki, herself, had felt moved, but she also had evidence. And, God willing, the evidence would convict Lucas Burke.

CHAPTER 98

YUKI SAID, "The People call Crime Lab Director, Dr. Eugene Hallows."

The doors swung open and Gene Hallows entered the courtroom. He was fiftyish, tall, stooped, and he looked off balance as he walked to the witness stand. Still only six months into the top job as head of the crime lab, the pressure was on him to step into Clapper's shoes both in the lab and in court.

Yuki approached him and smiled.

"Dr. Hallows, or shall I say Director Hallows, what is your background in forensic science?"

Hallows haltingly listed the key points in his résumé; his two PhDs in criminology from UC Irvine, his years with the crime lab in Chicago, his five years as deputy director under Chief Charles Clapper, and his recent promotion to director of Forensics. Now, he supervised two hundred investigators and scientists at the crime lab at Hunters Point.

Yuki asked, "Have you had a hands-on role in the Burke case?"

"Yes. From the discovery of the Burke baby through now."

Yuki took him through the elements of the investigation, underscoring the recovery of the razor used to kill Melissa Fogarty.

Yuki went to her table and Gaines handed her a brown eight-by-eleven envelope sealed with red CSU tape.

"Director Hallows, did you seal this envelope?" She handed it to him.

"Yes. That's my signature."

"Will you open it for us now?"

Hallows ripped open the flap, then tipped the envelope so that a small weighted plastic bag slid into his hand.

He handed it to Yuki, who held it up. Even through the plastic, the razor, with its carbon-steel blade and chrome handle, glinted in the light. This was it. This was the proof she'd needed, finally in her hand.

She said to Hallows, "Is this the straight razor used to kill Melissa Fogarty?"

"Yes, it is."

"Could you tell the court how you can be sure of that?"

He said, "Ms. Fogarty's blood is on the blade and in the hinge, and Lucas Burke's fingerprints are on the handle."

A buzz rose up in the room as Yuki entered the blade into evidence. She then handed the closed plastic envelope to the jury foreperson. While the jurors passed the sealed glassine envelope among themselves, Yuki brought two photos over to her expert witness.

"Director Hallows, let me show you two photographs. Can you describe them?"

"Photo one is an enlargement from the video of Melissa Fogarty's murder. It's the face of the assailant in the school parking lot. Number 2 is the photo of the defendant, Lucas Burke, taken when he was arrested five months ago. Because the facial details of number 1 are hard to discern without a trained eye, even with facial recognition software, we contacted a highly respected forensic photographic analyst, Dr. Werner Stutz. We asked Dr. Stutz to compare photo 1, with photo 2."

Yuki taped both enlarged photos on the whiteboard under their respective labels.

"Director, can you explain the similarities and differences between the two photographs?"

"Surely. What we're looking at is the result of a process of measuring and comparing facial features that's been in use for over two thousand years. However, Dr. Stutz's digital instruments are more precise than those used in antiquity."

Hallows continued. "You'll note his measurements written on the photos. Here and here, the distance between the corners of the eyes. Here, the distance from center of the eyes to tip of nose. Here, length of the bridge of the nose, point-to-point measurement between the cheekbones, and here, cheekbones to ear tips and lobes. As you can see, there are additional facial measurements."

"For the record, did Dr. Stutz reach a conclusion?"

"Yes. With 95 percent certainty, his expert judgment is that the two photos are of the same man."

"Not a hundred percent?" Yuki asked. She was 'drawing the sting,' bringing out the weakness in the evidence before opposing counsel could do it and nail her witness.

Hallows said, "The figure on the video was wearing

a knit cap to his eyebrows covering the tips of his ears. That's the 5 percent. In the comparison photo, the defendant is not wearing a hat."

"Thank you, Director Hallows. Your Honor, the prosecution rests. Your witness, Mr. Gardner."

CHAPTER 99

ALVAREZ AND I WERE in the back of a squad car speeding down the Strip from the Bellagio to the airport.

I couldn't wait to get home, but the job wasn't done. I said, "Sonia, I'm feeling lucky."

"Yeah. He was in surgery either very late last night or this morning. He can't have lawyered up. I know people in the ER."

I spoke through the grill.

"Officer, changing our destination to Sunrise Med. Can you take us there and wait?"

"Chief says we're yours, sergeant. Whatever you need."

Minutes later we were parked to the side of the ambulance bay that led to the hospital's emergency room. Alvarez and I were in our work clothes, badges pinned to our lapels. At our approach, the automatic sliders breezed open and we had a clear view of the ER, only moderately busy that morning.

"Crap," Alvarez said, looking to the head nurse at the admissions desk. "I don't know her."

"You be the good cop. If that fails, I'll be the badass."

The nurse looked up to see the two of us at her desk with badges on display.

"How can I help you, officers?"

Alvarez said, "My partner and I are San Francisco police working a case with LVPD. We need to speak with a patient who came in around midnight with a shoulder wound."

"Name?"

"Last known as William Marsh."

She ran her finger down the list, found him.

"Stay here. Let me get the attending."

A moment later, a tall thirtysomething man in a white coat over blue scrubs appeared at the desk.

"Marco, hey," said Alvarez.

"Hey to you, Yorkie. You back already?"

"No, no. This is my colleague, Sergeant Lindsay Boxer, SFPD. Boxer, this is Dr. Marco Ganz. Marco, we'd like to talk to our subject for a minute. William Marsh."

"He's out of surgery. Sleeping it off down the hall."

"Just need a couple of minutes, doctor," I said. "He killed someone last night, a girlfriend or a pickup. We need him to give us her name."

"Come with me."

We followed the doctor down the corridor to a room where cops stood on either side of the door. Dr. Ganz opened it. Burke was alone in the room, lying in the narrow hospital bed, IV in his arm. Monitors beeped out his vital signs.

Ganz said, "Mr. Marsh, you have guests for a couple of minutes. I'll be outside."

Burke had kicked off his blanket. He wore an open-backed hospital gown, white patterned with blue dots, matching socks, and his right arm was in a sling crossing his chest.

"How sweet," he said. "I appreciate the visit. Especially from you, Sergeant Boxer. You're worried about me."

"Anyone you want me to call for you?" I asked without inflection.

He didn't answer.

I said, "Okay, then. We're taking the next flight home. Anything you'd like to offer our DA? For instance, a confession to the murders of Tara and Lorrie Burke, and Melissa Fogarty. Make it convincing and I think he'll ask a favor for you with the Las Vegas DA."

"Well, that's an offer I can't refuse."

Sarcasm. Burke was cogent and awake, but his voice was slow. That would be from the Demerol dripping into his veins.

"Here's something for your DA, sergeant, dear. You're going to like it. I've been sleeping with Luke's child bride. For years. Luke didn't know. I even went to the wedding."

Was he making this up?

Burke smiled. I felt him padding around inside my head.

He said, "Lorrie was *my* daughter. Even you can trust me on this. I wouldn't kill that little girl. What do I think happened? I think Tara told Lucas the whole story, about Lorrie being my baby and all. And Luke lost it. My son has a murderous temper."

Damn it. He was lying, wasn't he? *So why did I believe him?* Had Lucas really killed his own loved ones as charged? Or had Evan Burke?

I could argue both sides—and I didn't like it.

Alvarez swiped at her cell phone and showed Burke the face of Jane Doe with a bullet hole through her forehead.

"What's her name? Her parents might like to know where she is."

"I…don't…know…"

Burke had stopped fighting the drugs.

"Why'd you shoot her?" I said into his face. *"Why'd you have to do that?"* His eyes opened.

"She wouldn't stop *screaming*."

"You shot her for screaming? She was fucking terrified."

"Okay, sarge. How's this?" There was a long pause, but I waited him out. He said, "I was tired of running. I wanted to stop…"

His mouth went slack. And then his eyes closed.

Dr. Ganz came into the recovery room.

"Get everything you need? Don't forget I told you he was sedated."

"Yes, you did," I said.

Ganz opened his arms and Alvarez went in for a hug.

I said, "Thanks, doctor," and left the building. I got into the cruiser and Alvarez was right behind me.

"Yorkie?" I said.

"That's what he calls me." She used her fingers to lift her bangs and rake them out of her eyes. "He says that I'm like a terrier. Once I get my teeth into something…"

I laughed, and then said to the guys up front, "Our flight boards in twenty minutes."

"Copy that, sergeant."

Alvarez and I buckled in and the car squealed out onto South Maryland Parkway. She said, "What do you think of Burke's version of the crimes?"

"I wish I knew. He gives Lucas a believable motive for murder. His dad was sleeping with his wife. Lorrie wasn't his daughter. People have killed for less. But Evan Burke killed that poor girl in front of our eyes—for no good reason. He might have talked his way through the exit door with his gun and a living hostage. He's a monster, but he's a smart guy. I don't understand the lapse of judgment. Oh, yeah. He wants to stop running.

"Honest to God, Sonia, we can't believe anything that psychopath says."

CHAPTER 100

UNITED FLIGHT 5274 was thirty thousand feet over Nevada.

I was looking out the window, thinking about Evan and Lucas Burke.

I no longer knew if Lucas had killed his wife and child and poor sweet Misty. Was Evan telling the truth when he said, "Those hits belong to Lucas." He'd said it with such conviction. But had I believed that Lucas was capable of murder because I'd wanted to? Because I'd seen the dead baby? Because I'd spent time with Kathleen? Shared a cup of tea with Misty, telling her to break up with Luke?

I couldn't work it out. Had we indicted the wrong Burke? I pictured father and son facing off and tried to choose the real monster—and then, without warning, I was crying into my hands.

I fumbled for my purse under the seat and couldn't reach it. My tears were coming harder, turning into sobs.

Alvarez was dozing in the seat next to me. There

was a paper napkin in the seat pocket in front of her. I grabbed it, pressed it to my eyes, and when the sobs abated, I blew my nose, jostling Alvarez awake.

"What?"

"Sorry. Go back to sleep."

She took a look at me and said, "Lindsay. What's wrong?"

I tried waving her off again, but she persisted.

Finally, I said, "I think I get it now."

"Get what?"

"Why Burke really shot his girlfriend in front of us."

"Tell me. Don't hold back."

A flight attendant rolled the cart to our row, offering snacks and beverages. I chose the breakfast burrito and a mini bottle of chardonnay.

Alvarez said, "Make that two."

After we'd been served, I lowered the window shade and unscrewed the top from my bottle of wine. Alvarez was still waiting for me to finish my theory on why Burke shot Jane Doe.

She shook my arm and said, "Speak."

"Okay. My theory goes like this. Burke saw Berney at the Bellagio. He rightly assumes that Berney is there for him. When we crashed his party at the Eagle, he put it all on red. Better to risk a murder charge in Vegas than in federal court."

"Mmm. Nevada has a death penalty," Alvarez said.

"Okay, say he gets a great defense lawyer, a local pit bull who's looking for a showcase trial. Burke could cook up a convincing story about the Jane Doe shooting and maybe win over the jury. If so, he'd get light time or no time. You *heard* him, Sonia. He can say anything, spin anything, with feeling.

I went on with my hypothesis.

"So, Burke says, 'The room was totally dark.'"

"It was," said Alvarez. "And noisy."

"Right. There's pounding music from the wedding dancers overhead, pots clanking and shouting in the kitchen. And of course, Burke says he and Jane Doe were doing some heavy breathing when his door was kicked in."

Alvarez said, "He could say she never yelled for help."

"They're having a good time, right? As Burke's lawyer tells it, his client didn't hear us knock. He didn't hear us say 'Police.' He was otherwise engaged. Then, the door is kicked in and Burke sees silhouettes with guns. What's he supposed to think?"

Alvarez said, "That we aren't room service. That he's a target because of his winnings. He grabs his piece and fires."

"Right, and now the girl in his lap is screaming. He tries to push her head down as he aims around her, toward the doorframe—"

"—but she pulls away or otherwise moves her head. Oh, noooo."

"You got it," I said. "She catches a round with her skull. Now, it's an accident. Manslaughter, not murder, and we cannot prove otherwise."

Alvarez said, "His lawyer calls it bad freaking luck."

"Burke's a gambler," I said. "Win some. Lose some. This could be the best bet of his life."

CHAPTER 101

NEWT GARDNER MOVED with the confidence and deliberation of a jungle cat as he approached the stand to cross-examine Yuki's star witness.

Gardner said, "Director Hallows, I just have a few questions for you. Regarding the razor that you say was used to kill Ms. Fogarty.

"Assuming the blood on the blade was Ms. Fogarty's—"

"It was."

"—and you assert that the fingerprints on the handle belong to Mr. Lucas Burke. Did I get that right?"

"Yes, that's correct."

"How long can fingerprints remain on an item like that?"

"As long as the surface isn't handled. Could be for quite a long time."

"So, if someone picked up the razor with gloved hands, and didn't wipe the handle, the fingerprints would be preserved?"

"If the person who picked up the razor wanted to preserve them, yes."

"Now, you saw the video of Lucas Burke leaving his house? And some twenty minutes later Tara Burke left the same house with the baby?"

"Yes, I saw that video many times. Frame by frame."

"Did you see Tara lock the front door?"

"No. Her hands were full."

"So, could Luke's razor have been taken from the unlocked house by a person wearing gloves who had an interest in preserving the fingerprints that were on it?"

"It's possible."

"So…" said Gardner, turning away from the witness, keeping the spectators and the jury waiting for him to finish his point, then spinning back around to give Hallows his fifteen-hundred-dollar-an-hour stare.

"We agree. If someone wearing gloves took Mr. Burke's razor from the house and the handle had Mr. Burke's prints on it, that someone could have killed Ms. Fogarty with it. And if that razor remained concealed by weeds for months, it would still have the victim's blood and the defendant's prints on it, correct?"

Yuki listened to Gardner lay out his case on Hallows's back. Hallows was a very good criminologist, but Clapper had blamed him for not searching the vacant lot sooner.

Hallows said, "I'm a scientist, sir. You're asking me to give definitive answers to a number of compounding possibilities, all untested. That isn't how I work."

"I'm asking you as an expert, director. Is this scenario possible?"

"It's possible."

"Okay. Now, the prosecution uses your

photographic analyst's work to substantiate their case. Is this type of 'photographic analysis' a science?"

"Facial analysis by measurement of features is not all that technical or theoretical."

"All right. For sake of argument, let's say that the method Dr. Werner Stutz is using is what's called the golden ratio. Its purpose is to establish perfect facial proportions for the standards of beauty. My eyesight is twenty-twenty and I can barely see the features of the unknown subject taken in the school parking lot now called photo."

"Dr. Stutz uses high-powered digital microscopes and calipers."

"Even so. You say this isn't a hundred percent dead cert match because the man in the parking lot was wearing a cap?"

"Yes. The knit cap covered 5 percent of his features."

"Okay. I follow," said Gardner. "So, here's the question. If my client closely resembles his father, and it's dark of night and the camera is a big box store item of C minus quality—"

"Objection, leading like crazy, Your Honor."

"Sustained. Save it for your closer, counselor."

"Sorry, Your Honor. The question is, if Dr. Stutz is using a flawed photo 1 to make his match, by definition this match is flawed. And that photo might be the defendant's father, Evan Burke."

Yuki stood. "Argumentative, Your Honor. Defense counsel is leading and argumentative and taking liberties with the court."

Gardner said, "Your Honor, the witness is trying to establish questionable methods as science."

Hallows wasn't having it. "If an experiment is repeated innumerable times with the same precise result, it's scientifically proven—"

Judge Passarelli said, "That's enough, everyone. Prosecution's objection is sustained. Mrs. Clemons, please strike defense counsel's statements from 'Okay, I follow.' Mr. Gardner. Do you have anything else for this witness?"

"No, Your Honor," said Gardner. "That's all."

"Ms. Castellano. Redirect?"

"Yes. Thank you. Director Hallows. Now, regarding the razor blade. You'd stake your reputation on the validity of the blood test and fingerprint analysis?"

"Yes. One hundred percent."

Yuki thanked Hallows and returned to her seat at the counsel table. She was shaken by the exchange but more sure than ever that Lucas Burke was a killer.

Would the jurors—all of them—see that?

Or would they be swayed by her theatrical opponent?

CHAPTER 102

YUKI WATCHED AS Newton Gardner—top-tier criminal defense attorney, showboat, media candy, and amateur wrestler—opened his case by calling his first witness, his client's ex-wife, Alexandra Conroy.

Gardner was gracious to the attractive woman and gave her the expected softball questions establishing that Lucas Burke could not have killed Misty because at the time of the teenager's death Lucas Burke was in Ms. Conroy's arms, sobbing over the loss of his child and his privacy.

The questions were neat and short.

"What time did Mr. Burke call you? Come to your house? What was his mood? When did you arrive at Carmel? When did Mr. Burke see the murder headlines? What did you do after that?"

Questions were asked and answered in about five minutes. Then Gardner turned the witness over to Yuki.

Conroy was the key witness for the defense, and Yuki covered the same ground Gardner had done.

But Yuki was coming from the opposite direction.

She asked, "Ms. Conroy, after so many months and the very emotional circumstances, how can you know for sure that Lucas was in your hotel room at eight o'clock that night?"

Ms. Conroy said, "I checked the time before my evening spa appointment because I was going to put in a room service order."

Yuki asked, "Did you place the order at eight p.m.?"

"No. I wanted to talk to Luke first."

"At what time did you place the order?"

"Later. Maybe nine or so."

Yuki went to her table and returned with a computer printout. She asked the witness, "Is this a copy of your phoned-in order?"

"I don't know."

"Can you read your name at the top of the page along with the time you made it?"

The former Mrs. Burke said, "I'm not wearing my glasses."

Yuki couldn't help feeling a flash of killer instinct as she homed in on Conroy, preparing to pin her with the truth.

She pointed out a line on the reservation sheet and said, "You placed your order at thirty-five minutes past midnight."

"Oh. Well."

Yuki continued.

"That's time enough for Luke to kill Misty at eight and drive back to Carmel by ten. Take a shower. Have a snack, maybe a drink. Watch, say, *Jimmy Kimmel*."

"Objection!"

"Sustained. Watch it, Ms. Castellano."

Yuki said, "Sorry, Your Honor. Ms. Conroy, do you in fact know whether Lucas stayed in your hotel room?"

Conroy said, "I'm not sure. Luke was very upset that weekend. I wanted to comfort him. That's what I did. I wasn't watching the clock."

Yuki said, "Thank you. That's all I have for this witness."

Judge Passarelli told Conroy she could step down, and Gardner called his next and only other witness.

"I call Lucas Burke."

Gardner helped Lucas around the counsel table without knocking over his chair, then released his client's arm and watched him take the twenty-yard walk to the witness stand on his own.

Yuki wondered what the hell Gardner could ask Lucas that could redeem him from Yuki's crushing witness interrogations. Would he break down again? Or did Gardner have a-get-out-of-jail-free card up his sleeve?

Whatever was about to happen, he was holding the hundred and forty–odd people in Courtroom 2C in absolute suspense.

The bailiff stood behind Burke, ready to assist him as he climbed the two steps to the witness box.

CHAPTER 103

WATCHING HIM, CINDY was still shocked at how much Lucas Burke, a fairly fit, fortyish man, had declined after five months in jail.

Gardner walked up to his client and said, "I have a few questions for you, Mr. Burke. I hope they will give you a chance to answer to the situation in which you find yourself."

"Ready and willing," said the witness.

"Fine. Did you, possibly with good reason, kill anyone? Your wife and daughter, your mistress, anyone else?"

"Absolutely not. It's true that my wife, Tara, and I were fighting. She was only twenty. She'd never worked for a living. She wanted a lot of clothing and accessories that we couldn't afford on my teacher's salary.

"We had fights, but not physical ones. We called each other names, and once, after her mother got her going, Tara threw a pot at me, but she missed. As for my little daughter..." Burke's voice broke and he covered his face with his arm. His shoulders shook.

Gardner said, "Take your time, Luke."

Burke put down his arm, cleared his throat, took a couple of sips of water from a plastic bottle, then said with a quavering voice, "I loved Lorrie more than anyone in the world. My little sister and my mother both disappeared more than fifteen years ago, and I'll never get over the loss of them. Lorrie reminded me of my sister, Jodie, when she was a baby. My heart is broken. I pray that Lorrie didn't know what was happening to her. That she didn't suffer."

"I'm so sorry about all of that, Luke. I must ask you about Melissa. You called her Misty."

"Misty was the sweetest young woman, but our relationship was doomed. She was eighteen. She should have gone to college. There was no way to make sense of our relationship except that we loved each other."

"Did you make a date to see Misty the night she was killed?"

"No, and if I had, she would be alive. We did often meet in the parking lot, but I didn't even know what day it was. Or even think about Misty. I had just been released from jail. The police were ransacking my house. I got into my car and just drove fast.

"Alexandra Conroy, my ex-wife, had called me when she heard about Lorrie. She lives only a couple of hours away. I wanted to be with her, just to talk. Although our marriage had died a long time ago, Alex always understood me. I called her. She said, 'Come.'

"I drove straight to her house. It was dark when I got there."

"And then what, Luke?"

"We talked. I cried for hours. Alex made a reservation for us, a weekend's stay at a resort in Carmel. We woke up early and drove to the resort. We spent Friday night, and late Saturday morning, in the breakfast room, I saw the paper with Misty's picture under a headline saying that she'd been murdered.

"Alex and I left the resort and drove directly to the police station in this building, where I was arrested for murders I didn't, couldn't have, would never commit. So help me, God."

"Thank you, Lucas."

Gardner turned his handsome face to the jury as if to say, *You see what kind of man he is. He didn't do it.*

"Your witness," Gardner said to ADA Castellano.

"No questions," Yuki said.

"Okay then," said Gardner. "The defense rests."

CHAPTER 104

THE JUDGE CALLED a twenty-minute recess, which gave Yuki some time to settle her nerves.

This was it. She was about to give her closing argument. She'd been rehearsing variations on her summation for months with Len Parisi, with Nick Gaines, and with her husband, Jackson Brady.

She swung her eyes to the back of the room and saw Brady standing beside Cindy's chair.

He gave her a smile and she returned one of her own.

She heard the judge call her name and felt the hush in the courtroom as if it were a chill breeze. Nick's note was in front of her: "Go get 'em."

ADA Castellano walked to the lectern and addressed the jury with all of the confidence she had.

"Ladies and gentlemen, as you know, this case is about the murder of two innocent young women and a baby girl, all of whom were intimately connected to the defendant, Lucas Burke.

"Mr. Burke claims to have loved them all and denies

his guilt, but the evidence shows that he decided, with malice aforethought, to kill all three.

"How do we know he did it?

"Mr. Burke has testified that his marriage was going up in flames. Tara was too spendy with her credit cards, and the defendant states that he couldn't afford this. He told her to grow up, to stick to the budget, and when she continued to overspend, he canceled her credit cards.

"She was angry.

"You heard Tara's mother, Kathleen Wyatt, who told you that Mr. Burke was abusive to her daughter. Tara denied it, but this is often the case with abused spouses, and this seems to be such a case. Fights, bruises, mounting anger.

"Mr. Burke already *had another* teenage girlfriend. We have introduced the note that he wrote to Melissa Fogarty saying that he wanted to marry her, but to date, no ring was forthcoming. Not only was this affair another sign that Lucas Burke's marriage vows were broken, but perhaps Lucas was feeling pressure from his girlfriend.

"Based on these financial and emotional circumstances, I believe even Mr. Burke would admit that he went to bed angry every night and woke up angry every morning. And maybe he could no longer contain that anger and had to take action before it destroyed him.

"On the Monday, Lucas Burke fought with his wife on what would turn out to be the last day of her life. Phone records show that Mr. Burke last phoned Tara at eleven that morning. They spoke for three minutes and he never called her again. Not even after their baby was found dead Wednesday morning. He never called her during that period of nearly a week when she was missing. Unlike Tara's mother, he didn't dog the police department, demanding that they inform him of progress in the search for his wife, and he didn't put up posters asking, 'Have you seen Tara Burke?'

"Lucas Burke knew where she was.

"We deduce that on that last call, he made a plan to meet with her purportedly to discuss their fight—but it was a ruse. He had a different idea. He met her at a romantic place overlooking the water, and killed her by drawing his razor blade across her throat.

"He then smothered his own baby with his hand. He tucked them both into Tara's car, put a stone on the accelerator and, after getting safely out of the car, he rolled it into the ocean, where it stayed until Saturday. According to our medical examiner, both Tara and Lorrie were dead before they hit the water.

"Ladies and gentlemen, there is an absence of contradictory evidence from the defense.

"You have heard from the head of our Forensics laboratory who examined the evidence, and we have shown you the murder weapon used to kill Melissa Fogarty.

"Ms. Fogarty's blood was found on the blade, and Lucas Burke's fingerprints were on that razor's handle. Furthermore, Lucas Burke was the last known person to see Tara and Lorrie Burke, and he went to great lengths to get rid of their bodies.

"Why did Mr. Burke go on a murder spree?

"We contend it was because he didn't want to be weighed down with other people's expectations. So instead of moving to a new location, he expressed the volatile personality he has shown us in this room.

"And he believed that he could get away with it.

"Mr. Burke's defense is common to police and prosecutors all over this country. We have heard it too many times. It's referred to as TODDI.

"That's an acronym for the words 'the other dude did it.' In this case of three dead souls who loved the defendant, the defense wants to blame the other dude, the defendant's father. Mr. Burke's father does not have a criminal record. He has not been introduced to this court in person or by way of other witnesses. In fact, the defense has not produced a single witness to support this theory of 'the other dude.'

"They can't.

"Only one person known to the prosecution had a motive to murder Tara and Lorrie Burke and Melissa Fogarty in the space of one single week. He's sitting right over there with his head down on the table.

"For reasons only the defendant truly understands, Lucas Burke did it. For the sake of his victims, and to keep this man where he cannot harm anyone else, please find him guilty of three murders in the first degree."

CHAPTER 105

JOE AND JULIE were waiting for me at the airport's passenger pickup zone, along with Martha. The gang was all here.

Julie hugged me around the waist until I got her into her car seat, Martha circled my legs, and Joe squeezed me with his big man arms and opened the passenger door for me.

I was dying to catch up with everyone, and to be absolutely honest, I wanted to tell Joe everything that happened in Vegas since he'd left there singing as he went down the escalator.

My phone played a little tune, and when I looked at the caller ID, I had to take the call.

"Chief Belinky?"

"Sergeant. I'm glad I was able to reach you."

What was wrong? Had Burke escaped? Shot someone else? Died?

"You just caught me," I said. "What's up, chief?"

"Evan Burke is in the ICU. Turns out he has some kind of lung infection. His immune system is down."

I motioned to Joe, 'Just a sec,' hoping the chief would just get to it. And then he did.

"Burke wants to see you. He has something to tell you—"

"He's a lying liar, and dangerous as the devil. ADA Yuki Castellano still wants to depose him."

"About that," the chief said. "Without knowing what Burke is going to say, and without his having requested a lawyer, it's too soon to bring in the DA's office, even with the trial of Lucas Burke ongoing."

As I took it all in, the chief continued.

"I'll make sure there's no way he can hurt you."

I didn't want to see Evan Burke again. I didn't feel safe, and yet the bastard was so compelling. Even while wounded and sick. Even with a dead woman's blood on his hands and his son charged with murder. I'd never met anyone like him, and I'd really had enough of him.

I could have used Alvarez's take, but she'd already headed back to the squad room.

I said, "I have to run this past my lieutenant, my chief, and my husband."

"I haven't cleared it with your husband, but your chief, your lieutenant, and your task force all want you to meet with this piece of crap."

"I'll call you back, okay?"

"Sergeant," the chief said. "It'll be short and easy. Plane. Cruiser to the hospital. Talk until you're done, then back to McCarran. Say yes so I can line up my ducks."

I'm a cop and a chief of police was asking me, as good as pleading with me, to talk to the shooter I'd seen commit murder.

"Geez."

"Close enough," said Chief Belinky. "I checked the

flights and there's one that'll get you here by five. A car will be waiting to pick you up."

I couldn't think of a good enough reason to turn him down and maybe, maybe I could help.

"Yes. Yes. Okay."

Belinky gave me the flight info. I hung up and told Joe the news. He backed Belinky.

"Linds. This could be your Ted Bundy moment. When you come home tomorrow, Bugs, Martha, and I will be here to meet you."

My family walked me back into the terminal. I showed Julie the huge metallic lights hanging from the ceiling. We bought her a T-shirt in the gift shop and a pink hoodie for Mrs. Rose. We consumed a fully loaded pizza in the food court, and then Joe and Julie waved good-bye to me at the check-in line.

I flew back to Las Vegas, wondering what the hell Evan Burke wanted to tell me. He was a magnetic character, but I didn't trust him at all.

CHAPTER 106

CHIEF BELINKY WAS WAITING inside the entrance to Sunrise Medical Center. He was in his fifties, wearing a blue suit, red tie, about five eleven with salt-and-pepper hair.

He came toward me and shook my hand with both of his.

"Thanks for coming, sergeant. I think you'll be glad you did."

I doubted that.

Belinky said, "Burke is cuffed to a bed in the ICU. He's doped up, on antibiotics, apparently his lungs are full of goop, but I still don't trust him."

He went on.

"I promised to protect you, and we've taken the following precautions. The stall has a glass wall. We can see everything and there's a camera overhead. Here's your mic. That'll record whatever he tells you."

"Excellent."

I clipped it to my lapel.

We took an elevator up a couple of flights and followed the arrows to the intensive care unit. Belinky continued to brief me.

"Officers are stationed outside the door. Keep it ajar when you go in. His good arm and ankles are cuffed. His right arm is unrestrained, but it's in a sling and you can see his hand. I've promised everyone with a shield in the state of California that you're walking out of that room unharmed."

"Thanks, chief."

"Now, this guy has not lawyered up and I would say he has no expectation of privacy, right?"

"Right. People are coming in and out of his room. It's a hospital."

"Good. We agree."

We were in the ICU ward and Burke's stall was visible because of the two beefy cops standing on either side of the doorway.

"Ready or not," I said.

I said hello to the two officers and took a moment to observe Burke through the glass. He was lying flat in the bed with his eyes closed, blanket up to his chin, his bandaged wing cradled against his body. I entered the stall, leaving the door open a crack.

Pulling a chair up to his bed, I called "Burke," and he opened his eyes.

"Oh. Is that you, sergeant? I asked for you."

"And here I sit."

He pressed a gadget within reach of his cuffed hand, and the back of his bed rose.

"Could you?" he asked, tipping his chin to the table near the bed. There was a glass of water with a straw. I moved the glass toward him so he could reach it and sip, and then he returned the glass.

"Thanks. They don't know what I've got, but it's

pneumonia and something else that I couldn't fight off and it's supposedly not contagious."

I said, "How's your arm?"

"It's been better."

"Well. I flew in to see you, Burke, because you asked to see me. What do you want to tell me?"

"I want to tell you that I've killed people in my life. Quite a few. Quite. A few."

What was this now? False confession for leverage? Or braggadocio?

"So, you want to give some families closure? Is that it?"

"I told you back at the cabin, sergeant. My son, Lucas, is also a murderer," Burke said. "He's a killer who started very young. His first victims were small animals, and years later, I'm pretty sure he took out Corinne and Jodie. He came home from school without telling anyone. Corinne and Jodie were never seen or heard from again."

"Still, not proof, Evan. Why are you telling me this?"

"Because. I don't know how much time I have left. I want to make sure that the story is told right."

"Got it," I said.

I didn't. These two Burkes were twisted and they'd twisted me. Senior didn't sound repentant for the girl he'd killed in front of me. What did he want?

I said, "Why don't you start at the beginning."

"All in good time," he said. "I'm thinking about what—"

Without warning, he jerked, coughed, inhaled noisily, and was seized with a terrible-sounding coughing fit. The wheeze alone sounded like an accordion with pleurisy. He couldn't grab at his chest or even roll because he was cuffed at the wrist and chained at the ankles.

I stood up to get help, but help had seen through the glass walls and came through in the form of a nurse, an aide, and the ICU doctor.

The nurse pulled a mask over Burke's face and I heard the hiss of oxygen. The doctor asked me to please leave.

She said please, but it was a direct order and I followed it.

Evan Burke had accused his son, Lucas Burke, of killing Corinne and Jodie Burke, but he hadn't shed any light on the triple homicide for which Lucas was now standing trial. As much as Yuki wanted to depose Evan Burke, that was not going to happen.

CHAPTER 107

NEWT GARDNER SAT with Lucas Burke in the seventh-floor client-attorney conference room, killing time until the jurors came in with their verdict.

The room was a cage the size of a cell, furnished with a small table and four straight chairs. Gardner sat across from Luke and put his hand on his client's arm. Luke was depressed, down and deep in the darkest part of himself, and Gardner hadn't been able to help him out of the hole. He'd told Luke that he'd been right to testify. He'd said that his delivery had been very moving. "Tell me I'm wrong, but I thought my closer was almost as good as yours," Gardner joked.

Luke couldn't crack a smile.

Gardner placed a shopping bag on the table.

"This's for you. Open it," he said.

Luke did so with no enthusiasm and took out a new shirt and a silk tie in reds and yellows, which Gardner thought would warm up his client's sallow complexion.

"Thanks. Put this on my tab, will you, Newt?"

"It's a gift. And I have something else for you."

Luke had asked him to find out where Misty was buried, and Newt had learned that she was in the Fogarty family plot in a cemetery in Grand Rapids, Michigan. Gardner contacted a friend who lived in the suburbs and asked him to go and take a picture of Misty's headstone.

Gardner took a photo from his briefcase and passed it to Luke, saying, "I hope this is what you want."

Luke stared at the photo of Melissa's headstone. It read "Beloved Daughter."

"She's home," said Luke. "In the family plot. She loved her father. Thanks, Newt. This is good."

"It's yours," Gardner said. "But don't get morbid. I fully expect the jury to find in your favor."

"It looks peaceful," Luke said. "Like being in your own bed, forever."

Gardner said, "May I remind you that you're only in your forties."

"Tara and Lorrie are in Kathleen's plot in Colman?"

"That's right. Will you please make an effort to look like the innocent man you are, a man who has been put through hell, for having had a spat with his wife."

Luke nodded. "How long before the jury comes in?"

"One never knows, but it's only been an hour."

"Thanks again, Newt. You've been great. I need to lie down."

After Luke had been escorted back to his cell, Gardner had a hallway meeting with the head guard, Sergeant Holmes.

Newt said, "Keep a watch on him, Larry."

"Will do."

"He's despondent."

"Gotcha."

"Here's my card," he said. "Call anytime."

Gardner believed in Lucas and that belief never wavered. He went to the elevator and pressed Down.

CHAPTER 108

DA LEN PARISI CALLED Yuki two hours after she and Nick Gaines had left the courtroom to tell them that the jury was back.

Yuki's stomach churned and fluttered as she strode up the corridor from the DA's suite to the courtroom where Gaines was already waiting at the counsel table.

Often a jury's quick return signaled a guilty verdict. But it wasn't always true. There was every chance that Lucas Burke's bawling that his father had set him up had worked on a juror or two. Yuki was thinking about other killers who looked pitiable when testifying when she heard her name. She turned to see Lindsay.

"Hey."

"Hey, you."

They linked arms and Yuki said, "It's standing room only in there, Linds, but please find a place. I want you there when the verdict is read."

Lindsay said, "Of course. I came looking for you. Dinner tonight, okay?"

"Okay. Either way."

Yuki watched as Lindsay squeezed in next to Cindy in the back row. The courtroom settled down.

Judge Passarelli banged his gavel until the room quieted.

He said to the jury, "Have you arrived at a verdict?"

The forewoman stood, said, "We have, Your Honor." She handed a slip of paper to the bailiff, a bored-looking man who lumbered over to the forewoman, then back to the judge.

The judge took the slip, turned it around and read it without expression, then handed it back to the bailiff, who walked it back to the foreperson.

The judge said, "Madam Foreperson, will you please read the verdict?"

Nick pushed his tablet over to Yuki. He'd drawn a question mark with rays coming off it.

Yuki scanned the faces of the jurors.

How had they decided? She couldn't read a one of them.

CHAPTER 109

CLAIRE, CINDY, AND I had picked up Yuki in the lobby of the Hall and bundled her into Cindy's Hyundai sedan for a chauffeured ride to the Women's Murder Club HQ.

Yuki sat in the front seat beside Cindy, turning to face me and Claire, lavishing us with her rapid-paced hardly stopping to breathe chatter that was both joyful and contagious.

I was elated for Yuki—hey, I was proud of the whole task force, especially Alvarez, still amazed we'd come back from the Las Vegas shoot-out without a scratch.

Yuki was saying that Red Dog had told her to relax while waiting for the verdict, but it had been impossible. "Every time I thought of floating on the calm sea, I pictured sharks swimming toward me and I just panicked. So, thanks so much, all of you guys, for, well, everything."

At five o'clock we were comfortable in our cozy red banquette in Susie's back room. Lorraine came over, her auburn hair in a pony, ballpoint pen tucked over her ear. She went straight to Yuki, and asked, "Did you win?"

Yuki nodded. "You know when I knew it?"

Four women asked, "When?" in unison.

Yuki said, "When the foreperson, that angel, read the verdict out loud. 'We find the defendant, Lucas Burke, guilty on count one—'"

Cindy chimed in, "Gardner polled the jury, and it was unanimous. They'd all voted guilty, guilty, guilty."

I couldn't remember Lorraine having ever touched any of us, but now she swept Yuki up from her seat and squished her in a hug, then said, "A pitcher of Margaritas on me, Yuki. Coming right up."

"Thank you, Lorraine. You *know* I need my tequila infusion."

"Beer for meeee," I shouted after her. "And chips."

"And menus," called Claire.

She looked rested, smiling and wearing pink, fully recovered from the surgery that had kept her out of work for months. Cindy had her laptop out on the table and had filed her story in the interlude between ordering and the arrival of food and drink.

Hours had passed since I'd shared a pizza with Joe and Julie at the airport. I was starving.

Margaritas, hot sauce, chips, and menus arrived along with a pitcher of beer alongside a frosted mug.

I filled my mug, lifted it, saying, "To Yuki, ace prosecutor."

"To you, Lindsay," she said, "and your task force for nailing Luke, that black-hearted killer. And to you, Claire, for standing your ground against Newt Gardner. And to you, Cindy, for sending Kathleen Wyatt to Lindsay in the first place and for covering the investigation and the trial of Lucas Burke and for being *on the record* with all of it."

Of course, we laughed. And we ordered too much food, and that balanced out the margaritas so that Yuki didn't sing and dance. When we were on the key lime pie course, I called Brady to come over and drive Yuki home.

Took him about ten minutes before he came through the door of the Caribbean café.

I said, "Brady, sit. Have a drink."

He said to Lorraine, "Dr Pepper and the check for alla this, please."

Minutes later Brady lifted his glass and said, "A more formidable murder club doesn't exist, anywhere." He drank the soda down, and when he was done he said, "I'm gonna take this little sweetie home now. Love all y'all."

The Women's Murder Club answered in unison, "Night, you guys. Good night."

CHAPTER 110

CLAIRE ORDERED AN UBER. I walked Cindy to her car, then caught a cab that was letting out a passenger just outside.

When my cab dropped me off on Lake Street, I felt buzzed, satisfied, and happy to be alive.

My husband, little girl, and best dog were all waiting for me when I blew through the front door. I was home, and even a hotel with a two-hundred-foot fountain playing show tunes and slot machines that could pay out a million dollars in quarters couldn't touch it.

Joe said no one had called, not Chief Belinky, nor Alvarez, nor any of the brass at the SFPD. A miracle. I read to my little Bugster until she told me, "You read like you're singing, Mom."

"Do I?"

"Uh-huh. I like it."

"I'll keep reading," I said, but Julie Bugs had fallen asleep in my lap.

I tucked her into bed, took a leisurely hot shower, changed into fresh pj's, and threw myself into bed.

It was past ten when I realized that I'd never turned my cell phone back on after leaving Susie's.

I got out of bed, grabbed my phone out of my bag, and that fast, Joe took it out of my hand. I protested that I had to check my calls, but he said, "You need to chill, Linds, and I'm the enforcer."

I knew he was right, but when my eyes flew open at 4 a.m., that nagging feeling was right there with me as if lit with neon lights.

What had Evan Burke wanted to tell me about his murders?

What did that son of a bitch want me to know?

I sneaked out of bed, found my phone plugged into the charger in the foyer, and checked my messages. Belinky had called me while I'd been with the gang at Susie's.

I played his message.

"Sergeant. Chief Belinky. Burke lawyered up. Call me."

CHAPTER 111

IT WAS ALMOST NOON when I reached Chief Alex Belinky from my desk in the bullpen.

I lowered my head so no one would interrupt me and gave my full attention to the LVPD chief as he said, "Sergeant, the rules of engagement regarding Evan Burke have changed. His lawyer is criminal defense attorney Randall Lanning."

I tapped Lanning's name into my laptop with one finger. There were about forty Google pages of Lannings in Las Vegas listings but I couldn't open them fast enough to read with comprehension and listen to Belinky at the same time.

Belinky said, "Lanning will depose you and Alvarez. The prosecutor is going to do the same and you'll both be called as witnesses against Burke at his trial."

"Inevitable, I guess."

"Burke is being arraigned on Monday—"

"Can I talk to him after the arraignment?"

"Doubtful. Lanning rightly told Burke not to talk to anyone but him. He is going to try to get Burke leniency. Lanning's good, but between you and me, he's got a rough job ahead of him."

"I'm trying not to scream, chief. If Burke hadn't had that coughing fit, if I hadn't been tossed out of the ICU, he would have talked to me. Maybe closed a couple of cases for us. He was saying, 'I've killed a lot of people.'"

"No names, right?" said Belinky. "My take on Burke is that he would have tried to work some kind of deal with you and then he would have reneged or angled for an even better deal. He's so twisted he could be making it all up."

"Can't dispute you on that."

"Our DA is Joseph Masci."

"I almost recognize that name."

"His father was Ray Masci."

"Mobster's best friend?"

"Very good. Ray was a lawyer for the mob back in the day. He defended all the big names in drugs, real estate fraud, money laundering, as well as your everyday murder of gangsters buried in construction sites or out in the desert.

"Like his father, Joe is tough, but he's a reformer. He could teach criminal law at his alma mater, but instead of a chair at Harvard, Joe is trying to rehabilitate the family name and the town. He's going to stay close to the Burke case, I'm guessing. And there's a fair chance he'll try the case himself."

CHAPTER 112

ATTORNEY RANDALL LANNING had wheeled his client into the crowded arraignment court that morning, finding it hard to grab a seat where he sat next to Evan Burke as they waited for their number to come up.

He knew the judge, Sarah Valencourt, and knew that like him she had a sense of urgency. An aisle seat became vacant and Lanning angled the bulky old wheelchair over to it and sat down.

At just after ten, his docket number was called and Lanning rolled Evan Burke's chair up to the bench. Burke hadn't said much to Lanning this morning. He seemed deep in thought, which was somewhat expected. Lanning had prepared him for the two possibilities.

Either a huge bail amount and zero chance of scratching up the required 10 percent for the bondsman, or he'd be denied bail altogether, which Lanning thought more likely.

A dozen rows in front of them, the judge sat high

on her bench. She polished off some paperwork, then looked down and around, apparently for Evan Burke, the man who had created a big stir in the media.

Judge Valencourt addressed Burke, but he was in his head, far away, and his attorney called his name, bumped the wheelchair with his knee.

Burke snapped to and answered the judge's question.

"Not guilty, Your Honor. This is a farce. A setup. The police know damned well that I didn't shoot that girl on purpose. My door was kicked in—"

"ADA Mintner?"

Lanning had gone against Tiffany Mintner before. She was smart and one of Masci's favorite ADAs.

She said, "Your Honor, Mr. Burke is a danger to the community. He is charged with the murder of an unarmed woman, and shooting at police officers. We intend to present those law-enforcement officers as witnesses at trial. Mr. Burke is also a flight risk and has evaded arrest in Nevada, California, and Oregon. Shall I go on?"

"I think that's enough, counselor."

"Mr. Lanning?"

"My client was shot by the police without warning. The victim's death was an accidental shooting. Mr. Burke has a home just outside Las Vegas and I recommend house arrest and police guard if necessary."

"Ms. Mintner? Bail?"

"No way, Your Honor. The best option for both the population and the defendant himself would be to remand him to the court and hold him for trial."

"So be it. Bail is denied. The defendant is remanded."

As Evan Burke was rolled out of the courtroom, he said to his attorney, "I want to make a deal."

"What kind of deal?"

"I have a lot to offer in exchange for a guilty plea that would bypass a trial."

Lanning wheeled the chair up to the elevator. The doors slid open and two people got out. Lanning held the door, and when Burke and his equipment were inside he pressed the Down button.

Lanning said, "Take some time to think about it, Evan. We should discuss what you have as leverage."

"Mr. Lanning. Randall. I might as well be in hell. Chained to the bed. Bedpans and needles."

"It's a hospital, for Christ's sake. You're sick."

"It's a hospital in hell."

He coughed all the way out to the street, and once he'd been transferred into the ambulance an EMT gave him oxygen. Still angry, Burke pounded on the ambulance window with his good hand until a sedative kicked in and he had to stop.

Lanning was going to have to find a way to manage his client or Evan Burke would be dead in the water.

CHAPTER 113

I'D OVERSLEPT FOR ONCE and the squad room was fairly quiet when I got there.

I wanted to talk with Conklin, Alvarez, Brady, but they were all out on a new case, a hostage situation involving a tender age child.

A new idea sparked.

Finding the last cardboard tray in the break room, I stuck three coffee containers into the holes, poured the java, and capped the cups. I then gathered up some fixings and took the elevator up to the sixth floor. I stared up at the lights behind the numbers and used the time to gather myself for what I hoped would be a useful meeting with Lucas Burke.

Sergeant Bubbleen Waters was behind the duty desk. I handed her a coffee.

"Oooh. Irish cream. Thanks, Lindsay."

I smiled. From our very first shared shift at the station, we'd liked each other instantly.

"I'm not above bribing a pal," I said. "Think I could have a few minutes with Lucas Burke?"

"Cheer him up, will ya? I can give you the cage until a lawyer wants it."

Five minutes later, Burke and I were in the attorney-lawyer meeting room. I tried to gauge his mood. He didn't look like the same man I'd met at Sunset Park Prep so many months ago. I offered him fresh brewed black coffee with an array of packets and little cream cups.

He drank it black and kept drinking until he had made it clear that I was going to have to speak first.

"I saw your father a couple days ago."

"Spare me. I'm going to be sentenced to life in prison and will do my best to forget I ever knew him. I'm going to invent a fictional family and he's not in it. Or maybe just bash my head against the cinder blocks. One clean hit should do it."

I moved past that image.

I said, "You know what happened with him? He was in a basement hotel room with a girl who was screaming for help. I kicked in the door and he shot his date through the back of her head."

"Interesting," he said, but he wasn't interested at all.

"I put a couple of shots in your father's shoulder."

"That was the best you could do?"

"Under the circumstances."

"So why tell me?"

He had gulped down the coffee. Getting some pleasure, I guess. I pushed mine over to him.

I said, "This has a lot of sugar. I drink it sweet."

"Fine. I'll take it. Did he tell you why he killed my wife, child, and girlfriend?"

"Nope. He's still saying that you did it."

Lucas got up and grabbed the bars of the cage with his cuffed hands.

"Guard! Guard!"

Still holding the bars, he turned to me, and said, "It wasn't me. I don't care what you believe. I was found guilty. I'm going to be sentenced in a week or so. I'll be put in protective housing for the next fifty years. At this point, I don't care what happens to me. I didn't kill anyone."

The guard arrived.

"Take me back to my cell."

Lucas Burke didn't say good-bye. He just walked out of the cage between the guards, the shackles around his ankles clanking as he rounded the bend.

I cleaned up the coffee remnants and tried to get a grip on my own feelings. I hadn't liked Lucas Burke, and I'd believed I had good reason not to. But I'd been haunted by questions since I'd come into contact with his father.

I'd had low expectations that he would confess to killing his wife and child, the girl he said he loved, but after meeting with him alone, hearing his voice, feeling his depression at losing everyone, I was surer than ever that he hadn't done it.

True to Berney's word, the FBI had made known its claim on the Evan Burke case. DA Masci was fully up to speed on the names of his family members both alive and dead, and that Burke had been on the agency's most wanted list. Which was why Burke had changed his name, his address, and his face. But he couldn't change the charges now stacked against him.

CHAPTER 114

RANDALL LANNING HAD CALLED Joseph Masci and told him that his client, Evan Burke, wanted to meet with him.

Lanning had expected a flat "I'll see him in court," but instead Masci said, "What does he want? I have a half hour free at three to hear from your client, who claims to be an unindicted serial psycho."

"He says he has something you're going to like, and you know, Joe, he wants to make a deal."

Lanning had conveyed the meeting time back to his client, who was still in the hospital. He added, "See if someone will give you a shave and a haircut."

"You ask them. I'm lucky to get a bedpan."

Lanning continued.

"I repeat, Evan. Negotiating with Joseph Masci is not a good idea. He's like a copperhead snake. He's venomous. And he's quick. If you insist on trying your luck, don't pop off. Think. Then, speak."

At three, Joe Masci was in his office when Randall Lanning trundled Evan Burke in.

Masci's assistant made everyone comfortable, and asked the boss, "Hold your calls?"

"I'll take emergency calls, but you decide, George. We won't be long."

Masci wasn't big, but he was muscular. He shook Evan Burke's left hand, gave it a good squeeze.

"I have ten minutes," he said, "and they're all yours. How can I help you?"

Burke said, "Thanks for your time. I don't know what you know about me, Mr. Masci. I'm a great man, an important man, and there's never been a killer on my scale. I kid you not. Hypothetically, I'm willing to do something that pains me. To admit that I killed Lucas's wife and child and that schoolgirl."

D.A. Masci was fully up to speed on Evan Burke's claim that he was an unindicted serial psycho. Masci knew the names of Burke's family members, both alive and dead, and that he had been on the FBI's most wanted list. Which was why Burke had changed his name, his address, and his face.

It was because of Evan Burke that Masci had spent that morning on the phone with a highly placed FBI special agent, J. Edward Bernstein, aka Berney, who said he'd be happy to take Evan Burke off the D.A.'s hands.

"And why, exactly, would you implicate yourself in a triple homicide?" Masci asked Burke now.

"I'd do it to save my son, my innocent son, Lucas, whom I hate."

Lanning started scribbling frantically on his legal pad as Burke continued to speak. This was the first he was hearing of his client's conflicting objectives.

"And that's barely the beginning. I'd confess to killing the girl at the Eagle as well as over a hundred murders in three states including Nevada with proof of death.

"I'd ask for a few comforts in exchange."

"Hypothetically, what comforts?"

"The death penalty is off the table. I get a private cell with TV and access to books and videos. Visitation rights for select people. Conjugal rights and a cell phone for good behavior."

"Chocolates on your pillow?"

Burke grinned. "Nah. But thanks for the offer."

"Anything else?"

"A time of day when the bathroom and shower are all mine."

Masci leaned back in his chair and gazed over Burke's head.

"And you would provide written proof of your kills?"

"Of course."

"Not interested," said Masci.

"What?" Burke said. "I said a hundred bodies plus the three in San Francisco. I'll give you those three now to show good faith."

"You killed your grandchild, daughter-in-law, and your son's girlfriend?"

"Yes. Yes. I'll say all of that. How and when and where now, and a hundred more I'll hold in reserve."

Lanning said loudly, "Evan, *stop talking*. Stop."

Masci took out a sheet of letterhead and wrote for a moment. Then handed it to Burke.

"Please read that out loud."

"I, Evan William Burke, do swear in the presence of my attorney and Joseph Masci, DA of Las Vegas County in the state of Nevada, and hereby confess to killing Tara Burke, Lorrie Burke, and Melissa Fogarty. My son, Lucas Burke, is innocent of these crimes. And at the bottom, Signed and Witnessed."

Masci pressed a button on his desk and his assistant came in. Randall Lanning squeezed and shook Burke's bad shoulder to make sure he was getting his attention.

"Yowwww."

Lanning turned his back to Masci and said, "*Evan, no. I said, do not do this.*"

Evan shook off his lawyer and said in a whisper, "I know what I'm doing."

Randall Lanning said, not whispering, "You don't want to sign that without a guarantee that you will not get the death penalty. I can draw it up, right on that paper—"

Burke said, "I said, 'In good faith.' I'm trusting DA Masci, and I'll give up the info about recent San Francisco murders—"

Masci said, "George, please bring this over to Mr. Burke and witness his signature. Then, have the tape of this meeting transcribed. Thank you."

When the signed document was back in his hand, Masci said, "Mr. Burke, I'll turn your confession over to the San Francisco DA and maybe he'll give your son a break. As I said a moment ago, I'm not interested in making any kind of deal with you. I like our case against you. Keep your secrets. We can only kill you once. Thanks for coming."

He stood, walked toward the open door, said, "Randall, I'll see you in court. I can hardly wait."

And then Joe Masci left the building.

As Randall Lanning wheeled his client out of the room, Burke said, "I think he's going to talk to Parisi. You heard him. But I have insurance in the form of a letter in my hospital room. It's for you to give to Cindy Thomas."

"Is that so?"

"Yes. Head crime reporter and she's up to speed on the whole deal. This is urgent, Randy. Do not open it. Send it by courier to Cindy Thomas so she gets it before I leave the hospital."

Lanning agreed, then added, "That's the last thing I'm doing for you, Evan. Find yourself another lawyer."

CHAPTER 115

RICH CONKLIN AND I went to MacBain's to have a quick lunch, and as luck would have it, we found a spot two tables away from the jukebox.

There was just enough background doo-wop to camouflage what we were saying, but we could still hear each other. Conklin told me that the little boy hostage had been saved, turned over to Child Protective Services, and that his father had been arrested.

"Dirtbag starved the little kid, beat him, said that when he learned to behave he was going to send him to summer camp. When a neighbor called the cops, he put a .38 to little Duane's head."

"Did you get in a punch?"

"If only."

Brady came through the doorway, looked around, saw me and Conklin. He came over and pulled up a stool.

"Hi, boss," said Conklin. "The kid is okay."

"Good work. Burke is dead."

I said, "What? Which one?"

"Ours. Lucas."

"Brady, that can't be true. I had coffee with him two hours ago."

"That'll mess with your mind for a while, Boxer. Tell me about that."

Brady lifted his hand to call Sydney over to the table. "I don't know what to order. I'm not even hungry. Syd, I need something to fill my belly when it's upset."

"Milkshake," suggested Conklin.

"I'm lactose intolerant. What kind of soup do you have?"

While Syd and Brady talked about soup, I put my bacon and cheese sandwich aside. A few minutes ago, I'd been dreaming of it.

Conklin was still working on his fries, but it was half-hearted and he gave it up. When Syd asked if we were finished, we said yes and she took the plates, left the beer.

I said, "Brady, what the hell happened to Burke?"

"His attorney."

"Newt Gardner killed him?"

"Sorry, I'm still trying to get my arms around it. Gardner bought him a jacket and tie for court. According to Sergeant Waters, he was fine after you left, and they took their eyes off him for a half second. He'd hid the tie under his jumpsuit. Made a slipknot — this is us putting it together after the fact. He gets into the top tier of his bed. Closes his eyes, right? When no one is around, he knots the free end of the tie to the bed frame and drops the fuck over."

I said, "I can't — he broke his neck?"

Brady nodded. "Body's with Claire by now. She'll let us know for sure if it was suicide."

I was shaking my head, going over my conversation with Burke.

Brady said, "What made you go up to see him?"

"Boss, I was looking for resolution."

"What did he say?" Rich asked.

"He said he didn't do it. He wasn't trying to convince me. He was dead inside."

Brady said, "Boxer. The guy was depressed and for very good reason, none of it having anything to do with you."

"He asked why I'd only shot Evan in the arm."

"Rich," Brady said, reaching into his jacket. "Why I'm here. This just came for Cindy with a rush on it."

Syd came back with a bowl of chicken noodle soup for Brady, and he handed Conklin the envelope marked "Rush. Urgent."

Conklin looked at the envelope, picked up his phone, tapped a contact.

"Cin? It's me. This will take two seconds. Can you meet us at MacBain's? Me, Brady, Lindsay. Yeah. Love you, too."

He disconnected the line.

"She's ten minutes out. On the way."

I said, "I'll bet she makes it in eight."

Conklin said, "I don't like this. What does Evan Burke want with Cindy?"

CHAPTER 116

WHEN CINDY ARRIVED at MacBain's, Syd set us up at a larger table away from the jukebox.

Cindy accepted the envelope from Brady, but barely looked at it.

"What's going on?"

Brady said, "Cindy, that's from Evan Burke. Apparently, he's a fan. And I have some news, off the record."

She said, "Can we please drop the cross-my-heart crap and just tell me. There are enough law enforcement out front of the Hall that someone will leak."

Brady said, "Lucas Burke took his life. End of sentence."

"He's dead? You're saying that Luke is dead?"

Brady said, "I do believe this is the first time I scooped you. Am I right?"

Cindy, open-mouthed, nodded.

"His body is at the ME's office. Maybe you can get something out of Claire. Okay. I have to go back, see Clapper. Try to put out some fires."

Brady paid for his soup.

"Cindy. According to Burke's lawyer, Evan wants to meet with you. He's at Sunrise Med in Vegas, maybe still in the ICU. Boxer and Conklin can go with you. As your friend, I do not want you to see this dude alone."

And then Brady was gone.

Cindy said, "I can't believe Lucas is dead. I mean I've been watching him for months. I hoped to interview him. I turn my back and he kills himself?"

I said, "I saw him this morning, Cindy. He was depressed, but he's been depressed since the day I met him."

"I gotta write the end of his story." Cindy stuffed the unopened letter into her bag. "I'll be at the ME's office."

"Hang on, Cindy," Rich said. "Read the letter."

"I'm gonna have a panic attack."

"Hon. Read the letter with your buddy and your lover right here. Then go see Claire."

"Fine."

Cindy picked up a bread knife and opened the envelope. She read, "Att: Cindy Thomas." She looked up and said, "This was written on copy paper with a felt-tip pen, dated today."

She skimmed the letter, sipped some water. Said, "What the hell is this? I've never met Evan Burke."

I said, "Is that a key taped beneath his signature?"

"Yes. So here's what he says, and I quote: *'I'm a master killer and in over twenty years, this is the first time I've been caught. That was half due to frustration, and half due to, I'm tired of doing all this work and getting zero credit. That, Cindy, is where you come in.'* Then, he says, *'Keep this key. If you want a story with headlines from here to eternity, pay me a visit at Sunrise Medical Center, Las Vegas. ICU. You look good in baby blue.'*"

Rich said, "Cindy. He's a subhuman liar."

"I'll call him up," she said. "Take it from there."

She kissed me on the cheek, Conklin on the mouth, grabbed her bags, and split.

"The boss is right that we should go with her," I said. I signaled to Sydney.

"You know, Rich, Evan claimed to me that he'd been sleeping with Tara for years. That Lorrie was his child."

"What? That's crazy. Is that true? Did you believe him?"

"I didn't believe a damned thing he said, but he got to me. What if *some* of that is true? Now, I'm having a sick feeling that he is going to confess to killing Lorrie, Tara, and Misty. And that would mean...Oh, my God."

"If true, that means Luke was wrongly convicted. That he killed himself because his father trapped him and there was no way out."

CHAPTER 117

THE ICU DOCTOR'S name tag read "R. Warren, M.D."

He was grizzled, harried, and gruff, telling Cindy that his patient was adamant about seeing her and he was going to permit this because he didn't want Evan Burke to stroke out.

Dr. Warren went on.

"You're not a relative. You're not even a friend. But this patient is restricted in unusual ways, and if spending five minutes with you makes him feel better, I just have to allow it."

Cindy said, "Five minutes? I just flew here from San Francisco."

"I might be talked into six, but that's it."

"Okay. Okay, doctor. Thank you."

She could see Evan Burke in the hospital bed, cuffed to the rails, IV dripping fluids into his arm, a nurse changing his bandages.

The nurse tapped his hand and Burke opened his eyes and turned his head. Cindy felt a shock, like she'd been struck by lightning. She mouthed "Cindy" and pointed to herself.

Burke held up a finger to indicate one minute. When the fresh bandage was in place and the nurse had refastened his robe, she stepped outside and said, "He's been waiting for you for two days."

"Are those handcuffs secure?"

"Yes, and those two policemen over there will be watching you. Don't sit close enough to him for him to…I'm not sure."

"Grab me, I guess."

"Just be careful, dear. I'll tap on the glass when your time is up."

The nurse exited and Cindy went in, took the chair, and sat back, out of reach.

"Mr. Burke. How are you feeling?"

"We don't have time for chitchat."

She said, "Would you mind if I record our conversation? That will save time."

"Go right ahead."

Cindy took out her phone, tapped the mic app, and held it in her lap.

"There's a lot to say, so I'm going to talk fast."

Cindy nodded.

"I've followed your coverage of this recent activity in San Francisco—Kathleen's hysteria, Luke's running away, Tara's car—all of it, and without going overboard. You're going to be famous one day."

"Thank you."

"And I'm going to help you. Or else I'm just messing with you. I'm capable of both."

Cindy wondered if he was for real or completely insane. Was he just mouthing off? Or was he giving her the story of her dreams? Could this even work? Whatever kind of spotlight Burke wanted, the

Chronicle wasn't going to go for it, but before she made the decision for Tyler and the board, she could play along.

"What is it you want to tell me?"

"I'm one of the greatest serial killers of this century and no one knows it."

Determined to keep him talking, Cindy tried not to show any emotion. Not to move her chair back. Not to even comment.

Burke said, "Try to imagine all of the words you've written in your career, but instead of them going out into the world, you've kept them all to yourself. Where's the fun in that?"

"And so now you want…"

"The spotlight, of course. I want to see my name in your paper. I want an agent. I want Al Pacino to play me in the movie. I want it all.

"I have a place in Lonelyville, out near Red Rock Canyon. I gave the nurse a map and permission for you to go into my place and take out my personal stuff. You only have twenty-four hours to do this.

"The shack is sold," said Burke. "I need to pay my lame lawyer. The new owners are taking possession in the morning. So if you want this story, you'd better get ready to load up your car. Any questions?"

"What's the nurse's name?"

"That's Nancy."

"How do I get this information?" she asked.

"Do you have the key?"

"Yes."

"Show me."

Cindy reached into the top of her shirt and pulled out a red waxed string lanyard with the key knotted into the loop.

"Good."

There was a tap on the glass.

Cindy turned, nodded, turned back to Burke.

"You're going to want a letter I've left for you in case somehow I check out of here before I speak to you. Get your letter and tell Nancy I need my catheter. Nice meeting you. And be sure to look under the bed."

He closed his eyes. Nancy signaled for her to come outside.

"You have a letter for me?" Cindy asked.

Nancy opened a drawer, hunted around, said, "Oh, dear."

There was a newspaper on the side chair near the desk. It was the *Chronicle*. Cindy picked it up, turned it over, and read the headline on the front page.

Her headline.

Convicted Killer Lucas Burke Commits Suicide

Cindy said, "Did Mr. Burke see this paper?"

"Oh, yes. He saw the story on the news and sent down for it."

"How did he react?"

"He seemed mad, then he laughed and said something like, "What a jerk." Then he complained that the handcuffs were rubbing his skin off. I told him he wouldn't be here much longer. Moving him out of the ICU and into a room later today."

Nancy handed the envelope to Cindy.

"Here you are, dear. Go with God."

Cindy thanked her and left the hospital. She had a lot to do and not much time.

CHAPTER 118

RICH AND I WERE in the waiting room twenty yards away from the core of the ICU and out of sight.

When Cindy turned the corner, she looked pale. Stricken.

"How did it go? What did he say?"

"How did it go? It was *Clarissa meets Hannibal Lecter.* He was cold, friendly, abrupt, welcoming, all in about five minutes. I would say he's as far away from human as you can be and still have a pulse. I know he has one because his *heartbeat* was on the monitor. And he knows about Luke. Listen, I might get sick."

I pointed to the ladies' room, but Cindy stayed with us.

Conklin said, "What did he want?"

"I'll tell you in the car."

We piled into our rented Outback and Conklin took the wheel. Cindy sat in front with him and I stretched out in the back seat. I called Chief Belinky and gave him the bare facts, that we had a permission letter and a line drawing of the location of Burke's house out near Red Rock Canyon.

"He's still chained to his bed, chief, but due to be moved out of the ICU and into a room today. I guess he's getting better. Talk to you soon."

Judging from the distance on the hand-drawn map, Burke's home was thirty miles from the Strip. Following Cindy's directions, we stayed on Route 95, the highway that cut through housing developments, across smaller roads and plain flat desert dotted with scrub.

I wouldn't have imagined Burke living this far from the coast. This far from anything.

Although I'd never been to a more desolate area, there was beauty here. Sunset. Mount Charleston in the distance backlit as the sky turned from blue to a vivid red and yellow and orange.

Rich pointed to an exit coming up at a left angle to the highway.

"That's it," Cindy said. "Good catch, Richie."

He took a hard left and we traveled, I'd say a half a mile, following real estate company arrows, crossing other narrow turnoffs, until a grim little shack was dead ahead in our headlight beams.

Rich pulled up to a small home that looked like Burke's place at Mount Tam. The structure was a hybrid of sorts; an old camper attached to a hand-made wood-frame house. There was a red-and-white sign on a post at the end of the drive reading "Sold by Patricia McNamee Real Estate." There were no lights on in the dwelling, no cars in the driveway, no traffic, only insect sounds as the sun melted in the distance.

I said, "Looks cozy."

Cindy laughed nervously.

Rich said, "Cindy. Stay here until we come to get you. Lock the doors."

My partner and I approached the house with flashlights and guns. We listened at the doorways and windows, pressed our ears to aluminum and wood siding.

It seemed that no one was home.

CHAPTER 119

IT WAS GREAT WORKING with Richie again.

We didn't have to speak as we circled the house, me to the left, Conklin to the right. We heard nothing, saw nothing through the windows, or in the yard and after checking the toolshed we executed the knock and announce protocol.

I knocked, called out, "Police! Open the door."

No answer. The front door was locked and there was a real estate lock box just outside the doorjamb.

Conklin called out "Police!" once more and louder. When there was no answer, he kicked in the door, right off the hinges.

I stepped in and flipped on the lights, which illuminated the entire four-hundred-square-foot interior, all visible from the doorway.

The main room doubled as a bedroom/sitting room with a built-in bed and a bookcase with a foldout writing surface for a desk, cubbyholes above it for filing. The camper section contained both the kitchen and bathroom.

Conklin and I cleared the dwelling, including the two closets and the shower stall. When we were sure it was safe, Rich stood up the kicked-in front door and called out to Cindy.

We stood aside as she stepped over the threshold and began her exceedingly well-earned treasure hunt.

She said, "What I'm looking for is supposed to be under this bed."

The twin-sized bed was made of a built-in rectangular frame tied into the floorboards. The mattress was centered on top, no room underneath for dust bunnies or anything else. Rich hefted the mattress out of the frame and leaned it against the wall. Inside the frame were two-by-four slats resting across the width of the bed, used to support the mattress. It took only a minute to lift them from the frame—and there it was.

A plain wooden chest, about the size of a child's toy box.

"Go ahead," I said to Cindy.

She stepped into the opening where the slats had been and tried opening the lid of the box. It was locked.

She said, "Oh. Right."

Pulling out a red string lanyard from inside her shirt, I saw the key that had been taped under Burke's signature. Cindy tried the key, and after a few wiggles, the lock clicked open.

Cindy lifted the lid and stared at the treasure inside. I saw three stacked leather-bound books with dates etched into the covers. I opened one and saw dated pages, covered in very small, very tight cursive writing.

Cindy pulled a large, bulging scrapbook from the bottom of the chest. When she flapped it open, we saw that it was filled with glued-down photos. All of the photos were of women, all smiling at the camera, all looking to be in their teens or early twenties, Burke's cramped handwriting under each; for instance, *Becky Weise, Catalina, 1998, tattoo around her ankle of birds and flowers. Roses are red. Summer is yellow. Neither of them last.*

Each photo was annotated with dates, names, or "unknown," plus maps to the places where Burke had presumably killed his victims and where he'd buried, dumped, or hidden their remains.

I looked to Cindy and saw tears streaming down her cheeks. I hugged her hard and tried not to cry myself. It was too painful. The scrapbook had transformed Burke's bragging and lying and sly intimations into real people; real people Burke had killed.

"What do I do?" Cindy said. "What's my first step?"

Conklin said, "Let me see that note from Burke, the one the nurse gave you."

He sat on the floor next to us and read the handwritten note, the map to Burke's house, and also something of a legal document.

"I, Evan William Burke, do hereby leave my possessions from my house in Lonelyville to Cynthia Thomas."

It was dated, signed, and witnessed "Nancy Shepherd, RN."

Richie said, "These books belong to you, Cin. But the information in here? It can't just go out online."

"No, of course not," Cindy said. "But which police?"

"I know what we should do," Rich said.

We rifled through the books on the shelves, the desk, too, and found more letters and an accordion file of photos, all of which we put into the wooden box. We tossed the drawers and closets and found other items of interest:

A key to a Sea Ray motorboat, the same model Wendy Franks had owned.

A luggage tag, monogrammed "SW," presumably for Susan Wenthauser, the young traveler killed before she could find her way home.

A picture of Misty Fogarty in her blue and white school uniform, taped to the inside of a kitchen cabinet. It was disgusting to think that he'd taken this picture and then killed her out of spite.

With the chest of evidence in the trunk, Rich drove us to a Lowe's about fifteen minutes away where we picked up a strong wifi signal in the parking lot.

And we made calls.

First to Brady, to let him know we were safe. Then I called Joe. He said, "Hang on," and connected us in a conference call. The next voice I heard was Berney's.

"We have Evan Burke's murder records," I said. "He gave them to reporter Cindy Thomas with a signed, witnessed document."

"May I talk to her?"

"Sure. Berney, this is my dear friend, Cindy," I said.

As Rich and I stepped outside to give Cindy some privacy, I could hear her saying, "I want *you* to have the material Burke has written. But when it's cleared, I will need it for publication." She was smiling when she handed the phone back to me.

I said good-bye to Joe and Berney, and then Cindy called her lawyer and friend, Bob Barnett.

Bob had represented Cindy when she'd written her true-crime thriller, *Fish's Girl*.

I put my ear next to the phone so I could hear, too.

"Bob, I'm in Las Vegas. I've got a blockbuster in the works, a true-crime story that reads like fiction."

Bob sounded delighted to hear her voice.

"Cindy, this is the Burke story? I've been following it. Avidly. As soon as you can, come to Washington so we can talk it over and make a plan."

"See you soon," she said.

We shared a group hug, then Rich started up the car and we headed back to the airport and home.

ACKNOWLEDGMENTS

With thanks for the advice of these exceptional people: Captain Richard Conklin, BCI, Stamford, Ct. PD, Lisa Raquel Pallack, forensic pathologist, Ulster County Dept of Health, NY, and our gifted researchers, Vivian Kahn, Heather Parsons, and Ingrid Taylar, who has been our West Coast sleuth for fifteen years. To Team Patterson: You are the best. And we are most grateful to Mary Jordan, who keeps the runway clear for takeoffs and landings and disappears random UFOs.

And we will always have fond memories of attorney, Philip Hoffman, partner, Pryor Cashman, LLP, NYC, who advised us on the trials in this and previous works. RIP, Phil.

ABOUT THE AUTHORS

James Patterson is the world's bestselling author. His enduring fictional characters and series include Alex Cross, the Women's Murder Club, Michael Bennett, Maximum Ride, Middle School, and Ali Cross, along with such acclaimed works of narrative nonfiction as *Walk in My Combat Boots*, *E.R. Nurses*, and his autobiography, *James Patterson by James Patterson*. Bill Clinton (*The President Is Missing*) and Dolly Parton (*Run, Rose, Run*) are among his notable literary collaborators. For his prodigious imagination and championship of literacy in America, Patterson was awarded the 2019 National Humanities Medal. The National Book Foundation presented him with the Literarian Award for Outstanding Service to the American Literary Community, and he is also the recipient of an Edgar Award and nine Emmy Awards. He lives in Florida with his family.

Maxine Paetro is a novelist who has collaborated with James Patterson on the bestselling Women's Murder Club, Private, and Confessions series; *Woman of God*; and other stand-alone novels. She lives with her husband, John Duffy, in New York.

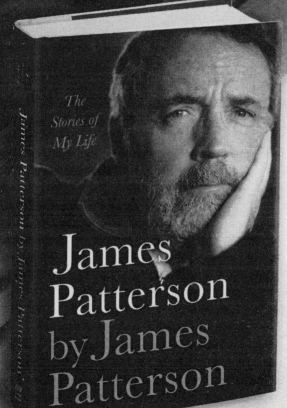

JAMES
PATTERSON
RECOMMENDS

JAMES PATTERSON
AND
BILL CLINTON

THE
PRESIDENT'S
DAUGHTER

"PROPULSIVE, EXHILARATING, AND
UNNERVINGLY BELIEVABLE." — KARIN SLAUGHTER

THE PRESIDENT'S DAUGHTER

I can't think of a more terrifying prospect than your child being abducted. And it is exactly that situation that I've thrown at former US president Matthew Keating. He has always defended his family as staunchly as he has his country. Now those defenses are under attack. A madman abducts his teenage daughter, turning every parent's deepest fear into a matter of national security. As the world watches in real time, Keating—a retired Navy SEAL—embarks on a one-man special-ops mission that tests his strengths: as a leader, a warrior, and a father.

THIS BOOK
WILL MAKE YOUR
JAW DROP

INVISIBLE

THE WORLD'S #1 BESTSELLING WRITER

JAMES PATTERSON
& DAVID ELLIS

INVISIBLE

Have you ever known something and no one believes you? It's the most frustrating thing and—in this book—deadly. Everyone thinks FBI researcher Emmy Dockery is crazy. Obsessed with finding the link between hundreds of unsolved cases, she has newspaper clippings that wallpaper her bedroom, and has recurring nightmares of an all-consuming fire. Not even her ex-boyfriend, field agent Harrison "Books" Bookman, will believe her. Until Emmy finds a piece of evidence he can't afford to ignore.

JAMES PATTERSON

JUROR #3

AND NANCY ALLEN

JUROR #3

As a thriller writer, I'm always creating powder-keg situations that push my characters to their limits. That goes for the citizens of Rosedale, Mississippi. Ruby Bozarth is a newcomer, both to this town in the Deep South and to the bar. Now she's tapped as a defense counsel in a racially charged felony. The murder of a woman from an old family has the upper crust howling for blood, and the prosecutor is counting on Ruby's inexperience to help him deliver a swift conviction. Then her case is rattled as news of a second murder breaks. As intertwining investigations unfold, no one can be trusted, especially the twelve men and women on the jury. They may be hiding the most incendiary secret of all.

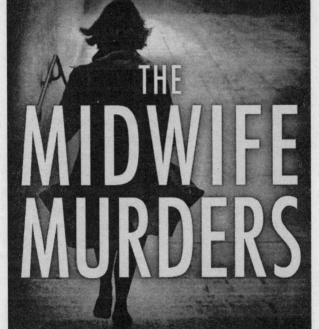

JAMES PATTERSON

THE MIDWIFE MURDERS

and RICHARD DiLALLO

THE MIDWIFE MURDERS

Imagine the outrage when new moms become the victims of two kidnappings and a vicious stabbing. To senior midwife Lucy Ryuan, nothing could be more heinous. Something has to be done, and she's fearless enough to try. Rumors begin to swirl, blaming everyone from the Russian Mafia to an underground adoption network. Lucy teams up with a skeptical NYPD detective to solve the case, but the truth is far more twisted than a feisty single mom could ever have imagined.

THE FIRST LADY

The US government is at the forefront of everyone's mind these days and I've become fascinated by the idea that one secret can bring it all down. What if that secret is a US President's affair that results in a nightmarish outcome?

Sally Grissom, leader of the Presidential Protection Division, is summoned to a private meeting with the President and his chief of staff to discuss the disappearance of the First Lady. What at first seemed an escape to a safe haven turns into a kidnapping when a ransom note arrives along with what could be the First Lady's finger.

It's a race against the clock to collect the evidence that all leads to one troubling question: Could the kidnappers be from inside the White House?

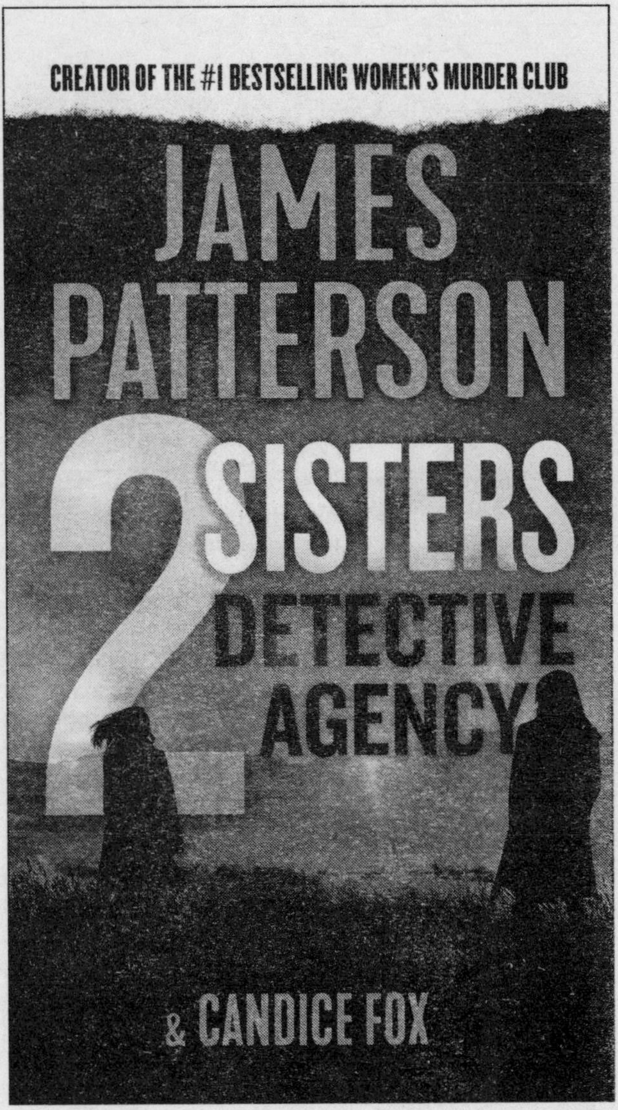
CREATOR OF THE #1 BESTSELLING WOMEN'S MURDER CLUB
JAMES PATTERSON
2 SISTERS DETECTIVE AGENCY
& CANDICE FOX

2 SISTERS DETECTIVE AGENCY

Alex Cross and John Sampson. Lindsay Boxer and Yuki Castellano. Rhonda Bird and Baby Bird—meet the first sister-led detective agency that gives bad guys a lot to be afraid of.

Attorney Rhonda Bird returns to her hometown after a long estrangement when she learns her father has died. There she makes two important discoveries: her father had stopped being an accountant and had opened up a private detective agency, and she has a teenage half sister named Baby. Baby brings in a client to the detective agency, a young man who claims he was abducted. During the course of the investigation, Rhonda and Baby become entangled in a dangerous case involving a group of overprivileged young adults who break laws for fun, their psychopath ringleader, and an ex-assassin victim who decides to hunt them down for revenge.

For a complete list of books by

JAMES PATTERSON

VISIT
JamesPatterson.com

 Follow James Patterson on Facebook
@JamesPatterson

 Follow James Patterson on Twitter
@JP_Books

 Follow James Patterson on Instagram
@jamespattersonbooks